"It's your show," Grant said, offering Avery a small smile.

"Thanks," she said softly. Her lips felt dry so she darted her tongue out to moisten them. Standing this close, she could see a flash of heat in the depths of his hazel eyes. Avery felt an answering warmth, a small coal of need that burned brighter the longer Grant watched her.

How would he respond if she placed her hand on his chest and pressed her mouth to his? She knew what the boy would do. How would the man react?

She never got the chance to find out. Quicker than thought, Grant dropped his head and kissed her, his lips warm and firm against her own. Avery inhaled deeply, the heady scent of Grant's skin making her head spin. She sank into the comfort of his kiss, her body celebrating the rightness of this moment, this connection. The bad taste of her memories faded as she teased Grant's tongue with her own, stoking his response as her own desire built.

* * *

We hope you enjoyed a sneak peek at the latest volume in Lara Lacombe's exciting miniseries, Doctors in Danger!

* * *

If you're on Twitter, tell us what you think of Harlequin Romantic Suspense! #harlequinromsuspense

Dear Reader,

People often ask where I get my ideas for a story. In this case, a scientific discovery made two years ago sparked my imagination. Researchers found a prehistoric virus trapped in the permafrost of Siberia, and when they thawed it out, they discovered it was still infectious! No need to panic, though—it only infects amoebas. As soon as I read that article, I knew the discovery would make a great premise for a book. Of course, I had to take a little artistic license here and there, but that's all part of the fun.

I hope you enjoy reading Grant and Avery's story. And maybe it's not so fictional after all—who knows what discoveries will be made in the future?

All my best!

Lara

DR. DO-OR-DIE

Lara Lacombe

HARLEQUIN® ROMANTIC SUSPENSE

Recycling programs
for this product may
not exist in your area.

ISBN-13: 978-0-373-40196-3

Dr. Do-or-Die

Copyright © 2017 by Lara Kingeter

Printed in U.S.A.

Lara Lacombe earned a PhD in microbiology and immunology and worked in several labs across the country before moving into the classroom. Her day job as a college science professor gives her time to pursue her other love—writing fast-paced romantic suspense with smart, nerdy heroines and dangerously attractive heroes. She loves to hear from readers! Find her on the web or contact her at laralacombewriter@gmail.com.

Books by Lara Lacombe

Harlequin Romantic Suspense

Doctors in Danger

Enticed by the Operative
Dr. Do-or-Die

The Coltons of Texas

Colton Baby Homecoming

Deadly Contact
Fatal Fallout
Lethal Lies
Killer Exposure
Killer Season

Visit Author Profile page at
Harlequin.com for more titles.

For Mom, with love.

Prologue

US Research Base, Fort Gilmour, Antarctica

"I think I've found something."

There was a pause, and Paul Coleson imagined the man on the other end of the line mentally translating his words. The language barrier was one of the downsides of working with the Organization, a shadowy group of men and women that operated under the cover of an internationally respected charity. Four months ago, Paul hadn't known they existed. He'd accepted their offer in good faith, seeing it as an opportunity to earn a little side money while working at the bottom of the world. But as time passed, their true intentions had become all too clear. Now he was just trying to make the best of a bad situation, cooperating in the hopes they would leave his family alone.

"Tell me more."

He shoved his free hand in his pocket and swayed back and forth on his feet. He'd learned that if he kept moving, the infamous Antarctic cold couldn't settle in his bones. Even though he spent most of his time inside, it was so damn cold in this godforsaken place he thought he'd never get warm again. "I isolated it from a core sample. So far, the results are promising." He tried to keep the excitement out of his voice, so as not to raise their expectations. They'd all known from the beginning that he was basically conducting a fishing expedition. Results were desirable, but not guaranteed.

Now that he had a potential lead, he didn't want to misrepresent his preliminary findings—if they thought he had found a suitable candidate and it turned out to be a failure, things would not go well for him. And even though this was his first time working for the group, he'd learned enough about their operations to know that overpromising and underdelivering was not a sound strategy.

Especially if he wanted to live.

"What results?" The man's voice was flat, with no hint of interest. They might as well be discussing the weather. But something told Paul that he had his contact's full attention.

He took a deep breath. "As I said, I isolated the agent from an ice sample. It thawed beautifully, and I've been testing it in cells." And now for the good news. "It's killed everything I put it in."

More silence, but he could practically *feel* the

man's focus sharpening. "How long does it take to kill?"

"Forty-eight hours."

The man made a noncommittal noise, and a creeping sense of unease made the hairs on the back of Paul's neck stand on end. He stopped swaying, his feet rooted to the floor as if glued there. His contact didn't sound too happy with those results. What more could the man want?

"We had hoped for a slower process. To make it more difficult to assign blame."

"Ah." He let out the breath he didn't realize he'd been holding and started moving again. "Well, keep in mind these are just cells in a dish. Once you start human trials, I think you'll find it will take longer, since the systems are larger and more complex."

Another silence, this time tinged with...*amusement*? What the—

"I think you mean when *you* start the human trials."

"What?" Paul couldn't keep the shock out of his voice, and he glanced around reflexively to make sure no one had overheard. The room was empty, but the interior walls were thin, something he'd do well to remember.

"That was not part of the deal," he hissed, careful to lower his voice. "I was just supposed to find potential agents and pass them along after doing the preliminary testing. No one said anything about human experimentation." His gut cramped even as he said the words, not because of any moral objections, but because of the increased risk of doing such experiments. He was already sticking his neck out pretty far, risk-wise. If they wanted him to start infecting people, he was almost guaranteed to get caught.

"The terms have changed."

"No," he snapped. "You can't."

As soon as the words were out, he realized his mistake. The man on the other end of the line laughed softly, and the menacing sound wrapped cold fingers around his heart.

"You are not in a position to bargain," his contact said, his voice lethally quiet. "You will conduct human trials, or we will sever our agreement." The tone of his voice made it clear that other things would be severed as well if there were any problems.

"What about the risk of exposure?" It was a long shot, but the only one Paul had left. Perhaps he could make them understand that having him conduct the experiments simply wasn't worth the risk involved. "If I'm discovered, the project is a failure."

"Then I suggest you work carefully." The words were final, and he realized any further objections would only anger the man. It wasn't a chance worth taking.

Resigned to his fate, he sighed quietly. "How many?"

"Pardon me?"

"How many test subjects do you need?" Best to clarify things now, so he could take care of everything at once. There would be no second chances. If this agent acted like he expected it to, the effects were going to be dramatic. People were going to panic, and it was quite possible the base would be quarantined, making it even more difficult to collect the data the group wanted. Attention would definitely be paid to this research outpost, which meant he had to work very, very carefully. It had to look like a natural event. If there was even a hint of deliberation about it, the spotlight would shine so hot and bright on the base personnel that there'd be no way for him to escape.

But maybe that was what they wanted... The thought made his blood run cold, and he almost missed hearing the man's reply.

"As many as possible."

Of course, he thought. *They want me to assume all the risk and get caught for my troubles*. The dawning realization lit a spark of anger, warming him from the inside out. He was the perfect scapegoat for them—once he'd been caught, people would stop looking for someone to blame, which meant the Organization would be free to continue operating as before.

Why didn't I realize it before?

The answer was instantaneous: money. He'd been blinded by dollar signs, and had jumped into bed with these guys for the sake of his family. Now it seemed they were going to be his downfall.

"Very well," he said, needing to get off the phone before his epiphany made him say something rash. Better for them to think nothing had changed. He didn't need their suspicion right now—things were going to be hard enough without worrying about the group coming after him.

"Call when you have additional results." His contact disconnected without another word, and Paul put the phone in his pocket with a sigh.

"Now what?" he muttered.

Two options loomed before him, neither one par-

ticularly appealing. He could lie and say he'd tried
to infect people but the agent hadn't worked. It was
a possibility. And it would keep people from finding out he worked for the group, which in turn would
spare him some rather uncomfortable questions and
time in prison.

Lying wasn't without risks, though. If the Organization found out what he'd done, they wouldn't hesitate to take their displeasure out on his children. Just
the thought of his kids in the hands of those men…
He shuddered and placed a hand on his roiling stomach to quell the incipient revolt. No, he couldn't take
that chance.

Which meant he'd have to set up the human trials.

He thrust a hand through his hair and began to
pace, his mind whirring with possible options. He'd
have to try out different routes of exposure, different doses of the agent. And then somehow keep track
of how people felt and when and if they developed
symptoms.

No, not people, he thought. *Test subjects*. Best
to start depersonalizing them now, since they were
nothing more than a data point from here on out.

And he'd do well to remember it.

Chapter 1

"Got a minute?"

Dr. Avery Thatcher glanced away from her computer monitor to find her boss, Dr. Harold Jenkins, standing in the doorway to her office. She waved him in with her free hand and swallowed her bite of yogurt before placing the spoon back in the container and pushing it to the side of her desk. Harold was a writer by nature, and every time she met with him he wound up jotting stuff down on a small notepad that she suspected was permanently attached to his palm. She'd learned early on in their working relationship to clear a space for him to use, and after five years the action was pure reflex. It was almost like a little dance, she mused now as she completed the familiar choreography.

He shut the door, then sat and patted his jacket

pocket for the ubiquitous accessory, but his hand came up empty. That was odd. Had he forgotten it?

Avery took a closer look at her boss and for the first time noticed the fine lines of strain around his eyes and a subtle tightening at the corners of his mouth. Something was definitely up, and Avery had a sinking feeling she wasn't going to like what he had to say.

"How are things?" He asked the question mechanically, and she could tell he was merely trying to observe conversational formalities before diving into the bad news. Her heart picked up the pace as she tried to imagine what he was going to say. The latest round of budget cuts had hit her division hard, and some contractors had been released because of the shortfall. Had the Centers for Disease Control cut the funding for her position?

The thought made her blood freeze. She loved her job as an epidemic investigator. Avery had made the unfortunate discovery during medical school that she was more interested in the diseases themselves than the actual patients. Working at the CDC had turned out to be the perfect way to combine her interest in infectious illnesses with her desire to help people. And since outbreaks occurred all over the country, she'd been sent to some pretty interesting places. It was the perfect job for her, and if she lost it… She shuddered, not even wanting to consider the possibility.

"Harold," she said, her voice calm despite her frayed nerves. "Please just tell me what's going on."

He frowned slightly. "Am I that obvious?"

She nodded and swallowed hard. "Do I need to update my resume?"

Harold blinked at her, clearly taken aback by the question. "No," he said slowly. Then understanding dawned. "Oh, it's nothing like that."

All the air rushed out of her in a gust, and Avery sank back against her chair. "Thank God," she said, closing her eyes. "You had me going there for a moment."

"Sorry about that," he said, sounding rueful. "You know you're my best investigator. There's no way I'm letting you go, even if I have to pay your salary myself."

His words went a long way toward quelling her anxiety. "Thank you," she said quietly. "That means a lot."

He waved away her gratitude and leaned forward. "There is something I need to talk to you about, though." He glanced back at the closed door, as if to reassure himself they weren't going to be overheard. "There's something going on in Antarctica."

"Are the penguins in trouble?"

Harold didn't even bother to smile at her lame joke. "The US has a research base there, Fort Gilmour. It's staffed year-round, believe it or not. Something strange has popped up."

"What kind of something?"

He shook his head. "Unclear at this time. But there have been several cases of an upper respiratory infection with some unusual symptoms."

Avery felt the familiar tingle of curiosity that came every time she heard about an outbreak. "Such as?"

"It starts as an uncomplicated respiratory infection—

cough, congestion, the usual. Some people recover, but those who don't go on to develop strange hemorrhagic symptoms."

Avery's eyebrows shot up. "Strange?" she echoed. What exactly did that mean?

He nodded. "Rather than the diffuse, systemic symptoms we see with something like Ebola, these patients only bleed out into their lungs. They essentially wind up drowning in their own blood."

A wave of sympathy washed over her as Harold's words sank in. What a horrible way to die. She could picture it all too easily and shuddered. Harold saw her reaction and nodded. "I know. I feel bad for them, too," he said.

"How many cases?"

"Ten so far, of which four people have progressed to the hemorrhagic phase and died."

"Damn," she said softly. "This bug isn't messing around." A 40 percent mortality rate was serious business, high enough to make any self-respecting doctor lose sleep.

"It's bad," Harold confirmed. "And to make matters worse, the hospital on the research base is having to handle everything alone. Normally, they can send critical patients to South America or Australia for treatment. But given the nature of this disease, those options are closed. No one wants these patients, especially since we don't know anything about this bug."

"That's terrible!" Outrage stiffened her spine and Avery sat upright. "How can they deny advanced medical care to people who desperately need it?"

Harold shrugged. "They're happy to air-drop supplies, but no one wants to be responsible for exporting this disease. The major fear is that bringing the patients off-base would allow the agent to enter into the commercial air travel system, and then we'd have a real problem."

He was right, Avery realized with a growing sense of horror. Even though she hated the idea of sick patients being cut off from the potentially lifesaving technologies of a major hospital, the last thing anyone wanted was a global pandemic of a hemorrhagic respiratory illness. Better to keep the sick all in one place, away from the general population.

And a research base in Antarctica was about as isolated as you could get.

"Where do we come in?" Was Harold telling her this to keep her in the loop, or was there something else going on?

"I need you to go down there and figure out what's happening. Right now we know next to nothing. We don't know what the disease agent is, how it's transmitted, the incubation period, infectious dose—it's a black box. We need answers."

Avery nodded slowly. It was a plum assignment, the type of work she loved. But there was just one problem… "Do we even have jurisdiction? This sounds like more of a thing for the World Health Organization rather than us."

"The WHO is monitoring the situation," Harold responded. "But since this is happening on a US base, we get the first crack at it."

Excitement thrummed in her belly, and Avery started making mental lists of everything she'd need to pack. "When do I leave?"

"Tomorrow," Harold said. "And I need you to keep

this assignment between you and me. Outside of a few key people, no one knows about this."

"Why the cloak-and-dagger routine?" Avery was used to a certain amount of discretion with respect to her assignments, but this seemed a bit extreme.

Harold sighed, and as his shoulders slumped he suddenly looked ten years older. A warning tingle slid down Avery's spine, and she held her breath, waiting for his reply.

"We're thinking this might be some kind of new influenza strain," he said, sounding almost sad. "And if that's the case…" He trailed off, and Avery nodded, understanding perfectly.

The majority of Americans thought that flu was merely a seasonal inconvenience, something to be endured rather than feared. Most of them had never even heard of the global pandemic of 1918, when between thirty and fifty million people had died from a particularly nasty strain. Since then, doctors and scientists had lived in fear of another massive outbreak, worse than the last. There had been a few false alarms over the years, but so far, humanity had managed to dodge a bullet. Still, researchers kept a close eye on influenza, and most would agree that it was just a matter of time before another virulent strain emerged to threaten the status quo. If it was happening now, panic and fear would sweep the globe faster than any virus, and the very fabric of humanity would be at risk.

Suddenly, Harold's caution made perfect sense.

"We are modifying response plans as we speak, working in conjunction with the WHO," Harold said softly. "We all hope this isn't flu, but we have to be prepared."

"Is the government going to cut off the base?" It was a drastic measure, but if there was a chance of this bug getting out into the general population, one option would be for the government to seal off the research base until the disease burned out. If no one went in or out, there would be no chance for the agent to escape.

Harold shook his head. "Not yet. But if this does turn out to be some new, supervirulent flu…"

"I know," she said softly. "We'd be stuck there." Worry gnawed at the edges of her mind, dampening her earlier enthusiasm. Did she really want to take on this mess, knowing there was a possibility she'd be stranded for an indefinite amount of time?

Her boss stared at her, sympathy welling in his eyes. "You don't have to go," he said. "Given the nature of this one, I can't force you to go to Antarctica when there's a chance you might get stuck there."

"It's okay," she said, dismissing the hypothetical outcome. If she focused on the potentially negative aspects of her job, she'd never be able to work again. There was always a chance she might get caught in a quarantine, or worse, get sick herself. Those were just some of the risks inherent in her line of work. She couldn't give in to the fear and worry now, not when there was so much on the line.

"Besides," she continued, "it's not like they'd forget about us. They'd do supply drops to keep us fed."

Harold acknowledged the point with a nod. "That's true."

"And if they do shut things down, can you imag-

ine the hazard pay I'd earn?" She winked at him,
hoping to lighten the mood. It was nice of Harold
to give her the option of refusal, but Avery couldn't
turn down this assignment. Identifying a new, virulent flu strain was the chance of a lifetime, and she
wasn't going to sit on the sidelines and let someone
else do all the work.

Harold smiled and shook his head. "I didn't think
you'd say no, but I wanted to give you the choice all
the same."

"I appreciate it. Is it just me?"

"No, there will be three other people accompa-
nying you—two nurses and a lab tech. I haven't met
any of them personally, but from what I hear they're
the best of the best."

Avery nodded, pleased to hear about the reinforcements. If the situation was as dire as Harold believed,
they'd need all the help they could get.

He stood, and Avery did the same. "I'll get your
itinerary sent over. You'll fly to New Zealand first,
and get set up with all the cold-weather gear you'll
need to survive the place."

"Oh, good." That was a load off her mind. The
Centers for Disease Control was located in Atlanta,
which wasn't exactly known for winter weather.
Avery didn't think she had a coat that could handle
a Chicago winter, much less the cold of Antarctica.
"What about medical supplies?" Since the base hospital was handling everything, they probably needed
a good restocking. "Can we get some antiflu drugs,
too, just in case?"

Harold nodded. "Draw up a list of medications

and supplies you want added to the manifesto. I'll see that it gets sent to the correct people."

"Thanks," Avery said, already turning her attention back to her computer. She pulled up a blank document and started typing, knowing there was no time to waste.

Containment suits, scrubs, respirators, bleach... Not to mention all the equipment she'd need to set up a field lab.

Harold walked to the door, but before he opened it, he turned back to face her. "Avery," he said, his voice serious.

She glanced up, tamping down a surge of impatience at the interruption. "Yes?"

"Be careful out there," he said, his gray eyes solemn.

Avery nodded, taken aback by his warning. In the five years she and Harold had been working together, he'd never once told her to be careful. For him to say so now drove home just how worried he was about the situation, and Avery felt a small weight settle on her shoulders. This case was different, she could already tell. And not just because of the exotic location.

"I will," she promised. "We'll get this thing under control and I'll be back here bugging you before you know it."

He tried for a smile, but it didn't reach his eyes. "I hope so," he said. Then he opened the door and left, closing it softly behind him.

Three days later...

"Dr. Jones?"

The words drifted through the fog of fatigue that

hung heavy over Grant's mind. "Hmm?" Not his
most eloquent response, but it was the best he could
manage with his face half buried in the pillow.

"The plane's landed."

"M'kay." The pillow was soft and cool under his
cheek and he stretched, relishing the sensation of
lying flat for the first time in days. He hadn't caught
more than a few snatches of sleep over the past week,
and now that he'd managed to collapse on a bed he
wasn't going to get up unless the hospital was on fire.

And maybe not even then.

"Dr. Jones?"

"Hmm?" Now he felt a flash of irritation. Why was
the nurse still here? She'd delivered her message—
why couldn't she just leave him in peace so he could
lapse into the coma his body so desperately needed?

"The expert from the CDC is here and wants to
meet you."

Damn. He was going to have to get up after all.

"M'kay," he muttered. He flipped onto his back,
then brought his hands up to his eyes and rubbed
vigorously. "I'll be right there," he called out, dismissing the messenger. She closed the door, leaving
him alone again.

Grant forced himself to sit up, knowing that if he
didn't it would be all too easy to surrender to sleep
once more. But since he was the chief doctor on-
base, it was his responsibility to brief the reinforcements about the "situation," as he'd come to think
of it. He preferred that to the more inflammatory
term *outbreak*.

Or *apocalypse*.

He stood and forced the exhausted hamster back

on the rusty wheel in his brain. Caffeine. He needed caffeine—industrial quantities of it.

He stepped into the small adjacent bathroom and flipped on the lights, wincing at the sudden brightness. A dull throb started up behind his eyeballs, but he ignored it. He'd learned from experience that medication didn't relieve his fatigue-induced headaches. Only sleep helped, and he wasn't likely to get that anytime soon.

A glance in the mirror told him he looked as rough as he felt. Too bad there wasn't time for a shower and shave—he certainly wasn't going to make a good first impression with his hair sticking out and a weeks' worth of stubble on his cheeks. He sighed, dismissing the issue. With everything else going on, he just couldn't muster up the energy to care about his appearance.

He stepped out into the hall and started down the narrow corridor. Every inch of available room was crammed with stuff—supplies, medical records, bedsheets. They couldn't afford to let any space go unused. When he'd first arrived, he felt claustrophobic and overwhelmed—how was he going to remember where anything was? But it hadn't taken long for him to learn the system, such as it was, and now he navigated the apparent chaos with ease.

He walked to the main desk, which faced the entrance to the hospital, expecting to find the new arrivals clustered around the door. But the small entryway was empty, along with the nurse who was on reception duty. Where were they?

The sound of voices drifted down the other hall and he turned and set off, wondering what they were doing. Maybe one of the nurses was giving them a quick tour of the facility? And it would be quick— with only twenty beds, they weren't exactly set up for the kind of cases they'd been getting lately. He shook his head, his mood sinking as it always did when he thought of the four patients he hadn't been able to save...

Fortunately, most of the beds were empty now. After the initial set of ten patients, they'd settled into a lull, and there hadn't been any new cases in the last three days. He hoped this was a sign the outbreak was over, but deep in his gut he worried it was only the beginning.

Despite the ten patients and four deaths, he knew they'd been incredibly lucky. Although this bug was nasty, it wasn't very contagious. That was the only thing that had saved the base. If the virus or whatever it was figured out how to jump from person to person? This whole place would be wiped out within a week. It was the nightmare that kept him awake, trying to figure out what he could do protect the researchers and staff toiling away here at the bottom of the world.

He hadn't protested when the base commander called the CDC for advice—he had his pride, but given the nature of this disease, he wasn't about to turn down help, especially not from people who had tackled this sort of thing before. He just hoped the guy they'd sent out would be easy to work with— people were already stressed and on edge, wondering when the disease would strike again.

The voices were coming from the small bay that held the dentist's chair and equipment. Dr. Farnly was their resident dentist, but he hadn't seen much work recently. Grant poked his head around the corner and was shocked to find a small group of people moving dentistry supplies and equipment and setting up what looked like laboratory instruments.

The two women and two men moved around the space like they owned the place. He opened his mouth to protest, but his gaze caught on a blond ponytail and the words died in his throat.

Avery?

His brain rejected the idea almost immediately, but his heart took a little more convincing. Of course it wasn't her—it couldn't be. But this woman, whoever she was, had the same color hair—a warm, golden mix of honey, sunshine and corn silk that Avery had worn in long waves cascading down her back. How many hours had he spent running his hands over the soft strands, stroking it away from her face as she lay with her head in his lap, both of them enjoying the lazy days of summer back when they'd been college students and their biggest worry had been what to do on Friday night?

This woman shifted and something in his chest tightened, her graceful movements yet another reminder of the woman he'd once loved. He realized now with the gift of hindsight just how stupid he'd been. But it was too late to make amends. Avery had moved on with her life and she deserved better.

Fresh grief welled up, but Grant tamped it down. He missed Avery, would always miss her. But he couldn't get bogged down in emotion now, not when so many people were counting on him to stay focused.

He shook his head to dispel the faint nostalgia that always appeared whenever he thought of Avery. He'd realized his mistake almost immediately after their breakup, and he'd spent days mired in the memories of their life together. But as the weeks and months had turned to years, he'd gotten better about keeping thoughts of her tucked away, only stopping to take them out and linger over them when he was alone. He certainly hadn't meant to indulge now, in the middle of the hospital.

It was the fatigue, he decided. His defenses were down, which was why he'd been blindsided by the sight of a woman with long, blond hair. Time to meet this expert and head back to bed for a long-overdue nap.

"What is going on here?" The question came out a little harsher than he'd intended, his emotions still too close to the surface for his liking.

One of the nurses glanced over and stepped to his side. "It's the CDC expert—they're setting up a temporary lab."

"You've got to be kidding me. We don't have the space for that!"

She shrugged and held up her hands in a kind of "what am I supposed to do about it?" gesture.

So much for the guy being easy to work with. He'd been here all of five minutes and was already reorganizing and repurposing space without asking permission. Grant eyed the small group, trying to pick out the man at the head of this little takeover.

"Who's in charge here?" he asked, glancing back and forth between a tall, skinny man in a blue scrub top and a stockier blond guy in a Harvard sweatshirt. *My money's on Harvard*, he thought, waiting for a reply.

"I am," came a distinctly feminine voice.

A very *familiar* voice.

Oh, God. It's not possible. Is it?

His heart beating double time in his chest, Grant turned and found Avery Thatcher staring at him, one eyebrow quirked up in that familiar, inquisitive expression he'd once loved. She stared at him for a moment, and he watched as her blue eyes flared wide in recognition. He couldn't see her mouth because of the mask she wore, but he was willing to bet she was biting her bottom lip the way she always had when something bothered her.

"Grant?" She sounded almost as incredulous as he felt, and she tightened her grip on the clipboard she held, her knuckles going white under her skin.

A tsunami of words rose in his throat, all the things he should have said ten years ago now jostling and vying for expression. He swallowed hard. "Hello, Avery. Long time no see." It was a lame greeting, but it was better than gawking at her like she was a ghost come back to life.

She was silent a moment, and Grant got the distinct impression Avery wanted nothing more than to turn her back on him and pretend he wasn't there. But she was too much of a professional to let her personal desires get in the way of her job. "Grant," she repeated evenly. "What a surprise."

He tried to laugh to dispel the tension, but the sound came out as more of a strangled wheeze. "I know, right? Of all the gin joints in the world…" He trailed off and Avery smiled politely—he could see her cheeks move under the paper of the mask, but the smile didn't reach her eyes.

"Indeed. So you're the chief here?"

He cleared his throat, happy to change the subject. Besides, what could he say to make up for the past? It would take more than a few bad jokes to reach her now. "I am. I take it you're the expert from the CDC?"

"I am," she replied.

A fierce burst of pride came out of nowhere and made him want to hug her, but he knew better than to try it. Even when they'd been undergraduate students, Avery always wanted to be the best. She'd worked hard to rise to the head of their class, and thanks to her talent and determination, she'd had her pick of medical schools. It was no surprise that she was now at the top of her field.

A hint of sadness tinged the edges of his vision as he studied her. If he hadn't been such a dumb kid, he would have been a part of her life all this time, would have celebrated her accomplishments with her. Instead he felt like a stranger, a realization made all the more painful, thanks to the closeness they'd once shared.

He deliberately turned his thoughts away from the past. "It's not airborne," he said, gesturing to her mask. "You don't need that." Her eyes were quite expressive, but he wanted to see the rest of her face so he could get a better idea of what she was thinking. Once upon a time he'd known all her expressions and had been able to practically see her thoughts based on how she held her mouth or lifted an eyebrow. Would he still be able to read her like that now?

Her eyes narrowed. "I was told the patients suffered extensive respiratory symptoms."

"That's true, but whatever is causing this disease doesn't seem to be transmitted through the air. Why do you think I'm still alive?" His tone was light, but she didn't smile.

She eyed him up and down, as if assessing the truth of his statement for herself. After a long moment, she lifted her hand and tugged the mask down, exposing her pert nose and full, pink lips to his gaze.

Grant felt the faint stirrings of desire as he stared at her mouth, remembering the feel of it against his own. Memories flooded his mind, assaulting his senses and overwhelming his thoughts. He fought to put them back in the box where they belonged, but in his sleep-deprived state, it was harder than usual to keep things under control. Desperate for a distraction, he cleared his throat. "What are you doing?" He gestured to the equipment being crammed cheek by jowl on the available counter space, and the boxes of what could only be lab supplies stacked on the floor.

Avery frowned slightly. "Setting up a field lab," she replied in a tone that suggested this should be perfectly obvious. She glanced over to where a man was unpacking a box. "No, put the PCR machine next to the sequencer, please." He nodded and moved to follow her instructions, and Avery turned back to Grant. "I was given a list of your lab equipment and brought some of my own to supplement it."

Her presumption lit a spark of irritation in his chest, and he seized on the emotion, grateful for the change in his internal focus. "And you just thought you'd take over our dentist's office?"

Avery glanced around the space, her expression making it clear she didn't think too highly of that description. "It's across the hall from your existing lab," she pointed out reasonably. "It seemed like the best location, all things considered. And I was told you haven't had a lot of demand for dentistry lately."

It was true, but Grant still would have appreciated a heads-up before they'd taken over the space. "By all means," he said dryly. "Make yourself at home, then."

"Thanks."

He stood there a moment, watching the men and women unpack. They moved quickly but competently, and as they worked he could see the organization of things take shape before his eyes. It was yet another example of the take-charge, can-do attitude Avery had always shown, no matter the circumstances.

Grant knew he should be relieved that reinforcements had arrived, but he still couldn't shake his annoyance at the sense that things were spinning out of his control. Dealing with this strange outbreak had been difficult, and the deaths of four of his patients had made him feel powerless, a sensation he hated. Having to work with Avery, the woman he'd loved and lost, was just the icing on the cake of this crappy situation.

"I was told you wanted to meet with me?" His voice held a slight edge he didn't bother to hide.

Avery glanced over at him, as if she'd forgotten he was standing there. "Yes. Do you have an office where we can talk?"

"Of course." Truth be told, it was more of a broom

closet than an office. But it was his space, and that was all that mattered.

She turned back and eyed the progress of her little group, apparently doing some mental calculations as to how much longer it would take them to finish setting up her domain. "Can I meet you there in half an hour?"

"Make it an hour," he said. That would give him enough time to take a quick nap, which would reset his brain and allow him to shore up his defenses against the flood of memories her presence had unleashed.

"Great," she said, sounding a little distracted. "See you then."

Grant recognized a dismissal when he heard one. He turned and was surprised to feel a faint sense of anticipation as he walked away. He'd really screwed things up ten years ago, and she hadn't hesitated to cut him out of her life. Despite all the reasons he shouldn't care, it bothered him that their relationship had ended so badly. Part of him had always hoped to see her again, to try to make things right now that time had dulled the sting of his actions for both of them. And while he knew there was no way to repair all the damage he'd done, it would be nice if he and Avery could part company on good terms this time.

Provided they both made it out of here alive.

Chapter 2

Avery took a deep breath and placed a hand on her stomach to still the butterfly wings fluttering inside. Why was she nervous? She was a professional, for crying out loud. She'd successfully worked numerous outbreaks in many different settings, ranging from small, isolated towns to major cities, and everywhere in between. She knew what she was doing, and she did it well.

Why, then, did she feel like a rookie on her first assignment?

It could be because she was working with a new team. The nurses and lab tech who'd flown in with her weren't new to outbreak work, but since Avery had met them all for the first time only a few days ago, she wasn't sure how they would jell together. Everyone seemed nice enough now, but she knew from experience that once the real work began, the stress level increased and tempers rose to the surface. It would be up to her to keep the team focused, motivated, and feeling supported.

It was a tough job, but nothing she hadn't done before. And in truth, she relished the challenge—it was part of what she loved about her work.

No, her jangling nerves had little to do with the task at hand and everything to do with the man she was on her way to see.

Grant Jones had clearly been surprised by her presence, and the feeling was entirely mutual. She closed her eyes, mentally adding up the time since she'd seen him last. *Ten years*, she realized with a small jolt. A lifetime ago.

She had to admit; the years had been kind to him. His light brown hair still held a bit of a curl; only now it was shot through with a few silver strands. He'd acquired fans of fine lines at the corners of his hazel eyes, but the arches of his cheekbones and his long, straight nose hadn't changed. His mouth still held that hint of mischief, too, as if he was always thinking of some private joke.

She couldn't say she'd missed him—he'd hurt her too badly for that. But now that she'd seen him once again, a small bud of curiosity began to bloom. What had his life been like over the past decade? Did he have a wife? Kids?

The thought of children was like a knife to her heart, and she quickly dismissed the idea. But her memories weren't so quick to fade...

I'm pregnant.

Two little words, and yet they'd changed everything.

Avery looked down as she washed her hands in the small bathroom, but the chipped sink and unfamiliar surroundings faded as the memory of another bathroom took its place...

It was her senior year of college, and she and Grant had their future all mapped out. They were both going to medical school—even though they'd been accepted to different institutions, Grant was already planning to transfer to be with Avery during his second year. They'd get an apartment together, study together, support each other through the trials and tribulations of school. And then, when they'd both gotten their MDs, they'd get married and live happily-ever-after.

That was the plan, until halfway through the year when Avery came down with a stomach bug.

Except it wasn't a normal illness. This one lingered for days, leaving her exhausted. Her stomach revolted every time she ate, giving her no choice but to spend a lot of time in the bathroom. For the second time that day, she knelt on the cold tile floor and wiped the sick off her lips with a wad of toilet paper.

Swallowing with a grimace, she stood and flushed the toilet, then made her way to the sink and reached for her toothbrush. Her gaze caught on the blue box of tampons on the counter and she frowned. How long had it been since she'd had to use them?

She searched her memory, her thoughts growing more frantic as she went further back in time. Her period was two—no, three—weeks late. Her heart in her throat, she skipped class and drove to the gas station across town. No way was she going to buy a pregnancy test at the campus general store—that would trigger all sorts of rumors she didn't want to deal with. Ignoring the knowing smirk of the teenage boy who rang up her purchase, Avery raced back to her apartment and locked herself in the bathroom. She placed the stick on the counter and closed her eyes, counting silently as she waited for her fate to be revealed.

It was the longest two minutes of her life. Gathering up her courage, she took a deep breath and opened her eyes.

Two lines.

She was pregnant.

Her first thought was denial. This isn't happening. *She and Grant were always extra careful—she took her pill religiously every day, and they used condoms, too. The last thing either one of them wanted was a baby right now, not when they had such big plans.* The test has to be wrong. *It was the only explanation that made sense, and she clung to it like a drowning man given a life raft. Her body shaking, she took the second one. And then the third and final test in the box. Ten minutes later, she had to admit the truth.*

The next few days passed in a blur. She went to class, pretended everything was okay. But inside she was numb, still trying to process this unexpected detour in her life's plan. Gradually, though, the shock that had left her frozen thawed, and she began rewriting her blueprint for happiness. She and Grant would get married now, and she'd move out to Cal-

ifornia with him so he could start medical school. She'd delay her admission for a year and then begin her own program once the baby was a little older. It wasn't an ideal situation, but they would make it work.

Her mind made up and a new plan in place, Avery decided it was time to tell Grant. She met him at the apartment he shared with two of his fraternity brothers, figuring it was better to break the news in private.

It went well, all things considered. Grant certainly wasn't excited about the news, but he wasn't angry, either. Looking back on it later, Avery realized his dominant emotion had been terror, which was understandable. But he'd put on a brave face and told her everything would be okay. Avery had left him after a few hours, knowing he needed some time alone to process the news.

She went to bed that night feeling hopeful, and for the first time she began to really wonder about the new life inside of her. Would it be a boy or a girl? Would it have her blue eyes, or Grant's hazel-green? And what about names?

A few weeks later, she started bleeding.

Faint at first, but as the day wore on it got heavier. She called her ob-gyn, who told her this was normal for some women. The reassurance made her feel a little better, but she still worried. A few hours later, she started cramping.

She tried to call Grant, but he didn't answer his phone. So she drove herself to the emergency room, and was alone when the doctor told her the news. Even today, Avery could still see his face when she closed her eyes. He was a young man, tall and lanky in green scrubs and wearing a white coat that was too big for his frame. He looked like a little boy wearing his father's clothes, and Avery kept waiting for the real doctor to show up.

"I'm so sorry, miss," he said, looking supremely uncomfortable. "But you're having a miscarriage."

The words stung, each one landing like a separate slap that left her reeling. She fought to hold back her tears, but it was no use. She broke down in the exam bay, the white curtain surrounding her bed doing nothing to muffle her sorrow from the rest of the ER. To his credit, the doctor didn't leave. He walked over to the bed and held her hand, his touch bearing witness to her pain.

After what seemed like an eternity, Avery somehow managed to get herself home and curled up in a ball on the bed. She didn't know how much time passed—didn't really care. Her whole consciousness was turned inward, focused on the internal workings of her body and the heartbreaking events in progress...

The door hinges squeaked and Avery came back to the present with a little jump. She smiled at the woman who walked in and received a polite nod in return. *Time to go*, she thought, twisting off the faucet. She couldn't very well continue to stand here, lost in bitter memories, now that she had company. Besides, she'd already spent too much time thinking about the past. Her shared history with Grant was painful, but she wasn't going to let it affect her current job. And if the shock on his face was anything to go by, he didn't really want to walk down memory lane, either. It seemed they were both on the same page, then. Focus on the problem at hand so they could each go their separate ways.

Avery stepped out into the hall and turned left. She could see the door to Grant's office from here, and despite her resolve to remain professional at all times, her stomach flopped about like a landed fish. Part of her wanted badly to tell him off—to let him know in no uncertain terms how much pain he'd caused her. But another, more rational part recognized that was a bad idea. It just wasn't worth the effort, and in the end it wouldn't bring her the satisfaction she craved. Better for her to stop looking back. She couldn't change the past, and if she got mired in memories she wouldn't be able to work effectively.

Was Grant having the same problem? *Likely not*, she thought with a soft snort. Unless she missed her guess, he'd moved away after college and hadn't looked back. And why would he? He'd dodged a bullet when she lost the baby—he'd made that much clear.

Avery shook her head, drawing deep inside herself for strength. She was going to walk into his office with her head held high and her shoulders back, and she'd keep her chin up for the duration of her stay here. She wasn't about to let Grant know how much the past still haunted her after all these years. No, she was going to project the image of a calm, capable professional, not a woman forever changed by his actions.

And maybe after a while, she'd believe it herself.

* * *

Grant sat behind his desk and took a deep breath, his mind going a million miles a minute. What was he going to say to Avery? The shock of seeing her had begun to wear off, but he still wasn't feeling terribly articulate. The last thing he wanted to do was say the wrong thing and increase the tension between them.

She definitely hadn't been excited to see him. He recalled the look on her face when she'd realized it was him, and a sense of shame made his skin prickle. It was his fault Avery looked at him like he was something stuck to the bottom of her shoe. Once upon a time they'd meant the world to each other. But a few careless words had killed her feelings and ruined his chances of ever finding happiness with her again.

He thought he'd managed to put that painful episode of his life behind him, but seeing Avery brought it all back up again, and Grant was surprised to find the heartache was still fresh, ten years later.

So much for time healing everything.

Should he just start with an apology and get it over with? *I'm sorry I said the miscarriage was for the best.* Straight and to the point. No way for her to misinterpret his words. It was a hell of an opener, but maybe it was the best approach. When a patient had an infection he didn't hesitate to use aggressive treatments. This wound had festered between them for far too long—perhaps it was time to air things out and start the healing.

Or maybe not.

Avery had always been a stickler for rules and protocol. She probably wouldn't appreciate him bringing up the past, especially since she was here in a professional capacity. It was one thing to talk about their shared history over a beer, quite another to discuss it as part of an outbreak investigation. It might be better for him to ignore the past and focus solely on current events.

Besides, it was entirely possible Avery had moved on with her life and no longer carried the burden of her loss.

Not likely, he thought, dismissing the prospect almost immediately. Avery wasn't the type to pretend something hadn't happened. Grant could still remember the look in her eyes, that haunted, hopeless grief eating her up from the inside... He shuddered, and goose bumps broke out along his arms. No, he did not think Avery had gotten over the loss of the baby.

But maybe she had found someone new and started a family. The thought filled him with equal parts pleasure and dismay. Grant would never wish for her to be unhappy, but the idea that she'd moved on with her life stung, especially since he certainly hadn't.

He'd dated a few women over the years, but his heart really hadn't been in it. He made a point of warning the women up front that he was not the marrying kind, but they always seemed to take it as a challenge, like they would be the one to change his mind. The experience left a bad taste in his mouth, and so he'd chosen to remain single rather than break someone else's heart.

Had Avery been wearing a ring? He closed his eyes, trying to remember. But all he could recall was her face, those bright blue eyes growing cold when she realized who he was...

Grant shook his head to clear the memory and focused on his immediate problem. What should he say to her? He glanced at his watch, and his heart kicked hard against his breastbone. She was going to be here any minute, and he still had no idea how to talk to her.

A knock on the door told him he'd run out of time. He'd just have to wing it, and let her take the lead. No matter what had happened between them, they had to work together now. He wasn't going to be the reason this investigation failed.

"Come in."

The door swung open and he stood to greet her, gesturing for her to take the seat across from him. "Sorry it's so crowded," he said as she maneuvered into the small space. The room was a narrow rectangle, carved out from the slightly larger staff break room. Grant's desk sat at the far end, opposite the door. Bookshelves lined the walls, crammed full of texts on every conceivable medical subject. It was a testament to the preinternet days when a base physician needed access to information on a wide variety of conditions. As Grant had already learned, there was no telling what might walk through the door.

Avery glanced around, taking it all in as she moved forward. Her eyes landed on the cot shoved to one side of the room, topped with a tangle of sheets. She quickly looked away again, and Grant felt a sudden stab of embarrassment. Why hadn't he thought to make the bed? She probably thought he'd turned into a slob.

"It's cozy," she said, the corner of her mouth lifting in a half smile as she sat. Grant did the same and promptly forgot how to breathe when she leaned forward to pull something out of the bag she'd set at her feet. The V of her scrub top gaped open, giving him an unobstructed view of her lovely attributes. His face heated and he turned his head, looking for something—*anything*—else to focus on while he willed his body's response to go away. Of all the inconvenient times to be reminded of her as a woman... Dozens of memories rushed in, overwhelming him with visions of them together. His hands on her. Her hands on him. Her mouth— He shifted in his seat and cleared his throat, then eyed the bottle of water on his desk. Would it be too obvious if he dumped the contents into his lap?

"Everything okay over there?"

Grant glanced back to find Avery watching him, a curious expression on her face. Damn. He was going to have to be more careful about controlling his reactions around her. Thanks to their shared past, she could tell when something was bothering him.

"I'm good," he said. "Just had a little tickle in my throat." He unscrewed the cap on the water bottle and took a healthy swig to lend more credence to the lie.

She nodded, apparently accepting his answer.

"How have you been?" Grant asked. He knew she'd probably rather talk about the outbreak, but he wasn't going to be able to focus until he knew more about her life and what she'd been up to in the last decade.

"Just fine, thanks." She kept her head down, flipping through the notebook in her lap.

"That's good." He paused, but when she didn't speak again he forged ahead. "I guess you live in Atlanta?" That was the location of the CDC's headquarters, so it stood to reason she'd live there.

"Yes." She continued to flip pages, the rustle of paper the only sound in the room.

"Ah, apartment or house?" he asked, needing to fill the awkward silence.

Avery apparently found her place in the notebook and looked up. "Apartment. Look, Grant. I appreciate the chitchat, but let's just get down to business, shall we?"

"Sure," he said, nodding in agreement. "I'm just glad to see you're okay."

She smiled, but the expression didn't reach her eyes. "I'm great. You look fine, too. And now that we've established that, I think we'll both be better off if we focus on the outbreak."

She was right, of course. And really, he should be relieved that she didn't want to spend time going over their past. But part of him was disappointed—how was he going to apologize if she didn't want to talk about the elephant in the room?

"What can you tell me about this outbreak?"

"It started two weeks ago," he replied automatically, shoving aside his personal concerns. There would be time enough to chat later, once he'd hopefully figured out how to broach the subject. "The first two patients presented on the same day, a few hours apart."

"Can you tell me about their symptoms?"

"Low-grade fever, congestion, mild cough. Typical upper respiratory stuff. It's the kind of thing that cycles through here on a regular basis, so I gave them the usual treatment and sent them on their way."

"And then what happened?" Her pen flew across the paper as he talked, taking notes on everything he said.

"The rest of the patients presented in the same way over the next two days. I put out a notice, reminding everyone to focus on hand-washing, cover coughs and sneezes, that kind of thing. But I didn't realize anything was wrong until the third day."

Avery pulled another piece of paper from her bag and consulted it. "That's when Patient Zero came back?" she asked, referring to the first patient.

"Yes," Grant confirmed. "And he looked like death warmed over."

One of Avery's eyebrows lifted. "Is that your official clinical opinion, Doctor?" There was the slightest hint of amusement in her voice—not enough for a stranger to register, but Grant picked up on it. He gave her a little smile of acknowledgment and was gratified to see her own mouth curve up slightly in response.

"Indeed," he replied solemnly. "Fever of one hundred and five degrees, productive cough, bloody mucus. Not to mention, his eyes were bloodshot— he'd ruptured the capillaries from coughing so hard."

Avery grimaced. "Poor guy."

"Yeah." Grant shook his head, remembering that sick feeling in his gut he'd gotten when the man had stumbled back in. "And to top it off, he said his pain was an eight on a scale of one to ten."

"What did you do?"

"Started him on a febrifuge and pain meds. His

chest sounded crackly, so I ordered a chest X-ray. Came back almost entirely whited out."

Avery's eyebrows lifted. "There was that much fluid in his lungs?"

"Oh, yeah. I'll get you the medical records for all the patients so you can see the results for yourself. But essentially he was drowning in what I later learned was blood."

It was a sight he'd never forget, a scene from a horror movie burned into his brain, made all the more terrifying because it had really happened. The man's cough had grown steadily worse, and two hours after his admission, he'd begun to gag. They'd rushed to clear his airway only to find a rising swell of blood trying to escape. As he suffocated before their eyes, the team had flipped him onto his side. A torrent of blood had gushed out in a wet splatter on the floor, and a hot, metallic stench had filled the air.

Grant swallowed, clearing the memory of the smell from his tongue. "He died a few hours later," he said softly. It always rankled to lose a patient, but it was doubly hard here. There was a finite number of people on the base, and Grant had made it a point to introduce himself to everyone. Even though he hadn't known the man well, he did remember exchanging pleasantries with him whenever their paths had crossed.

Avery was silent for a moment. "It sounds like a very difficult case," she said, a note of sympathy in her voice.

Grant nodded. She understood. Even though Avery didn't practice medicine anymore, she was still a doctor and would have lost patients in med school. There were some cases that stuck with you,

and Grant knew the death of the four men in this outbreak would haunt him for years to come.

"After he died, I tracked down the other patients
who had presented with the same initial symptoms.
I hoped this was just a one-off, but unfortunately,
three others progressed too rapidly for us to save. I
wanted to send the other six to South America for
treatment, but my request was denied." He shoved a
hand through his hair and tried to keep the bitterness
from his tone. "As soon as people heard what this
thing does, they refused to take them. Didn't want
to risk it spreading."

If he looked at the situation dispassionately, Grant
understood the decision. Better to contain the pathogen here, where there were a finite number of potential victims. If this thing spread into the wider
world, it could be a species-ending infection. But
Grant hadn't had the benefit of detachment. He'd
touched those people, held their hands, comforted
them as best he could. It was personal for him, and
he was still angry his patients had been left to the
mercy of a medical center that wasn't equipped to
handle this kind of disease.

Could the four victims have been saved if they'd
made it to a larger hospital? It was a question that
would undoubtedly dog him for a long time...

"I heard," Avery said, a note of sympathy in her
voice. "For what it's worth, I think it was a crappy
thing to do."

He jerked one shoulder up. "Fortunately, we caught
the other six before they bled out into their lungs.
They got pretty sick, but at least they're not dead."

"What kind of drugs did you use on the ones who survived?"

Grant leaned back and ran a hand through his hair again, exhaling through pursed lips. "What *didn't* we try is the better question. I pumped them full of anything I thought might help—steroids, antivirals, antibiotics, epinephrine, versed, Plasma-Lyte, albumin—you name it, I tried it."

"Do you have any idea if one of the drugs was responsible for saving the other patients?"

He shook his head. "At that point, I was just trying to keep them alive. I don't know if it was the combination of the medication, the supportive care or the fact that we caught them early enough that allowed them to survive."

"Probably all three factors," Avery said. She laid her notebook on his desk and set her pen down, then leaned back and met his eyes. "It sounds like you did a hell of a job."

Her praise washed over him like warm summer rain, and he wanted to close his eyes and savor the feeling. He had always respected her opinion, and it meant a lot to know that she thought his actions had been appropriate. "Thank you," he murmured.

There was a flash of warmth in her eyes, there and gone in the space between heartbeats. "You say there have been no new cases in the past three days?" she asked, getting them back on track.

"No. At least, no one has come to me with symptoms."

"And none of the staff that treated the patients have been affected?"

"No. I think we really dodged a bullet here. What-

ever this thing is, it doesn't seem to be very contagious. Otherwise, the whole base would have come
down with it by now."

Avery tilted her head to the side, apparently considering his words. "Possibly," she said. "But we
don't know what the incubation period is. For all we
know, more people have already been infected but
haven't started to show symptoms yet."

A cold chill washed over Grant as the implications
of her suggestion sank in. "My God," he whispered.
"This thing could be a ticking time bomb."

"Let's hope not," Avery replied, her mouth set in
grim lines.

"What do we do now?" That helpless feeling was
starting to creep up on him and he pushed it away.
They would come up with a plan, and it would work.
It had to work. The alternative was unthinkable.

Avery sighed quietly. "I'd like to look at the patient
files for all the cases. We need to identify common
behaviors or exposures that might tell us something
about where they picked up the agent. Do you have
any samples we can analyze to try to identify the
pathogen?"

"I think there are some blood samples left, but I
don't know what state they're in now."

"That's fine." She waved away his concern. "The
tech I brought has a reputation as a miracle worker.
We'll see if she can find anything."

"What can I do?" Grant wasn't going to just sit on
his hands while they worked. He would go mad if he
didn't have something to do, some way to contribute
to the investigation. Even though he'd only been on-
base a few months, he felt a sense of ownership of the

place. Not in a material way. But this was his home for the next few months, and these were his people. It was his responsibility to take care of them, and he'd already failed four times. Logically, he understood those deaths were not his fault. His internal score-keeper saw things differently, though, and he felt a strong need to redouble his efforts. Perhaps he could somehow make up for their deaths by saving others.

Avery eyed him across the desk, her expression assessing him as if she was trying to determine what he could handle. "First of all, I need you to get some sleep. You're no good to me exhausted."

He couldn't stop the laugh that rose in his throat at her unexpected order. "That obvious, huh?"

"Quite." She gathered her notebook and pen and stood, and Grant rose to his feet, as well. "Come find me after you wake up."

He waited until she got to the door before asking the question burning in his mind. "Can we stop this thing?"

Avery paused and glanced at him over her shoulder. "If we're lucky," she said, suddenly sounding as tired as he felt. Then she walked out of his office, closing the door softly behind her.

Chapter 3

"I have results." Paul glanced around out of habit, but there was no one nearby to eavesdrop on his conversation. Still, it didn't hurt to be cautious…

"I'm listening."

He took a deep breath, feeling very much like he was about to step out onstage in front of a roomful of people. Would his contact be impressed with his results? Were his findings dramatic enough?

Only one way to find out…

"I was able to infect ten people. All became symptomatic, and four died within forty-eight hours after showing signs of illness."

"What about the other six?"

"They survived. But I'm not sure if they suffered permanent damage. I haven't been able to see them yet."

The man on the other end of the line made a non-committal sound, and Paul felt his stomach clench. *I did what you asked. What more do you want from me?*

He heard a muffled noise and imagined the man had placed his hand over the receiver, likely so he could talk to someone nearby. A few seconds later, he was back.

"It is not enough."

Despair washed over Paul and he put a hand against the wall to steady himself. "What do you mean?" he asked softly.

"We need more information. You must infect additional people."

"But..." He stopped, knowing his protest would fall on deaf ears.

Apparently, his reluctance came through loud and clear. "Now is not the time to back away," his contact said, a note of steel in his voice. "Finish the job, or your family will suffer for your incompetence."

It was the first time they'd explicitly threatened his family. He'd known it was coming, but a sense of bone-deep terror gripped him nonetheless. Not for the first time, he kicked himself for getting involved with this group in the first place. The promise of financial security was not worth the cost, but he'd been too desperate at the time to recognize it.

"Very well." There was no other acceptable answer, and they both knew it.

"We have arranged for you to have some assistance."

"What?" He couldn't hide his incredulity. How was that even possible? He wasn't aware of any in-

coming flights scheduled in the near future, so how on earth were they going to bring someone in? Unless they were already on-base…

Just how many people were working for this shadowy organization? And did they all have the same mission? His mind spun with possibilities and questions, but he knew better than to ask.

"He will reveal himself to you soon. I think you will find him quite helpful."

"Excellent," he lied. Any "assistance" was likely a spy in disguise, sent to make sure he complied with his orders. It was just another subtle tightening of the noose wrapped round his neck.

"Report back in a week. We look forward to hearing your progress."

There was a click followed by the loud drone of a dial tone. Paul tucked his phone back into his pocket and rubbed his hands together, chafing some warmth back into his frozen fingers. It was cold in the storage room. Hell, it was cold *everywhere*.

Seven days. That didn't give him much time. Frustration gnawed its way up his chest, filling him with the urge to hit something. Every time he did what the Organization asked, they told him it wasn't enough. They kept moving the goalposts on him, making it impossible for him to meet their expectations. It was enough to drive him insane. If this was a normal situation, he'd simply walk away. But nothing about this was normal, and Paul knew if he burned this bridge, he wouldn't be the one to pay the price. The kids had already been through so much. He couldn't risk them—not now, not ever.

He closed his eyes, seeing the faces of the ten men

he'd infected. Nice people, all of them. Friendly and decent, the kind who probably had families of their own back home. Paul's heart tightened at the thought and a swell of regret surged, threatening to drown him. What had he done?

Needing a distraction, he grabbed his phone and pulled up the most recent picture of his family. There they were, all smiling into the camera, squinting a bit thanks to the sun. Noah was getting so tall, and the dark shadow of a sprouting mustache on his upper lip drove home the fact that his son was no longer a little boy. His younger daughter, Lisa, still had a bit of baby fat clinging to her slight frame, but he could see the promise of the woman she would become in the slope of her brow and the angle of her jaw. They were growing up so fast. And while he hated knowing he had killed four men, he consoled himself with the knowledge that they were adults who had lived their lives. It was a hard thing he had done, but he couldn't let his sympathy for relative strangers outweigh the promise of his children's future.

One week, he thought grimly. Time to go back to work.

Avery glanced at her travel alarm clock for what felt like the millionth time that night. While she normally didn't have trouble falling asleep in a new place, she was too keyed up to relax right now. She was itching to dive into the investigation and figure out what exactly was going on at this frozen research base. If this really did turn out to be a new strain of influenza, then her work would go down in medical history, right up there with the men and women who had studied the Ebola virus or HIV. It was an exciting thought, and she allowed herself a moment to imagine how this case could push her into the upper echelons of her field.

Part of her recognized how strange it was to be so excited about a disease, and such a nasty one at that. She truly didn't want anyone to suffer, and she felt bad for the families of the four people who had already died. But she knew the best way to honor the patients who had lost their lives was to dive in and figure out how to keep others from sharing their fate.

And if the work went well and she happened to wrap things up quickly? That would be the icing on the cake.

Seeing Grant again had been unnerving, to say the least. She felt like a snow globe that had been violently shaken, her previously settled emotions all stirred up and swirling around like so many white flakes. It was frustrating to revisit a period in her life she'd thought was over. She'd worked hard to process her grief at losing the baby and the pain of their breakup. Slowly, but surely, she'd put the pieces of her heart back together and had moved on, always looking forward, never daring to look back for fear she would get sucked into the black hole of despair again. Escaping it once had been hard enough—she didn't think she would get so lucky a second time.

Now, thanks to the emotional upheaval Grant had triggered, she was forced to question if she'd really dealt with her past at all, or simply ignored it long enough that the pain was no longer so fresh. After all, if she'd truly gotten over the losses, seeing Grant shouldn't have such a powerful effect on her.

She flipped onto her back with a sigh and burrowed under the down comforter, grateful for the warmth in the chilly room. It was the shock factor, she decided. That was why he'd gotten under her skin again. If she'd known he was here, she could have mentally and emotionally prepared herself to see him. Instead she'd been blindsided by his sudden appearance and hadn't had time to throw up any mental buffers. Now she knew what to expect.

She closed her eyes, determined to get at least some sleep tonight. But her brain wouldn't cooperate. Question after question popped into her mind, preventing her from relaxing. And to her great dismay, most of her curiosity was focused on Grant. Had seeing her again affected him the same way? Did he ever think about her and the baby she'd lost? Or had he jumped into another relationship and put her out of his mind and heart completely?

The thought stung and she blinked hard against the prickle of incipient tears. "Stop it," she muttered, taking a deep breath and harnessing her emotions. Grant's private life wasn't any of her business, and she needed to remember that. Still, she hadn't seen a ring on his finger… Did that mean he was single?

Doesn't matter, she told herself firmly. She was here to do a job, not reconnect with her old flame. They'd had their chance once. No need to make the same mistake again.

If only she could get her body to understand that.

While her mind was busy dealing with unwanted and unwelcome memories, the rest of her had suffered no such troubles. No matter what had happened in the ten years they'd been apart, Grant still looked very much the same. He was a little leaner, a little harder maybe, but those broad shoulders, hazel eyes and long nose hadn't changed. As soon as she'd seen him her body perked up, all the nerve endings coming to life and making her feel like a live wire.

Being so close to him in his office hadn't helped, either. The small room had smelled like him, that familiar combination of soap and a hint of spice that she knew from experience was the scent of his skin. Once upon a time, the smell of him had been enough to make her weak in the knees. She was less affected by it now, but it still made her stomach do a little flip.

Just ignore it. She couldn't allow herself to see Grant as a man, or else she would make the mistake of wanting him again. And that was a distraction she simply couldn't afford.

Of course, it was easy to tell herself she was going to keep things professional. Quite another to actually follow through. Especially since she had firsthand knowledge of what it was like to be with him... She felt a phantom caress on her thigh and recognized it as the ghost of his touch from long ago. They had been very good together, a fact that her body was all too keen to point out. The few men she had gone on to date after Grant had been nice enough, but they hadn't been *him*. And even though he'd broken her heart, he was still the standard to which she compared them all. It wasn't fair or logical, but feelings generally weren't, particularly where he was concerned.

What she wouldn't give to talk to Olivia or Mallory right now! Her two best friends knew her history with Grant and would know just what to say to help her deal with this unexpected complication. She reached for her phone, trying to calculate the time difference between Antarctica and Washington, DC, where Olivia Sandoval lived. Would her call wake Olivia up?

"Probably," she muttered, setting the phone back down. Besides, at this time of night, Olivia was likely snuggled up with her fiancé, Logan. They'd been neighbors for a few years, but things had really developed between them during Olivia's most recent medical charity trip to Colombia. In a bizarre turn of events, a drug cartel had tried to blackmail Olivia into smuggling cocaine back into the United States. Desperate, Olivia had turned to Logan for help. He and his colleagues at the DEA had hatched a plan to outmaneuver the cartel, and fortunately, their gamble had paid off.

Avery still couldn't get over Olivia's stories, and she was so glad Logan had been there to keep her safe. Even though she hadn't met the man yet, she had spoken to him over the phone. He seemed like a genuinely good guy, and she'd never heard Olivia sound so happy before.

Avery didn't want to dampen Olivia's joy with her own sob story, so that left her other best friend, Mallory Watkins. Mallory was a little tougher to get in touch with, thanks to her job as ship's doctor for a major cruise line. It was probably for the best—if she actually spoke to Mallory, it would be too difficult to hide where she was and why. And since Harold had cautioned her to keep the investigation quiet, she probably shouldn't tell anyone off-base about it. But Mallory did always respond to emails…

Avery grabbed her phone again, squinting as she stabbed at the maddeningly tiny letters with her fingertip. It took forever, but she managed to type out the most important details, namely that Grant was here and she didn't know how to deal with him. She pressed Send and leaned back, feeling a weight lift off her shoulders. Of the three of them, Mallory was the most practical. She'd have the perfect advice for dealing with this situation.

Now Avery just had to find a way to pass the time until she responded.

Sleep would be the best choice, but her mind refused to cooperate. Now that she had sent Mallory her worries about Grant, she was free to focus on the details of the investigation. And even though her limbs felt heavy with fatigue, Avery knew she wouldn't be able to rest until she'd at least looked at the patient records. The pathogen was still out there, and she couldn't afford to waste any time. Too many lives were at stake.

She sat up and reached out to flip on the small lamp located on the night table, then kicked the blankets off and swung her legs over the side of the bed. Even though she was wearing sweatpants and thick socks, the air in the room was still too cold for her liking. She had cranked the heater in the small, dorm-style room as high as it would go, but she was so used to the warmth of Georgia that the lingering chill in the air was enough to make her shiver. Eyeing the stack of folders sitting on the narrow desk opposite the bed, she decided working under the covers was the only way to stay warm.

"How do these people stay here for months on

end?" she muttered. It hadn't been a full twenty-four hours yet, and she already felt like a Popsicle. She couldn't imagine staying for months, the way most of the researchers did. But she might have to do just that if it turned out there was a new strain of influenza here. Better to be a little cold than risk introducing this disease into the wider world. Still, she hoped it didn't come to that.

She grabbed the folders and snuggled back under the blankets. It wasn't worth wasting energy worrying about a possibility that might not happen. First, she had to isolate and identify the bug. Then they could deal with the repercussions, whatever they may be.

It only took a few minutes for Avery to get sucked into the work, her tiredness and concerns about Grant fading into the background as she lost herself in the clinical language of the medical records. There was a lot of information in the files, including detailed descriptions of symptoms, medications administered and patient responses. She was immediately struck by the severity of the symptoms and the rapid speed of decline for some of the patients. Avery was used to the realities of diseases, but even the dry, dispassionate medical vocabulary couldn't disguise the horror of what these patients had suffered. Whatever this pathogen was, it didn't pull any punches.

But where had it come from? Pathogens didn't just materialize out of thin air. If this really was a new strain of influenza, her best bet was to look at the birds of Antarctica. Normally, such viruses circulated through migratory bird populations such as geese and other waterfowl, and in urban settings it was often found in chickens and pigs. But none of those creatures lived on this continent, which meant she'd have to go beyond the normal understanding of the virus. Antarctica had penguins. Was it possible the virus was native to those birds?

The more she considered the idea, the more it made sense. Penguins were an isolated group—since there wasn't a lot of regular human interaction, the virus might have been circulating through the population for years before making the jump to a hapless researcher. And if the virus didn't cause disease in the birds themselves, no one would think to make a connection between a sick researcher and his study subjects...

Her fingers flying, Avery flipped through the medical records, searching for background information on each patient. The first page of each file was a basic biographical sketch, and she skimmed through them all, hoping to find that at least one patient was a biologist of some kind who interacted with penguins or any other type of bird on Antarctica.

A moment later, she leaned back with a sigh, disappointment settling in her stomach like a small lead weight. None of the patients appeared to have had contact with any type of wildlife, at least not according to their histories. The patients ranged from astrophysicists to support staff, and the one thing they had in common was that their job duties were all localized on-base. Since Antarctica wasn't exactly teeming with points of interest, it was unlikely any of the men had ventured away from the comforts of civilization. How, then, had they become infected?

A biologist could still be involved, she mused. Perhaps someone had contracted the virus and exhibited a mild infection, or no symptoms at all. It wasn't unheard of for some pathogens to remain quiet in a host, effectively turning a person into a silent spreader of the disease—Typhoid Mary, the woman who had unwittingly spread typhoid fever throughout New York City in the early 1900s, was perhaps the most famous example of this phenomenon. But given the severity of symptoms displayed by the ten patients, she rather doubted that was the case here. This virus—if it really was a virus causing the infections—seemed incredibly aggressive. Based on the medical records, this appeared to be more of a scorched-earth type of pathogen rather than a live-and-let-live bug.

"So we have a dangerous, unknown pathogen on the hunt for new hosts and a base full of potential victims," she muttered. "What could possibly go wrong?"

And who else is infected? It was tempting to think that three days without a new patient meant the outbreak was over, but Avery refused to fall into that trap. Without knowing the incubation period of this pathogen, she had no way to determine if other people had been infected and had yet to develop symptoms. Even the virulence of the pathogen didn't necessarily provide any clues. Until she knew the identity of the pathogen, it might be better to assume more patients were forthcoming. She made a mental note to talk to Grant about it in the morning—perhaps they could put out a base-wide notice, informing people to come to the hospital at the first sign of illness no matter how mild the symptoms. Better to be inundated with cases of a seasonal cold than miss one or two patients with a more serious condition…

Stifling a yawn, Avery rubbed her eyes and rested her head against the frame of the bed. She should really try to get some sleep if she wanted to be at all useful tomorrow. It was tempting to spend the night working, but logically she knew she had reached the limits of what she could accomplish with the information she had. Tomorrow she'd interview the surviving patients and talk to Jennifer, the lab technician, about any preliminary results she'd obtained.

And as for Grant?

She shook her head, frustration rising as she pictured his face, still handsome after all these years. It wasn't fair that he looked good to her now, in spite of everything that had happened between them.

But the thing that bothered her the most was the hold he retained on her. One of the things Avery liked best about her job was the logic behind it—disease outbreaks had a cause, and by working methodically, she could usually identify the source and respond accordingly. No emotion required. But the situation with Grant wasn't like that. He complicated things, made her feel when she didn't want to. No matter how much she wished otherwise, he'd gotten under her skin again.

She just couldn't let him know.

"Higher, Daddy!"

Grant smiled and gave a little push, just enough to make the swing rise a few more inches. His little girl was turning out to be quite the daredevil, and while he appreciated her sense of adventure, he couldn't shake the ever-present fear that it was going to get her hurt someday. He knew he couldn't protect her forever, but he wasn't ready to let her go just yet...

She laughed, and the joyous sound burrowed into his chest and made his heart swell. She was so perfect he ached every time he looked at her. With her long blond hair and bright blue eyes, she was the very picture of her mother. But he was in there, too—she had his nose, and he recognized his stubborn streak in some of her more difficult moments. His daughter was a force to be reckoned with, and he knew without a doubt she was going to change the world.

She'd definitely changed his world.

"*Can I go on the slide now?*"

She let her feet trail along the ground, slowing the arc of the swing with each pass. Without waiting for his response, she launched herself from the seat as the swing made another upward trek, her long, lean body flying through the air, hair trailing behind her like a golden kite. His heart shot into his throat as he watched her come down, his arms already reaching for her, though he was too far away.

He needn't have worried. She landed on her feet, graceful as a cat. She shot him a triumphant grin he recognized all too well, then took off for the slide, confident he would follow.

"*Grant!*"

He turned to find Avery standing at the fence. He waved, and she gestured for him to come to her. The slide was only a few feet away, so he walked over to meet Avery, wondering why she didn't just come into the playground to talk to him.

He was halfway to the fence when he heard his daughter's cry. "Daddy!"

The panic in her voice froze his blood and he whirled around, his eyes scanning the area for her. Gray mist rose from the ground, shrouding the playground and turning the once-bright day into a realm of shadows.

She screamed again, this time in pain. Grant ran over to the slide, but she wasn't there. She began to sob, the wrenching cries filling his ears and tearing out his guts. He searched the playground, trying to wave away the fog as he moved from one station to the next. But there was no sign of her. Desperation clawed up his spine as he explored, and he had the sudden, horrible thought that she was gone.

Still, her words echoed all around, calling out to him as he moved. Where was she? Why couldn't he see her?

"Grant!"

Avery's voice cut through their daughter's cries. He turned back to the fence to find Avery clutching the little girl to her chest, one hand on her head, the other supporting her body. Avery's eyes bored into him, bright and accusing. What had he done? He took a step toward them, but she jerked back, taking their daughter with her.

"No," he said, reaching out for them. "Please, let me see her."

But his words fell on deaf ears. For every step he took, Avery retreated, carrying the little girl farther and farther away. He stopped moving, but Avery didn't. She held his gaze as she continued to back up, her pace measured and unhurried. Grant could only stand there, helpless, as the two people he loved most in the world were swallowed up by the swirling fog.

Just before they vanished from sight, his daughter turned to look at him. Even from a distance, he could see the tear tracks on her cheeks, and his heart clenched with the need to touch her, to soothe her worries and make everything okay again. The look she gave him was one of confusion, as if she was trying to figure out who he was and why he was standing there. She opened her mouth, and the wind carried her whispered question back to him.

"Daddy?"

Grant shot up in bed with a gasp, his arms outstretched, reaching for the little girl who wasn't there.

Had never been there.

His breath gusted out in a loud sigh and he lay down again, the pillow damp against the skin of his neck. He kicked the covers off, welcoming the relief of the cool air on his sweaty body. The dream lingered like a greasy film on his skin, a coating that covered him from head to toe in a claustrophobic embrace.

This wasn't the first time he'd dreamed about Avery and their child. Sometimes he saw her holding a baby. Other times, the child was older, like tonight's encounter. But he always pictured a girl.

There was no way to tell if the baby had been a girl or a boy—the miscarriage had happened too early in the pregnancy for them to know the sex. But deep in his heart, Grant thought it was a daughter they had lost.

And it was *their* loss.

He didn't pretend to know what it had been like

for Avery. He could imagine how she had felt: the pain, both physical and emotional, knowing the life inside her was dying. At the time, he'd still been adjusting to the news that she was pregnant. He hadn't yet formed any kind of attachment. But she had. And he'd known from the look in her eyes that she'd lost a piece of her soul along with the baby.

It had taken him longer to feel the ache. At first, he'd been so overcome with the pain of losing Avery that he hadn't really thought about the miscarriage. But the knowledge of it had stayed with him, quietly eating away at his heart like water dripping on a stone.

In his darker moments, he liked to torture himself with thoughts of what their daughter would have been like. It would have been her tenth birthday this year. There would have been a party, of course, complete with cake and balloons. He could picture it now, Avery carrying in the frosted confection, topped with two rows of glowing candles. Mary—he'd always liked the name Mary—would lean forward, closing her eyes tight to make a wish before blowing out the candles. It would have been a wonderful day, full of laughter and love. The kind of day he hadn't had in… well, forever, it seemed.

Did Avery ever think about the what-ifs? Of course she did, he realized immediately, shaking his head at the absurdity of the question. How could she not? But did the road not taken haunt her like it did him, or had she made her peace with the future they'd never have?

Part of him wished he could make the dreams stop. They weren't regular enough to be considered recurring, but every time he had one it stayed with him for weeks, casting his life in shadow. It didn't take a shrink to figure out why he'd had one tonight. Should he tell Avery? Would she forgive him if she knew he hadn't just walked away and forgotten about the baby? How would she respond if she knew he regretted the loss of their child every day?

I'll tell her tomorrow. He didn't want to upset her by bringing up painful memories, but his pride demanded he try to make her understand that he wasn't the callous bastard she'd thought him to be all these years. Perhaps it was selfish of him, but he wanted her to acknowledge his pain, to consider that maybe, just maybe, she'd underestimated him then.

It wouldn't change the past, but it might help him sleep better at night.

Chapter 4

"You're here early."

Avery looked up and blinked at him, and Grant could tell by the look on her face he'd broken her concentration. "Sorry," he said, sliding into a seat across from her. She had set up an office of sorts in the staff break room, and when he'd walked in she was busily poring over pages and typing notes on her laptop.

"It's okay." She gave him a quick once-over before returning her focus to the glowing screen in front of her. "You look better today."

"I feel better," he confirmed. "It's amazing what a little sleep will do." He didn't mention his dream, recognizing the time wasn't right. Yet. He took a sip of his coffee and noticed the dark circles under her eyes and the faint lines of fatigue around her mouth. "You should try it yourself."

She ducked her head. "I know. Believe me, I tried."

"Was your room okay?" She was down the hall from him, a fact that had pleased him when he discovered it this morning. If her quarters were anything like his, the room was small and no-frills, but serviceable enough. He'd stayed in far worse places, and he was willing to bet she had, too.

"It's fine." She frowned a bit, as if reconsidering. "The wardrobe isn't big enough for my coat, but other than that, I can't complain."

"I usually throw mine on the bed. Extra warmth that way."

"Good call. Is it always so cold?"

Her question caught him off guard and he laughed before he could stop himself. "You are in Antarctica," he pointed out.

Avery blushed, her pale cheeks turning a pretty shade of pink that made him think of roses. "I know," she muttered. "I just thought it would be a little warmer inside, that's all."

"Just be glad you're here in the fall," he remarked, taking another sip of coffee. "From what I hear, the winters are brutal."

"How long have you been here?" She sounded genuinely curious, and a small spark of hope kindled to life in his chest. If she was interested in his life, maybe he could segue into talking about the issues that really mattered. It was a long shot, but he chose to see her question as a sign she might be willing to listen to him…

"A few months. It took me several weeks to adjust to the cold. I've been in some chilly places before, but this is unlike anything else. It's a cold that seeps into your bones and freezes you from the inside out."

She nodded. "I'm beginning to understand that. Do you see a lot of frostbite?"

He leaned back, trying to keep a smile off his face. Avery was talking to him, really talking, and about something totally unrelated to the outbreak. He didn't know how long this apparent truce between them would last, but he was going to savor every minute of it. "Not as much as you'd think. The researchers and staff here take the temperature very seriously. Most of the time, they're very smart about going out with proper gear. Every once in a while I'll see someone who stayed out too long or had a gear failure, but they usually get to me before true frostbite has set in."

She cocked her head to the side. "So, what does your normal case look like?"

"Usually, it's an uncomplicated upper respiratory infection. That's why I didn't worry when the first cases presented—it looked like the normal crud that makes the rounds. Seems like everyone gets it at one point or another during their stay. I also have patients with lacerations, the occasional broken bone or sprain. But generally speaking, the people here are pretty healthy."

"I'd guess they would have to be, to survive out here for long."

He acknowledged her point with a nod. "The people who come out here are different from the general population. They tend to be pretty fit and have a well-developed sense of adventure. They also tend to be more willing to take risks, which results in some of the accidents. But you're right—there aren't really any couch potatoes here."

Avery's eyebrows drew together in a frown. "Which means this disease is pretty serious. If it can kill four previously healthy people in a matter of days? We're looking at something big."

"So what you're saying is it could be even worse if this thing infects your average American?"

She nodded, and the look in her blue eyes was grim. "Much."

Apprehension made the fine hairs on the back of Grant's neck stand on end. He hadn't really considered that aspect of things. He'd been so focused on the base population he hadn't stopped to think how different they were. But now that Avery brought it up, he realized she was right. This bug, whatever it was, would burn through the chain-smoking, cheeseburger-eating populace with a vengeance. It was yet one more reminder of how crucial it was they contain this thing here and now.

He gestured to the stack of folders next to her computer. "Have you had a chance to look at the medical records yet?"

"Yes." She leaned back in her chair and let out a small sigh. "Not that it's done me any good."

"Is something wrong with the records?" Grant sat up and reached for the top folder on the stack. If they were incorrect or compromised in any way, he needed to know about it. He'd never had trouble with the staff before, but everyone had been so exhausted and stressed while treating the sick that mistakes may have been made.

"No, they're fine as far as I can tell," Avery replied. "I just haven't been able to find any information that looks like a smoking gun." She smiled ruefully. "Of course, it's never that easy."

Grant studied her a moment, noting once again the marks of her sleepless night. "Have you eaten yet?" He knew from experience that food and caffeine made a world of difference, especially when he'd gotten little to no sleep.

"Ah, no," she said, sounding suddenly guarded.

"Aren't you hungry?" He was determined to push against the walls she kept throwing up—it was the only way to make progress.

She dropped her gaze and focused on the papers in front of her, apparently finding them fascinating. "I'm fine."

It was a lie and they both knew it. Grant opened his mouth, gearing up for the whole "breakfast is important" spiel, but he needn't have bothered. Her stomach let out a loud rumble that made her blush again. She glanced up at him, her expression resigned. "Any chance you didn't hear that?"

He grinned. "Nope. Come on. You need to know where the mess hall is anyway." Despite the seriousness of the situation on-base, they still had to eat.

"I saw it on the map," she said, but he could tell by her tone it was only a token protest.

"And now you're going to experience it firsthand." He pushed his chair back and stood. Seized by a sudden impulse, he held his hand out, offering it to her to help her stand.

Avery stared at it for a moment, and he could practically *hear* the thoughts churning in her head as she considered how to respond. Grant just stood there, hand outstretched, knowing if he pushed at all she would back away.

Finally, after what seemed like an eternity, Avery slipped her slender hand in his. The touch of her skin hit him like a jolt of lightning, and a current of sensation traveled from their joined palms up his arm and into his chest. His body rejoiced, recognizing the familiar feel of her skin against his. It was something he never thought he'd experience again, and he relished it.

Need slammed into him, and he wanted so badly to pull her close and embrace her. This small touch wasn't enough to satisfy him—he wanted, needed more. But he forced himself to keep his grip loose. If he gave in to the desires coursing through him, Avery would run and never look back.

She rose gracefully to her feet and slipped her hand from his. The loss of contact hit him like a blow, but he smiled, hoping Avery hadn't noticed how much the brief touch had affected him. Bad enough his internal equilibrium had just been rocked—he didn't need Avery to know that one soft brush of her skin had been enough to wreck the control he'd spent the last ten years building.

He waited while she donned her coat and handed over her gloves and cap. "Where's your gear?" she asked, zipping up the coat.

"Hanging on a hook by the front," he responded. "I'll grab it on the way out. You can start keeping your stuff there, too, if you like."

"That would be nice," she said, tugging the gloves

on. "I haven't been here long, but I'm already kind of tired of hauling all this stuff around."

Grant took his empty coffee mug to the sink and rinsed it, then set it on the rack to dry. "It is a lot to keep track of, but you'll be glad you have it once we step outside." He led her from the room and down the hall, pausing to shrug into his own gear. "Ready?"

"As I'll ever be." If the look in her eyes was anything to go by, she was already starting to regret she'd said yes. Fortunately, her innate sense of manners would presumably keep her from backing out now.

"Trust me, you're going to enjoy this," Grant promised. He shoved open the door and stepped into the cold rush of air. "Carter makes the best cheese omelet on the continent."

Avery lifted one eyebrow, the corners of her mouth turning up. "Quite an accomplishment, I'm sure. Although I doubt the competition is that stiff."

"You'd be surprised," he said. He felt a little bounce in his step and realized for the first time since the outbreak he felt…hopeful.

He slid a glance at Avery, her face barely visible under her knit hat and the hood of her coat. It was amazing how being around her had changed his entire mood. Even though she was clearly still upset with him, he found her presence calming. And she seemed to be softening toward him, little by little.

He looked up at the cloudless blue sky and took a deep breath. The air was refreshingly cold, and the chill chased away the last vestiges of fatigue and made him feel ready to face the day.

He was glad he'd taken the time to sleep; he was going to need all his energy to stop this bug.

* * *

Avery looked around as they walked, trying to match what she saw with the map she had studied so carefully on the plane over. She'd known on an intellectual level the base was fairly large, but actually seeing it in person gave her a whole new level of appreciation for the men and women who had built this place and who worked here today.

Grant led her down what appeared to be the main thoroughfare—a wide, unpaved avenue lined with buildings. There was a surprising amount of color in the scene, as the buildings were painted in vibrant shades of blue, red, green and even orange. It gave the place a cheerful quality and she couldn't help smiling to herself as they passed by.

Grant noticed her expression and turned to see what she was looking at. "The colors," she said. "I guess I didn't expect so much color here. I thought it would be very…white."

"Ah." He nodded in understanding. "I thought the same thing. Kind of a nice surprise, isn't it?" He smiled at her, his cheeks dimpling in that familiar way she loved. Her knees wobbled reflexively, a reaction she could not control and wouldn't bother trying to deny. It seemed that no matter what her brain said, her body was determined to throw good sense out the window where Grant was concerned.

"It is," she replied. They came to the end of the street and Grant turned right. Avery moved to follow him but then caught sight of the view spread out before them and stopped in her tracks.

A thin dusting of snow covered the ground, shimmering in the sun like a carpet of diamonds. The land stretched out in front of her, curving in a gentle slope down to the water beyond, where she could see the waves lapping at the frozen shore. It was unlike anything she'd ever seen before, and Avery's breath caught as the stark beauty of Antarctica sank in.

For the first time, she could understand why people came here, why they were willing to stay for months on end. There was something so primal about the place, and yet the seemingly barren landscape was endlessly fascinating. Each dip and curve, each jut of rock and splash of water, they all added up to create a majestic vista that was almost too amazing to be real.

She wasn't sure how long she stood there, mesmerized by the view. Gradually, she became aware of Grant standing next to her, patient and quiet as she soaked it all in.

He must have sensed when she came back to herself. "Beautiful, isn't it?" he said softly.

Avery nodded. "The word hardly does it justice."

He didn't reply, and she appreciated his silence. There was no need for words just now, and he seemed to understand that as well as she did.

After a few more moments, she turned to face him. "Thank you," she said simply.

He arched an eyebrow. "For what?"

"For letting me have the view." She shivered a bit, suddenly realizing how very cold it was. She'd been so enchanted by the scenery she hadn't noticed the temperature, but now she was acutely aware of every frozen finger and toe. Grant was probably feeling the same way, and yet he hadn't said anything, hadn't tried to rush her along or encourage her to move. He'd simply stood next to her, waiting while she processed the magic and wonder of this strange place.

It was a gift, made all the more surprising because she hadn't expected it from him.

"It was my pleasure," he said. There was an odd note in his voice, but before she could catch a glimpse of his face, he turned and held out his arm. "We should probably get inside. I'm starting to feel a bit cold."

For a split second, Avery debated asking him if everything was okay. But Grant was right—it was cold, and she didn't want to stand outside talking when they could be eating.

They walked about a hundred feet before Grant stopped in front of a red building. He yanked open the door and ushered her inside, following close on her heels.

The first thing Avery registered was the warmth of the place. It wrapped around her like an old, comfortable blanket, and she let out her breath in a sigh of relief. Her skin began to tingle as she started to thaw, a sensation that was both slightly painful and oddly pleasurable after the harsh temperature outside.

She inhaled deeply, drawing in the tantalizing scents of freshly baked bread, hot coffee and frying bacon. Her stomach let out another rumble, and Grant chuckled softly behind her. "I think you'll be able to find something you like here," he said, leading her into a large room filled with dining tables and chairs.

At the far end of the room was the kitchen area, and as they approached, Avery saw it was divided into several stations with different options presented at each location. The hot-food station offered scrambled eggs, omelets, pancakes and waffles. There was a large self-serve cooker of oatmeal nearby, complete with bowls of brown sugar, raisins and carafes of milk. A little farther down, she spied a cooler with yogurt and juices on offer, and next to that was a spread of fresh fruit laid out on chilled plates. The final station held baskets of muffins, bagels and slices of bread, along with a selection of jams and spreads. Overall, it was an impressive amount of food, and her stomach celebrated at the sight.

"I can't believe there's fresh fruit here," she murmured.

Grant nodded. "We get deliveries every week during the summer," he explained. "There's still a couple of weeks left before those will shut down for the winter. But some of the produce is grown on-site in the greenhouse."

"Impressive." Her respect for this place just kept growing. Avery hadn't had a lot of time to read about the ins and outs of daily life at the base before flying in, and she hadn't known what to expect. But it seemed that things at the end of the world were really pretty normal, almost boring even.

Except for the whole disease outbreak issue.

She and Grant made their selections and he led her to an empty table in the corner, away from potential eavesdroppers.

"So," he said, smearing butter on his toast. "Since you didn't find anything in the medical records, what's your next step?"

Avery took a bite of her omelet and closed her eyes in pleasure. Grant was right—it was excellent. She took another bite, savoring the combination of hot cheese and herbs, all wrapped up in fluffy eggs that practically melted in her mouth.

She opened her eyes to find him watching her, his expression satisfied. "Told you," he said, a little smugly.

Yesterday, his attitude would have rubbed her the wrong way. But Avery couldn't bring herself to be annoyed with him, especially after his display of patience while she dallied outside.

It hadn't even been twenty-four hours, and Avery already felt more relaxed around Grant. He exerted an almost magnetic pull on her, and it was so tempting to slide back into their old roles. They'd been good together once, and her nostalgia for that idyllic time in her life was a powerful force. Grant wasn't making it easy to forget, either. She knew he hadn't meant anything when he offered his hand to help her stand up, but just the brief touch of his skin against her palm had sent her heart rate soaring and had made her breath catch in her chest.

Now his confident grin triggered an answering flutter deep in her belly. Once more, she was uncomfortably aware of Grant as a man, rather than a colleague. It was a trap she couldn't afford to fall into.

Time to change the subject.

"Since the medical records weren't as helpful as I'd hoped, I need to interview the patients."

Grant nodded, accepting the conversational shift without comment. "A couple are still in the hospital. I'll help you track down the ones who have been released."

"That would be great." She wanted to conduct the interviews as soon as possible so she could start sifting through their responses in an attempt to identify any common exposures the patients had all shared. Had they eaten the same food, used the same bathroom, gone to the same research site? Since they still didn't know how people were getting infected with the mystery pathogen, she couldn't rule anything out.

"Want some help with the interviews?"

Avery chewed another bite of omelet while she considered his offer. On the one hand, it would be nice to have another set of ears present to make sure she didn't miss anything. And since the patients all knew Grant, they might be more willing to open up about private or otherwise potentially embarrassing behaviors that may have exposed them to the bug.

But if she said yes, it would mean spending more time around Grant. Sitting next to him and feeling the warmth radiate off his body. Listening to the easy rhythm of his breathing. Hearing his voice and seeing him interact with his patients. Could she handle that much exposure to him and still keep her head, or would she surrender to the whims of her body and allow her attraction to him to continue to grow unchecked? It was a possibility that was both appealing and appalling in equal measure.

In the end, her practical side won out. She was here to do a job, and she owed it to the patients and the people who had died to work as quickly and effectively as possible. If that meant dealing with a little personal crisis, so be it.

She nodded. "I'd appreciate that, yes."

Grant's eyebrows lifted, and she could tell her acceptance had surprised him. But he recovered quickly. "Great," he said, scooping up another bite of food and nodding to himself.

"Do you think the patients who recovered would volunteer to donate some blood?" Jennifer, the lab tech, would be able to take those samples and use them to help her identify the bug. It was a painstaking process, but if she was as good as her reputation suggested, she'd be able to get results soon.

Grant shrugged. "I'm sure they'd be happy to help. To be honest, I think they're relieved to be alive, and I bet they're willing to pitch in to keep other people from getting sick."

Avery chewed another bite, hoping he was right. She'd worked outbreaks where people couldn't wait to help the investigation, as well as those where patients wanted nothing more to do with the medical establishment. It could go either way, which was another reason having Grant along would be a bonus. He was a member of the community, more likely to be trusted than an outsider such as herself.

"Hey, Doc."

Avery looked up as a man approached their table. His dark hair was cropped short and his skin was pink and windblown, indicating he probably spent a lot of time outside. He limped a little as he walked, and Grant frowned at the man.

"David. Ankle bothering you again?"

David glanced down, then looked back up with a shrug. "No more than usual."

"Why don't you stop by the clinic today and I'll see if there's anything I can do?"

"Oh, I don't know about that," David responded. "Don't want to catch anything." He winked, but there was a note in his voice that made Avery think he wasn't entirely joking.

"I think we're past that now," Grant said, avoiding Avery's gaze.

David nodded, but his expression remained doubtful. He cast a curious glance at Avery. "Who's your friend?"

"Ah, this is Avery Thatcher. She's from—"

"Atlanta," Avery interrupted, sticking out her hand. She didn't mind people knowing she worked for the CDC, but she'd hoped to make an official announcement, rather than let the information spread through the base via gossip.

David shook her hand and gave her a kind smile. "Welcome to Antarctica. Be sure to keep an eye on this one here," he said, nodding at Grant. "He's trouble."

"Believe me, I know," she replied dryly.

"I'll let you finish your breakfast," David said, taking a step back from their table.

"Be sure to come see me today," Grant said, taking a sip of his coffee.

"Will do." David left them with a wave, and Avery turned back to face Grant.

"Do you think we should have a town hall type of meeting? Introduce me to the people here, let them know what's going on?"

Grant appeared to consider the suggestion. "That's a good idea. I know people have been worried. They could use some reassurance." He glanced in the direction David had taken, but the man was already long gone.

"How soon can you set it up?"

Grant tilted his head to the side. "A couple of hours."

Avery forked up the last bite of omelet. "Let's do it." She pushed back from the table, anticipation fluttering to life in her belly.

Time to go to work.

Paul sat at the back of the dining hall, arms crossed over his chest as he listened to the base doctor drone on about the outbreak. How it was contained, that they hadn't seen any new cases in three days and there probably wasn't anything to worry about. Little did he know...

He'd infected a few more people yesterday. Not many—just the three he'd shared a drink with at the base bar last night. Just like with the first set of people, he'd bought the last round, a gesture they'd appreciated. He had a reputation as being a friendly guy, so no one had suspected his motives or looked twice at their drinks after he'd carried them back to the table. And while his stomach had cramped a little as he watched the men sip their beers, he knew there was no help for it. His contact had made it clear the lives of his children were at stake, and that was a sacrifice he simply wasn't willing to make.

If the pattern held, the men would start to feel bad tonight, and they'd likely head to the hospital tomorrow. At that point, the good doctor would realize the bug wasn't really gone after all...

The woman sitting at the doctor's table stood up, introduced herself as Avery Thatcher from the CDC. He leaned forward. *That* was interesting. She'd been sent to investigate the cause of the disease and hopefully identify its source. That meant she'd be asking a lot of questions.

His heart started to pound, and blood whooshed through his ears, making it hard to hear what she was saying. How long would it take for his name to come up? For people to remember spending time with him right before they got sick?

He felt suddenly light-headed and leaned forward in his chair, taking a deep breath. The risk of detection had always been there, but he'd assumed the doctor and his staff would be so busy caring for patients they wouldn't have time to figure out where the disease was coming from. But now that the CDC had sent an investigator, it was only a matter of time before his part in the outbreak was discovered.

Although…maybe the three he'd infected last night wouldn't live to talk to the woman or the doctor. It was possible. After all, four out of the first ten people he'd infected had died. It wasn't a stretch to imagine the latest group would suffer the same fate.

A small voice in his head wondered when he had become the type of person who wished for others to die. But he ignored the thought, ruthlessly slamming the door on what remained of his conscience. He didn't have the luxury of morals anymore, not when his children were at stake.

"You must be Paul."

He jumped at the unexpected voice and glanced over to find a man sitting in the previously empty seat next to him. He'd been so distracted by his own thoughts, he hadn't registered the man's presence until he'd spoken. *Thank God I wasn't talking to myself!*

"Ah, can I help you?" Who was this guy? Paul

had definitely never seen him on-base before. And why did he talk as if they'd already been introduced?

"Actually, I think it's more a question of me helping you."

Awareness began to dawn as the man's words sank in. This must be the "help" his contact had said was forthcoming. Paul gave him a quick once-over, taking in his pale skin, light blue eyes and dishwater-blond hair. The man looked like he was on the verge of fading into the background, and Paul experienced a flash of doubt: Had he really never seen this man before, or had his appearance simply not registered?

"What's your name?" He didn't like the fact that a stranger knew how to find him in a crowd. What else did the man know?

"Call me Jesse."

Paul frowned. The way he spoke made it sound like he hadn't really answered the question. Was Jesse his actual name or just a cover he was using while on-base?

"Well, Jesse, what exactly do you think you can do to help me?" No way was Paul going to talk about what he'd done out in the open, especially not with a man he'd just met who might or might not be working for the same organization. Maybe he was being overly paranoid, but it was possible Jesse was actually some kind of mole who was canvassing the crowd, trying to find out what people really knew about the outbreak.

"You're off to a good start here," Jesse said, nodding faintly at Dr. Jones, who was now asking people to cooperate with the disease investigation. "But we need to take things to the next level while there's still time."

Paul glanced around to make sure no one had overheard, but the chairs around them were empty, and the few people seated nearby appeared totally absorbed in what the doctor was saying. "What do you mean?" he said quietly.

"The Organization requires more data," Jesse replied. He faced forward, his expression rapt. Anyone who looked would see a man focused on the presentation in front of him, not someone quietly plotting to expand the outbreak of a devastating new disease.

Paul ground his teeth together, biting off the retort that first sprang to his lips. "I know what they want," he said tightly. "But there are limits to what I can do."

Jesse slid him a glance before returning his gaze to the speakers. "Of course," he said pleasantly. "Which is why I'm here. My role on the base makes me uniquely suited to assist your efforts."

Despite his reservations about the man, Paul was curious to know more. "What do you mean? What do you do here?"

Jesse inclined his head, nodding at the doctor and the woman standing in front of the group. "I'm part of the outbreak response team. I arrived with Dr. Thatcher yesterday to assist in the investigation."

"My God," Paul whispered. He truly was a wolf in sheep's clothing. It was terrifyingly perfect. To have one of the people on the investigation team actively working to thwart their efforts? The consequences were almost too awful to contemplate. The people on-base didn't stand a chance now.

Provided Jesse didn't get caught.

Paul gave him another look, viewing his unremarkable features with a new appreciation. He looked like the last person anyone would suspect, and since he was actually a member of the team tasked with beating the disease? Paul couldn't have asked for a better assistant.

"Is this your first assignment?" It was one thing to look innocent, but if he made a rookie mistake it would jeopardize the whole endeavor.

Jesse nodded once. "Just like you," he said, a subtle note of challenge in his tone.

"I guess we both have something to prove," Paul said easily. He didn't bother explaining that his first assignment would also be his last. Working for the Organization was proving to be more trouble than he'd anticipated, and the sooner he wriggled free of its clutches, the better.

Jesse nodded. "Will there be another group soon, or do I need to step in?"

Paul bristled at the implication he couldn't do his job, but he tamped down the response. He and Jesse were going to have to work closely together, and it wouldn't do to start off on the wrong foot.

"Tomorrow at the latest," he replied. Jesse's eyes widened briefly, and Paul felt a surge of satisfaction at his response. *That's right*, he thought. *I'm not as incompetent as you thought.*

"Very nice," Jesse murmured. "Should we set up additional events?"

Paul shrugged. "Maybe we should wait and see how the next ones play out."

Jesse appeared to consider his suggestion. He nodded. "Very well. I will be in touch." He stood, and

Paul realized the meeting was over. The scrape of chair legs on tile filled the room as people rose to their feet and began to shuffle out. He watched as a clump of people formed around the two doctors at the front of the room, the small crowd doubtless wanting some personal reassurance that they were not in danger.

If they only knew...

Jesse was uniquely placed to help his efforts, a fact that brought him a small measure of relief. With Jesse's help, the success of his mission was practically a foregone conclusion. More important, though, the safety of his children was no longer so precarious. The realization made the tight knot in his chest ease a bit, and his muscles relaxed for the first time in days.

Briefly, he wondered what the Organization had told Jesse. Did his instructions differ or had they told him the same thing? Get more data. Not for the first time, Paul wished his contact had provided clarification. How many more people did he have to infect? When would the Organization be satisfied?

Part of it was out of his hands. His tenure at the base was coming to an end in a few weeks, so time was a limiting factor. Somehow, though, he doubted that would be seen as a legitimate excuse for failure. He wasn't worried yet; given the results thus far, there was no reason to expect he wouldn't be able to get the Organization the information it wanted before he left.

Especially now that he had a partner.

Chapter 5

It took a little time, but Grant eventually made it back to the base hospital. The town hall meeting had gone well, all things considered. A crowd had gathered after his talk, everyone wanting a personal word or needing to ask a question. Their behavior hadn't surprised him—people were naturally worried—but he felt like he'd done a good job of assuaging their fears.

For now, at least.

If the outbreak really was over, tension on the base would ease the longer they went without a new case. But if Avery was right, and the disease was simmering undetected in the population... He shuddered, half afraid to even think of the possibility for fear his attention would make it come true. It was superstitious, he knew, but he didn't like to dwell on such a terrible prospect.

He'd sent Avery back to the hospital ahead of him. She'd been patient while they were swarmed after the meeting, but she'd been so eager to get started interviewing the recovering patients, Grant had practically felt her vibrating as she'd stood next to him. As soon as there had been a break in the crowd, he'd motioned for her to go ahead of him. She'd shot out the door, pausing only to cast a grateful look over her shoulder as another person walked up to bend his ear for a moment.

Now he stood at the nurses' station, ostensibly filling out paperwork. In reality, though, he was sneaking glances at Avery as she sat by a patient's bedside, notepad in her lap and expression attentive.

It was the same look she'd worn when they had studied together in college—one of total absorption, all her attention focused on a single topic. It was a strategy that had served her well in school, and her ability to tune out the world and immerse herself in a subject had also served him well, in their more private moments.

He shifted his weight, feeling suddenly warm. He couldn't afford to indulge in those memories of Avery—she'd made it very clear she only wanted to interact with him on a professional level. If he showed even a hint of remembering the intimacy of their former relationship, she'd probably ignore him for the remainder of her stay on-base.

The problem was, the more time he spent with her, the more attention his physical desires demanded. He wished he could turn off his responses, but his body operated on an instinctive level that was not subject to the control of his mind. Even something as subtle as a whiff of her spicy, orange-scented shampoo was enough to set his heart racing and flood his brain with memories of their time together.

Was it the same for her? Was she having to fend off memories left and right? Or was she unaffected by him and the reminder of the past they shared?

Probably. She had the strongest will of anyone he'd known. Once Avery made up her mind to do something, it was as good as done. And since she'd made no secret of the fact that she wanted to keep their interactions superficial, he doubted she was suffering from the same small physical betrayals he was subject to every time they got within three feet of each other.

Part of him was glad to know he could still *feel*. Part of why he'd taken the job on-base was for the thrill of practicing medicine in such a remote location. Since he hadn't been able to emotionally connect with anyone in years, he'd decided he might as well enjoy an adrenaline rush or two. For a long time, he'd thought he was broken. That the breakup with Avery and the loss of their baby had left him so destroyed he wouldn't ever be able to truly love anyone again. It was a hell of a thing to realize he'd been wrong, especially when he couldn't do anything about it.

But the worst part of all? He had no right to feel that way about her. To remember what they had shared. To think about the future they had planned, and how different his life would be now if only he hadn't been so stupid.

If only…

* * *

"I'm losing the baby."

He blinked, trying to process her words through the haze of fatigue that weighed him down. He'd been in the bathroom all night with a stomach bug and had crashed hard sometime midmorning. He hadn't heard the phone ring, and when he'd woken to throw up again, he'd found her message that she was going to the emergency room. He'd tried to call her back but she hadn't answered. Convinced she must be dying, Grant had stumbled out to his car and raced over to her place, his heart in his throat.

"But you're okay, right?" She looked fine, but he needed to hear her say it, needed her to confirm that, yes, she was perfectly healthy. He'd spent the drive over imagining a set of terrible possibilities, and even though he could see for himself that she looked normal, he wanted her reassurance.

She blinked up at him, her eyebrows drawing together in a frown. "Did you not hear what I just said?" Her voice cracked a little and she sniffed, lifting her hand to knuckle away a tear. He winced, realizing how insensitive his question must have sounded. But truth be told, he cared more about Avery than the baby. In fact, he didn't really think of it as a baby yet—it was still just this abstract idea he was trying to wrap his brain around.

He hadn't told Avery that, of course. He wasn't stupid. But the news she was having a miscarriage didn't elicit much of an emotional response in him. How could it, when he still hadn't come to grips with the fact that he was going to be a father?

Judging by her tearstained face and swollen, red-rimmed eyes, Avery was not nearly so detached.

He searched for something to say, but the past twenty-four hours of illness and lack of sleep made his brain fuzzy. Still, he knew he had to do something. Avery was clearly hurting, and it was his responsibility to make things better. That was his job—to take care of her, to fix the problem.

Normally, he had no problem taking care of things. But right now? He was totally out of his depth.

He sat next to her and tentatively put his hand on her shoulder, unsure if she would welcome his touch. She sat straight for a moment, then let out a shuddering sob and leaned over to press her face into the curve of his neck. Her tears were hot against his skin, and his heart cracked as he listened to her cry as if her world was coming to an end.

"Avery," he murmured, running a hand down her back. "It's going to be okay."

She didn't reply, but he thought he felt her shake her head. "We'll have other babies," he tried, hoping to distract her from the current situation. It was true—they were going to get married, and they'd already talked about their future two-point-five kids and dog and how they would all frolic in the yard framed by a white picket fence. Maybe if he got her to focus on that, she'd realize there was still something for her to look forward to.

"I wanted this baby." Her voice was low, barely above a whisper, but he heard her all the same. Her words hit him like a punch to the gut, and he sucked in a breath. She couldn't be serious; it had to be the pregnancy hormones talking. The timing was all

wrong for them. And even though he would never wish for her to lose the baby, a small part of him was...relieved? No, that wasn't right. But he couldn't deny he felt a little lighter somehow, knowing they now had more time to prepare themselves before becoming parents.

"Avery," he said slowly. How could he make her understand? What could he say to convince her it was going to be okay?

She shook her head again, dismissing his feeble attempts at comfort. A knot formed in his chest as he realized he didn't know what to do to help her. Helplessness and bile swirled in his empty stomach, and he had the sudden urge to be sick again. He had to do something, say something to make things better.

Grant pressed his lips to her hair and took a deep breath. The familiar orange-spice scent of her shampoo calmed his nerves, eased the tightness in his chest. "Everything will be all right," he said softly. There was a small pile of crumpled tissues on the bed, stark white against the dark blue sheets. He stared at the sad little pyramid, absently stroking her back as she cried. "Maybe this is for the best."

She stiffened suddenly against him, and he realized a second too late that he had said the wrong thing. "I mean—" he said quickly, trying to explain. But it was too late.

Avery shoved him away and scooted to the other side of the bed, putting as much distance as possible between them. "What did you just say?" Her voice was lethally quiet and still weighted with tears.

He groped for the right words, feeling them drain

from his mind like sand through a sieve. "We weren't ready for a baby yet. You know that."

She stared at him as if he was a stranger. Emotions swirled in her eyes, but she remained eerily still as she processed his words. Grant shifted on the bed, the silence between them growing thick and heavy. Finally, Avery shook her head.

"Get out."

Fear was a sudden, sharp spike through his heart. He didn't want to leave her alone, not like this. They'd never parted ways in anger before, and he didn't want to start now. "Avery, hear me out—I didn't mean it to sound like that."

She was immune to his plea. "Get out," *she repeated, her tone flat and final.*

Grant sighed, knowing he had lost this battle. Not wanting to upset her further, he stood. "I'll give you some time," *he said.* "But I don't want you to stay angry with me. I'll check in on you later."

"Don't bother."

Worry made the skin on the back of his neck tingle. "I know you're mad at me right now, but we're still partners. I'm not going to abandon you while you're going through this."

Avery shook her head. "No. We're done."

"What?" *Shock made his body lock up, every muscle and joint freezing in place. He stood stiff and unyielding, feeling like he'd just been struck by lightning.* "You can't be serious."

Avery's eyes were cold and empty when she looked at him. "You're not who I thought you were. We're finished."

* * *

"I'm finished."

Grant jumped a little at hearing Avery's voice so close. He glanced over to find her standing at the counter, her expression slightly puzzled as she studied him. "You okay?" she asked. "You look a little pale."

"Ah, I'm fine," he lied. He hadn't thought about their last conversation in a long time, and it was a little unnerving to find the memory of it was still so fresh. He swallowed hard to dislodge the lump of emotion in his throat. "How are things here?"

"Good. I just finished interviewing Rob, and I'm hoping to talk to Marshall next."

He heard her voice but didn't really register what she was saying. Instead Grant found himself staring at her, the memory of her tearstained face superimposing itself on her present appearance. God, he'd been such a jerk! But he hadn't been thinking straight. How could he explain that to her? There had to be some way to make her understand. She'd rejected all his calls in the days after their argument, and his letters had been sent back unopened. But now that she was here, in front of him, surely he could convince her to listen?

But the words didn't come. Once again, he felt helpless, like a man stranded in the middle of nowhere. He could see where he wanted to go, but he couldn't figure out a way to get there.

Maybe he never would.

Frustration rose in his chest. What was wrong with him? By all objective measures, he was an intelligent guy. Why couldn't he find a way to communicate something so important to the woman who'd once been the center of his world?

"Grant?" Avery's soft hand on his arm jerked him out of his head. "Are you sure you're all right?"

"I'm fine." It came out a little harsher than he'd intended, and Avery pulled her hand away as if his skin had scalded her. Grant softened his voice. "Sorry. I was just stuck in my head there for a moment."

She nodded, accepting his explanation. Getting lost in thought was a trait they both shared, and Avery had never given him a hard time about it. She'd always been very understanding, not like the women he'd dated more recently. They always seemed to take it personally when he retreated into his thoughts. But not Avery. She recognized it as part of who he was, and he'd done the same for her.

"Did you get any good information from your interview?" He hadn't bothered to tag along while she talked to Rob. The man was notoriously talkative, and no subject was off-limits. If anything, Grant's presence probably would have distracted Rob into one of his characteristic conversational tangents, making it even harder for Avery to get her questions answered.

A faint smile ghosted across her lips. "I hope so," she replied. "I certainly got a lot of information, and now I just need to comb through it and see if anything stands out."

"I can help you with that," he said, the words popping out of his mouth before he could think twice. Avery eyed him curiously, and Grant kicked himself mentally. He wasn't trained in epidemiology, and she knew it. But it gave him an excuse to be around her, a need that grew stronger with every passing hour. It was almost a compulsion, tugging at his guts and occupying his mind so he couldn't settle, couldn't think of anything else until she was nearby again. Maybe his subconscious was trying to help him out. If they spent enough time together, surely he would find the words to fix things between them?

"I might take you up on that," she said. "In the meantime, I should probably go talk to Marshall."

"I'll come with you," he volunteered. Avery lifted an eyebrow and he rushed to add, "He's kind of shy. He might open up more if I'm there." It was the truth, but it sounded like a lame excuse. Grant felt like he was back in high school, asking a girl out on a date for the first time. *Please don't say no...*

"I appreciate it," Avery said. "I'm going to take a quick bathroom break and grab a cup of coffee. Want one?"

"Sure. Thanks." A little bubble of hope rose in his chest as he watched her walk away. She seemed to be softening toward him, little by little. Would it be enough in the end?

Avery sank onto the bed with a sigh, happy to be off her feet. The winter boots she'd been given in New Zealand were great at keeping her feet warm, but it was going to take some time to get them properly broken in.

Today's interviews had gone well. She'd managed to talk to the three patients who remained in the hospital and hoped to speak to the other three survivors tomorrow. Nothing had jumped out at her yet, but there was a lot of information for her to sift through.

Hopefully, after she'd talked to all the patients, a unique exposure would reveal itself, but she wasn't going to get her hopes up. The relatively small size of the base meant people interacted with each other and the facilities on a regular, ongoing basis. Any kind of exposure would likely be shared by multiple people, and since only a few had fallen ill, it was going to be difficult to determine where, exactly, this bug had come from.

She gently toed her boots off, wincing a little as they slid across developing blisters. Maybe she could get some bandages from Grant in the morning. Her traitorous stomach did a little flip at the thought of him. To her surprise, working with him today had been…nice. She had thought their past would get in the way of effective teamwork, but that hadn't been the case. He seemed just as determined as she was to ignore their shared history, and they had managed to fall into an easy back-and-forth rhythm during the patient interviews. Being around him again felt right, and for the first time in years, she felt complete.

Their breakup had cast a shadow over her life. It was something she'd managed to ignore at first, but over the years, she'd grown to accept the fact that her life would forever be marked by that event. Her relationship with Grant had changed her in so many ways. She knew what true happiness felt like, what it meant to love someone totally and completely. He'd made her feel safe and cherished, and knowing he was beside and behind her had given her the courage to try new things, both academically and personally. Their time together had been some of the best years of her life.

And losing him had very nearly wrecked her.

It wasn't just the fact that her best friend and lover was gone. What had stung the most was finding out his true feelings about the baby.

She'd known he wasn't thrilled at the prospect of being a father. The timing wasn't right for them, but she had figured they would make things work. They were a team, and they could handle life's challenges together.

Looking back, she couldn't really blame him for not being too upset at the news of her miscarriage. After all, she'd been the one carrying the baby. She'd been the one to feel the effects of early pregnancy, to know on a cellular level that things would never be the same again. For Grant, the baby had been an abstract concept—she hadn't even started to show yet, so he could hardly be blamed for feeling a little detached.

No, in the end, it was Grant's relief that had made Avery realize she could no longer be with him. He'd tried to hide it, but she'd seen the way his body relaxed at the news, the tension draining out of him with his breath. And then when he'd tried to tell her that losing the baby was for the best? Her heart had snapped into pieces, the jagged edges making her soul bleed along with her body.

The memory of it brought tears to her eyes, and she blinked them away before they could fall. No matter how much her body liked being around Grant again, she couldn't afford to forget why things had ended between them. He had hurt her before. She wasn't going to give him the chance to do it again.

But what if he's changed? The question popped

into her head without warning, and try as she might, she couldn't ignore the thought. It was possible, she conceded. She certainly wasn't the same person she'd been ten years ago. Was it really fair to expect that Grant hadn't changed, as well?

Mallory had said as much in her email. Avery's best friend had even gone so far as to suggest it might be time for Avery to forgive "the stupid mistake of a dumb kid." Avery knew her friend was right—it was time to let her anger go. But that was easier said than done.

Besides, her forgiveness wouldn't really change anything. Even if by some miracle she was able to overcome the hurts of the past, she and Grant lived very different lives now. She had a stable, steady job in Atlanta. He was working a temporary position at the bottom of the world. Who could say where he was going to go next?

Moving quickly in a feeble attempt to stay warm, Avery shucked off her clothes and donned the sweats she wore as pajamas. Then she dove under the covers with the notes she'd taken from today's interviews. Time to start digging into the information and hopefully get a better idea of where and how these patients had contracted the disease.

She spent a few minutes making lists and organizing points. The work was soothing, and thoughts of Grant and their past fell away as she lost herself in the intellectual puzzle. This was the part of the job she loved most—identifying patterns, picking out the common threads that ran between patients. Sifting through a million seemingly insignificant actions to find the one or two that resulted in a life-changing event for these patients. Most people found it mind-numbingly boring, but there was something about the process she loved. It was logic, pure and simple, immune to any emotion or personal whims.

Time flew by as she read over the interviews. By this time in her career, she'd done enough of them that she had the questions memorized, but she forced herself to read every word. Complacency was the enemy, and if she relaxed her standards, who knew what important detail she might miss?

The men she'd spoken to today were fairly ordinary, except for the fact that they worked on a base in Antarctica. But other than that, there weren't any glaring risk factors to explain why they, out of all the people here, had become sick. They ate pretty standard stuff, although she would still need to further investigate the cafeteria and its food-prep areas. Still, if the contagion was being spread through the chow hall, she would have expected many more cases by now.

The patients all worked on different areas of the base—one of them studied ice core samples, one was doing astronomy work and the third was considered support staff, an employee whose responsibility was to keep the facilities running and in good repair. Since they had such varied jobs, it was unlikely their exposure had occurred while they performed their regular work duties.

How, then, had they encountered the pathogen? Each one of the men had assured her they weren't sexually active. All three of them were married, and while she knew that didn't stop some people, Grant had privately told her he didn't think they were fooling around with anyone on-base. Assuming that was the truth, it meant the bug wasn't spreading via sexual transmission.

At least not yet.

She dove back into her notes, paying special attention to what the men had eaten in the days before falling ill. Patient recall of specific meals was always a bit spotty, but perhaps they had all eaten something that had been contaminated?

She scanned their responses, but nothing jumped out at her. One of the men was a strict vegetarian, while another appeared to be allergic to anything green. Avery sighed and ran a hand through her hair. She'd known this wasn't going to be easy. Hopefully, after she spoke with the other three patients tomorrow, she'd have a better idea of where the pathogen was lurking on-base…

Avery leaned back in her chair, enjoying the stretch and pull of her tired muscles. A quick glance at her watch confirmed it was well past time for her to go to bed. A good night's sleep would give her fresh eyes and make it easier to find the patterns in the data.

She moved to sweep the pages of her notes into a pile, but something caught her eye and she paused. The bar. One of the men had mentioned having a drink at the bar before falling ill…

No, she realized, flipping through the pages. Not just one of the men. All of them had shared a drink on the same night, right before getting sick.

A tingling sensation zinged down her back, and she sucked in a breath. Coincidence? Perhaps. But something told her she was on the right track.

According to their responses, all three men had met for a drink at the base bar approximately twenty-four hours before they experienced the first symptoms of the disease. They'd all had beer and eaten peanuts, but nothing heavier. And according to Rob, the first patient she'd interviewed, there had been a fourth man at their table: Paul Coleson.

Avery frowned at the name, not recognizing it from the list of victims or survivors. Who was Paul Coleson, and why had he remained unaffected by the disease when the three men he'd shared a drink with had not been so lucky?

It wasn't unusual for some people to exhibit immunity to a given pathogen. Thanks to genetics, luck or a combination of the two, some people never contracted an illness, no matter how often they were exposed. Was Paul such an individual? And if so, would he be willing to undergo tests and provide them with samples? If they could study his blood, perhaps they could isolate and identify antibodies or other factors that protected him.

Avery's heart rate picked up at the thought— could they be close to a treatment or even a cure for this scourge? *Not so fast*, she reminded herself. She couldn't afford to let her excitement get the best of her. This was a promising lead, to be sure, but she was a long way from the end of her investigation. Still, she was glad to have a new direction to explore.

I have to tell Grant. The thought popped into her head like it was the most natural thing in the world, and with it came a pang of longing. Once upon a time, talking to Grant had been as easy as breathing. He'd been her best friend, her confidant, sometimes even the voice of reason when she wanted to do something crazy. It had taken her years to get out of the habit of thinking of him whenever something exciting happened in her life—it was only natural that seeing him would remind her of that closeness.

Avery pushed aside the nagging sense of nostalgia along with her notes, and instead focused on the growing list of things she needed to tackle tomorrow. Finish the interviews, track down Paul Coleson, check in with the lab tech and see if she had made any progress with the patient samples... She reached over to flip off the light sitting on the bedside table, but before she could reach the lamp there was a soft knock on her door.

The unexpected sound made her freeze, her hand still outstretched. Was she hearing things? The knock sounded again, a little louder this time. No, there was definitely someone at the door.

She climbed out of bed, frowning slightly. It was late—who would want to talk to her now? Maybe it was the lab tech, Jennifer. She'd been working hard all day, and perhaps she had made some progress she wanted to discuss.

Avery opened the door and her greeting died on her lips. It wasn't Jennifer who stood on the threshold. It was Grant.

He wore a long-sleeved black shirt that clung to him like a second skin, outlining his broad shoulders and muscled arms to perfection. Thin cotton pants rode low on his hips and skimmed his thighs, leaving very little to the imagination. The years had been kind to him, and she felt her cheeks warm as her gaze drifted over his body.

"Hey," he said quietly. If he noticed her blatant perusal of his muscles, he didn't show it. "I just wanted to stop by and make sure you had settled in okay. I meant to check on you yesterday, but I didn't get a chance."

"Um." Her brain screamed at her to respond, but her tongue felt too big for her mouth. Why did he have to look so damn good? He wasn't even trying!

He lifted an eyebrow and tilted his head to the side. "Avery?"

"Yeah." She shook her head. "Yes. I'm fine." She sucked in a breath and was treated to the scent of warm male skin and clean sweat. "Did you just work out?" It was a ridiculous question, but at least she was stringing words together in a coherent manner again.

He nodded. "Remind me to show you where the gym is tomorrow. It's actually in this building." He shifted a bit, and Avery's gaze caught on the play of his muscles under the fabric of his shirt.

"Sounds good." She crossed her arms over her chest, grateful the thick material of her sweatshirt hid her body's reaction to seeing Grant like this.

"So…" His voice trailed off and Avery indulged in a brief, highly inappropriate fantasy. *Why, yes, I'd love for you to come inside. I agree, it is hot in here. I think we're both wearing too many clothes…*

"Do you need anything?" She tuned back in, and his question nearly made her groan. *It's been too long*, she thought. The fact that she was fantasizing about Grant only proved it was well past time to end her current dry spell. As soon as she got back to Atlanta, she was going to make time to date again.

"I'm okay." Her brain came back online and she straightened. "Actually, I have something to tell you."

"Oh?"

She nodded. "Why don't you step inside for a minute? I'll show you my notes." No sense in having this conversation in the hall.

Grant walked in and she turned to grab the files still on her bed. She riffled through the pages until she came to the section she wanted him to see. "I think I may have a lead." She turned and handed the notes to Grant, pointing out the patients' responses to her questions. "It seems the three men I interviewed today all remember sharing a drink with a man named Paul Coleson right before they got sick. I checked the names of the other patients, and Paul never got sick. He might be naturally immune, which means we're that much closer to finding a treatment or even a cure for this thing!"

Grant studied the pages for a second, nodding slowly as he read. Avery suddenly realized how much smaller the room felt with him in it. Warmer, too.

She shifted her weight from one foot to the other. Maybe she should have waited to discuss this with him tomorrow, when he was wearing something a little less distracting. From this angle, she could see the curve of his buttocks outlined by the thin pants. Her fingers itched to pinch him, the way she had done back when they were dating. *Stop it*, she chided herself silently. She placed a hand on her stomach, hoping to quell its distracting fluttering. She and Grant had a job to do, and she couldn't allow her hormones to hijack her focus.

Even though he smelled even better now that he was standing so close.

"Do you think the men were infected at the bar?" He glanced up at her now, his hazel eyes intent.

She lifted one shoulder in a shrug. "I'm not sure yet—it's too early to say. But I definitely want to check it out, perhaps take some samples for analysis."

He nodded thoughtfully. "I doubt they're still serving the same batch of beer, but it's worth looking into."

"Do you know Paul Coleson?"

Grant shook his head. "I can find him, though. Do you want to talk to him tomorrow, or wait until after you've interviewed the remaining three patients?"

Avery considered the question for a moment. If she talked to the other men first, she could discover if they, too, had shared drinks with him before falling ill. It would be even more compelling evidence that Paul was immunologically special. And really, would it hurt to wait? There weren't any active cases on the base right now, so the need to develop a potential treatment wasn't vital. Perhaps it was best to wait, to really build her case before approaching him in the hopes she could ensure his cooperation with a deluge of facts.

"I think I'll wait," she said, nodding to herself as she confirmed her decision. "Talking to the other patients will give me a more complete understanding of the situation, and that will help me identify what questions to ask when I do meet with him."

"It's your show," Grant said, offering her a small smile that made her stomach flip. She stared up at him, feeling the pull of his gaze like a physical hand on her shoulder, drawing her closer to him.

"Thanks," she said softly. Her lips felt dry, so she darted her tongue out to moisten them. Grant's eyes dipped down to follow the gesture, and his chest expanded as he drew in a breath.

Standing this close, she could see a flash of heat in the depths of his eyes. Avery felt an answering warmth start low in her belly, a small coal of need that burned brightly and began to expand the longer Grant watched her.

Her awareness of Grant felt simultaneously familiar and foreign, a strange combination that piqued her curiosity and made her want to get closer. How would he respond if she placed her hand on his chest and pressed her mouth to his? She knew what the boy would have done. How would the man react?

She never got the chance to find out. Quicker than thought, Grant dropped his head and kissed her, his lips warm and firm against her own.

Avery inhaled deeply, the heady, potent scent of Grant's skin making her head spin. She sank into the comfort of his kiss, her body celebrating the *rightness* of this moment, this connection. The bad taste of her memories faded as she teased Grant's tongue with her own, stoking his response as her own desire built.

A low, rough sound rumbled from his throat, and he threaded his arms around her, pulling her forward until her body was flush against his chest. Her curves flattened against the long, hard planes of his body, the increased contact between them making her already sensitive skin tingle with a pleasurable ache.

She needed to touch him, needed to feel the heat of his body with her own hands. She scrabbled blindly for the hem of his shirt and yanked it up, then slid her palms along the muscles of his back. He hummed in appreciation as she raked her nails lightly across his skin. Her answering smile was pure feminine satisfaction, and she didn't bother to try to contain it.

Grant's hands roamed across her body, caressing and squeezing and teasing in equal measure. He slipped one hand under the waistband of her sweatpants to cup her bottom, his palm a warm weight against the curve. He pressed, and Avery rose to her tiptoes, moving her hands from his back to thread them through his hair. It was how they had always kissed—Grant anchoring her against his body, her hands gripping the back of his neck in a silent acknowledgment of their shared need. For a split second, Avery lost all sense of time, and the years melted away, taking her back to the days when their relationship was solid and uncomplicated, a foundation she'd planned to build her life on.

She wasn't sure how long they stood there, entwined and lost in the feel of each other. It just felt so *good* to be in his arms again, and a growing part of her wanted to stay there forever. Grant seemed happy to agree. His kisses had lost the frantic edge of need and had shifted into an almost lazy sampling, as if he was settling in for a long getting-to-know-you-again session.

Languor stole across Avery's body, making her bones feel liquid. The edges of her body seemed to soften and blur, molding to Grant's frame. The familiar reaction nearly made her cry—he was the only man who'd had this effect on her, and her inability to find such a connection again had left her feeling broken. Now she knew for sure her body hadn't failed her. Rather, her heart simply needed Grant to be complete.

He leaned back and stiffened in her arms, then cursed under his breath. "Oh, God, I'm sorry."

Avery frowned, his reaction unexpected. "What's wrong?"

Grant raised his hand to her face and used his thumb to swipe across her cheek. A cool trail followed the gesture, and Avery realized with a sudden jolt that she *was* crying.

"Avery…" He trailed off, guilt and remorse stealing over his features. "I'm so sorry. I never meant to hurt you. Again," he added softly.

She dashed away the tears and shook her head. "No," she said, wanting to reassure him but not knowing what to say. "I'm fine." He eyed her skeptically, so she gave him a small smile. "Really, Grant. I'm okay."

"You're crying." This was said in a tone that made it clear he considered her tears to be a sign of distress. And normally, they would be. But how could she explain the rush of joy that had filled her when she'd realized she was capable of feeling again? Should she even try?

In the end, she settled for a white lie. "I don't know why I started crying. To tell you the truth, seeing you again has made me a little emotional. I guess I'm still trying to work through that."

He nodded, his gaze serious. "I know what you mean." He dipped his head, then glanced back up at her. "I feel the same way," he said, sounding a little shy.

"Sounds like we both have some things to think about." And now that he was no longer kissing her, the voice of doubt in her head was back and screaming for attention. Was she crazy, latching on to him again without any thought for the potential consequences? There was no happy ending for her here, and she'd do well to remember it.

"At some point, we need to talk."

No. The denial was instant and final, a shield thrown up to protect her heart. She did not want to discuss the circumstances of their break-up. It had taken her a long time to move on, and nothing could be gained by looking back. Avery had made her peace with her losses—best to leave the ghosts alone.

But she could tell by the determined glint in his eyes that Grant was resolved to have the conversation. Knowing she wasn't going to be able to convince him otherwise, she decided her best defense was evasion. "Can we do it later? It's pretty late, and I know we both need to rest."

He studied her for a moment, and she had the distinct sensation he could see through her words. For a second, she thought he was going to challenge the excuse, but then he nodded thoughtfully. "You're right. Big day tomorrow. For both of us."

He stepped back and reached for the handle of the door. "Get some sleep," he said gently. "I'll find you in the morning." It was part farewell, part promise, and Avery's traitorous heart skipped a beat at the thought of seeing him again in a few short hours.

She nodded. "Sounds good."

Grant gave her a final, enigmatic smile and closed the door softly behind him. Avery sank onto the thin mattress of the bed, her breath escaping in one long gust. There was no point in denying it any longer—Grant still held sway over her, body and mind. It was a complication she didn't need or welcome, but there was no way she could ignore the effect he had on her.

More important, though, she had to find a way to distract him, to keep him from starting that talk he'd suggested they have. Her libido offered up several propositions in that department, but she ignored the possibility of getting physical with him. If she slept with Grant, it would only further complicate matters. She was just going to have to keep him at arm's length while she was here—it was the only way to protect her heart.

Richard rubbed his eyes, hoping to ease the ache in his temples. His head had been pounding all afternoon but he hadn't been able to take a break. There was too much work to be done. As one of the maintenance workers on-base, he had to make sure the infrastructure was sound and able to withstand the rigors of an Antarctic winter. And since bad weather was only about six weeks away, his to-do list grew longer by the day.

He took a sip of coffee and winced as the hot liquid slid across the sensitive tissues of his throat. It was another annoying development in his day, likely because he'd spent most of his time outside, checking the anchor points of the rooftop satellite dishes across the base. The air was warm compared to what it would be like in a few weeks, but there was still a definite chill that settled over him and clung to his body like a second skin. Even though he'd been inside for the better part of an hour, he still felt cold— hence the coffee.

He shuffled down the aisles of the small general store on the base, searching for a bottle of aspirin. Just a couple of pills and a good night's sleep and he'd be right as rain again.

"Hey, Rich. How's it going?"

He plucked a bottle from the shelf and turned to find Cindy Dalton approaching with a friendly smile. She was one of the scientists doing astronomy research, and he'd recently helped repair one of the sensors her group used in their work. It hadn't been a terribly difficult job, but his efforts had apparently rescued several weeks' worth of data, and the team had been so grateful they'd promised to name a star after him. It was one of those moments that made the daily slog worth it and reminded him why he chose to work at the bottom of the world.

Richard smiled back, genuinely pleased to see her despite his headache. "I'm doing all right, thanks. How are you?"

Cindy stopped midstride, her eyes widening as she heard his voice. "You don't sound so good," she said, her tone full of concern. "Are you sure you're okay?"

He nodded. "Just a cold," he assured her. Talking made his throat itch, but he fought the urge to cough, knowing it would only make him sound worse.

Cindy didn't seem convinced. She eyed him cautiously, clearly reluctant to come any closer. "Maybe you should go get checked out." She eyed the bottle of aspirin in his hand. "Dr. Jones did ask everyone to stop by if they felt sick at all."

It was true, but Richard was reluctant to go to the base hospital. Even though he knew this was just a normal cold, there was a small, scared part of him that wondered if the mystery disease was back.

I'm fine, he told himself firmly. *It's just a regular case of the base crud.* He got one every year about this time—it was truly nothing to worry about.

He lifted the bottle and shook it gently, causing the pills inside to rattle. "I think I'll give this a try tonight," he said. "If I still feel bad in the morning, I'll head to the hospital." The tickle in his throat grew worse and he gave in to the urge to cough, emitting a thick, wet sound that seemed to come from the depths of his lungs. He shook his head, fist pressed against his mouth as he swallowed a gobbet of phlegm. Maybe he should pick up a decongestant, too…

Cindy took a step back, her hand lifted as if to ward off any germs. "I hope you feel better soon," she said, practically tripping over her own feet in her haste to get away from him.

Richard sighed, feeling self-conscious. He really couldn't blame Cindy for her concern, given the recent events on the base. He should probably get to his room quickly so he didn't cause anyone else undue alarm.

He paid for the medication, somehow managing to hold back a cough as he handed over a few bills. The urge was growing stronger, though, his throat demanding the temporary relief it would bring. He grabbed his change and raced outside, succumbing to a fit of coughing that left him feeling light-headed. When it was over, he leaned to the side and spat, clearing his mouth of the slime he'd produced. It left a foul, metallic taste in his mouth, and he took another gulp of coffee in an attempt to wash it away.

He took a step, but his head was spinning so badly he almost fell to the ground. Seeing no other alternative, he leaned against the wall of the building, ignoring the chill seeping through his coat. It took several minutes to recover, but he finally regained enough of his equilibrium to start the trek back to his quarters. His body ached from the cold and the day's physical labors, and he felt as though his shoes were lined with lead. The bottle of aspirin in his pocket jangled with every step, promising relief as soon as he made it inside.

Finally, after what seemed like an endless journey, he opened the door to his quarters and stepped inside. It was a few more steps to the kitchenette, and he poured himself a glass of water. His hands shook as he opened the pill bottle, and he dropped several tablets on the floor as he fished out a few. No matter. He could pick them up tomorrow.

The bitter taste of the pills barely registered as he washed them down with a gulp of water. Then he stumbled over to the bed, not even bothering to take off his shoes before he pulled the blankets over himself.

Tomorrow, he promised, shivering slightly as he waited for the bed to absorb his body heat and warm up. *I'll feel better tomorrow.*

Chapter 6

Grant smothered a yawn and took another sip of coffee. It was the only thing keeping him going this morning, as he hadn't slept much the night before.

It was his own fault, really. What had he expected after kissing Avery?

More important, what had he been thinking?

He'd meant to take a little more time, for them to get to know each other again before trying to make a physical connection with her. But she'd looked so damn appealing standing there in her sweats, her hair pulled back in a messy ponytail and her makeup smudged from the long day. Seeing her look so un-polished and *real* had hit him right in the gut and ignited a need that had burned through his self-control.

Even so, the relative public nature of the hallway had been enough to hold him in check. But then she'd invited him inside her room, where there were no prying eyes…

He knew she hadn't asked him in to seduce him. And truth be told, he had found her discovery interesting. It hadn't taken her long to find a possible break in the case, which was further proof of Avery's intelligence. It wasn't a surprise, of course. He'd always known how smart she was, and seeing her in action now made him feel proud of her all over again. She was a truly remarkable woman, and he'd been lucky enough to be a part of her life.

Once.

He might have been lucky a second time, but his amateur, fumbling attempt had likely cost him any chance he might have had with Avery. She'd kissed him back, at least initially, and her body's response had made his heart soar and given him hope that she still had feelings for him. But then he'd tasted her tears, and the unexpected dash of salt on his tongue had made him realize the magnitude of his mistake. Avery might enjoy kissing him, but her heart wasn't in it.

As he'd lain awake in bed last night, staring up at the ceiling, he'd been tempted to suggest they enter into a no-strings-attached affair. They'd been good together in college—things would likely be even better between them now, if the kiss had been any indication. But almost as soon as he'd had the thought, he rejected it. He wanted Avery so much it made his hands ache to touch her. But he wanted all of her, not just her body. He was willing to offer her his heart and soul again. If she couldn't do the same, he'd rather live without any part of her.

He reached for a stack of patient charts, wanting to check on the three men still in the hospital before Avery got started on her interviews. He'd promised to accompany her, and even though that had been before the kiss, he still meant to be there while she talked to the last three surviving men. Hopefully, she would be willing to overlook his mistake so they could continue to work together. And as soon as time allowed, they could sit down and clear the air. Even though she hadn't said anything, he could feel the weight of their past hanging over his head. It was time to put things right between them.

It didn't take long to complete his rounds. The three men were the only ones staying in the hospital, and fortunately, they were growing stronger by the day. They were also growing impatient to leave, which was another good sign. He promised to spring them all tomorrow, provided the results of a final blood panel were within normal limits. He left them grumbling about the offerings of daytime television and headed to the staff break room to meet Avery.

His heart drummed hard in his chest as he approached the doorway. How was she this morning? What should he say about last night? Should he apologize again, or pretend nothing had happened? Maybe it was best to let her take the lead—the last thing he wanted was to cause her any more distress. Her tears had always twisted him up inside, and he hated to be the reason she cried.

He paused in the hall and took a deep breath. *Just be cool*, he told himself. If only he knew what that meant!

He stepped inside and found Avery standing at

the counter at the far end of the room, her back to him as she poured herself a cup of coffee. "Hello," she said, not turning around.

"Morning. How'd you know it was me?"

The spoon chimed against the porcelain of her cup as she stirred in cream and sugar. With a final tap on the rim of the mug, she placed the spoon in the sink and turned to face him. "I smelled you," she said simply.

He flushed, feeling suddenly self-conscious. "Do I stink or something?" He sniffed discreetly at his shirt—he'd showered and put on a fresh-ish pair of scrubs this morning, but maybe he wasn't as clean as he thought.

She smiled, clearly amused at his discomfort. "No. But you've used the same body wash and detergent for years. I could wear a blindfold and still be able to pick you out of a lineup."

"Well…" He trailed off, at a loss for how to respond. Part of him was thrilled that she had noticed such a personal detail; surely she wouldn't have commented on it if she was still upset with him for last night? But he didn't want to say the wrong thing and spoil the moment. "Uh, no sense in changing something that works," he said with a shrug.

"Where are we meeting for our first interview?" She took a sip of her coffee and leaned back against the counter.

"I thought we could talk to him in here," Grant replied. He nodded at the table. "There's room for the three of us to sit comfortably, and you have plenty of room to spread your stuff out and take notes."

Avery nodded. "Excellent." She bent to pick up her

tote bag and set it on the table along with her coffee. Grant watched with a growing sense of amusement as she pulled out her notebook, several pens and a small recorder, and arranged them all just so on the table.

When she was done, she glanced up and caught him staring. Her cheeks went pink and she looked away. "What?" she said, sounding adorably defensive.

"Nothing," he said, not bothering to hide his smile. "All set?"

She nodded. "I'm ready. Are you going to bring him in?"

"Yeah." Grant checked his watch. "He should be here any minute. I'll go grab him." He stepped back into the hall and headed for the entrance, hoping to snag Dave, their first interview of the day, as he walked in. Sure enough, the door opened as he approached, but it wasn't Dave who entered. Instead a man stumbled inside, nearly falling as he crossed the threshold.

Grant reached for him instinctively, grabbing his arms to keep him upright. The man turned his head to the side and let loose a torrent of coughing, and the deep, wet sound made Grant's guts turn to water. He'd heard that same cough before.

The disease was back.

Avery took a sip of coffee and flipped to a clean page in her notebook, ready to jot down anything that struck her as important during the interview. She recorded the responses to make sure she didn't miss anything, but taking notes helped keep her focused.

Anticipation made her stomach flutter, overcoming the brief spurt of awkwardness she'd felt at seeing Grant. She'd spent most of the night thinking about his kiss and imagining the million different ways things might have progressed if she hadn't started crying.

But in the end, it didn't matter. "What might have been" was nothing more than a pointless thought exercise that caused her to lose sleep, and given the situation on-base, she needed her rest. The lull in cases of the mystery disease was too good to be true, and experience had taught her it probably wouldn't last. Virulent pathogens didn't just suddenly disappear— whatever was the cause of this ailment was probably lurking in the base population, and it was only a matter of time before a new case emerged.

Which made talking to the survivors all the more crucial. If the first group of patients had all visited the bar in the days prior to falling ill, she could start to narrow the focus of her investigation and hopefully hone in on the source of this bug. She needed to find where it came from and where it was hiding so she could protect the other people on-base.

Avery made a mental note to stop by the lab after the first interview. Jennifer, the lab technician, had been working with blood and tissue samples, and Avery wanted an update on her progress. Was she getting any closer to identifying the pathogen? Even knowing something as simple as whether they were dealing with a virus or a bacterial organism would help her channel her energies in a more productive way.

She took another sip of coffee, hoping the caffeine would kick in soon. It was shaping up to be another long day—

A shout rang out and she jumped, spilling coffee over the rim of the cup and onto her fingers. She shook off the hot droplets and rose to her feet, glancing cautiously behind her. Footsteps pounded as someone—or someones, she realized—raced past the door. Something was going on, and given the response, it couldn't be good.

She poked her head out into the hall to find a cluster of nurses standing in the entryway of the hospital, all focused on the floor. Someone was clearly in need of attention, but who? Was it Grant? Her heart lurched at the thought, and she started walking toward the commotion before her brain had a chance to catalog all the reasons why he was probably fine.

As she approached, she heard his voice, urgent and low, rise above the scrum. Relief washed over her, but it was short-lived. He glanced up as she neared the group, and the look on his face made her stop dead in her tracks.

"Stay back," he warned. His mouth was set in a grim line and the worry in his eyes was plain even from a distance.

Only one thing could trigger such a reaction from Grant. Avery craned her neck to see through the crush of bodies and caught glimpses of a man being loaded onto a gurney. He moaned as they lifted him, and his body shuddered as he coughed over and over again in a racking spasm that sounded incredibly painful. Something fluttered to the floor, and she spied what appeared to be a bloody tissue, apparently dropped by the man as the staff arranged his body on the bed.

She glanced back at Grant, who read the question in her eyes. He nodded, and the bottom dropped out of her stomach.

The reprieve was over.

Her first thought was to rush over and try to talk to the man while she still could. Given the fatality rate of this disease, it was entirely possible he might not survive. If she were to have any hope of figuring out how he might have been exposed, she needed to speak with him now, before he could no longer talk. She took a step forward, determination making her heedless to the danger. But before she could get much closer, Grant held up his hand and scowled at her.

"Don't come over here." His tone brooked no argument and her body obeyed before she could think twice.

"I need to talk to him," she insisted.

He nodded, resignation entering his eyes. "I know. But I want you suited up before you get anywhere near him."

It was the right thing to do, even if it did cost her time. Not knowing what to expect, Avery had brought along several biocontainment suits to use to protect herself and her staff from contracting the disease. The bulky plastic armor was cumbersome and hot, but it made it safe for her to handle specimens, interact with patients or work with the disease agent. Jennifer had been wearing hers from the beginning to protect herself as she tried to isolate the pathogen. Avery hadn't bothered to put hers on, since she hadn't been around any acutely ill patients.

Until now.

The realization that she might have already been exposed made her stomach cramp, and a growing sense of panic gripped her heart, urging her to run, go now, put on the suit, protect herself. She fought to control her breathing, knowing the fear would only make her sloppy. She hadn't come close to the man— the likelihood she had been exposed was small.

But Grant couldn't say the same.

Her dawning horror must have shown on her face, because he smiled sadly and nodded as the nurses wheeled the patient away. "Go put your suit on," he said quietly.

"But what about you?" A painful lump formed in her throat and she swallowed hard in a vain attempt to dislodge it. The man had been coughing violently and Grant had been right there by his face trying to help. Had his altruistic instincts doomed him to a terrible fate?

"I'll be all right," he said, a little gruffly. "I've treated this thing before without the special getup. This will be no different." But she saw the flash of fear in his eyes and knew he was worried about his own exposure.

"We brought extra suits," she said. "I want you to wear one."

He nodded. "Lay it out for me and I'll get it in a bit. I have to stabilize him first." He nodded in the direction the patient had gone, and a weight formed in Avery's stomach as she realized he meant to examine the man wearing nothing more than a pair of gloves and a white coat.

"But, Grant—"

He cut off her protest with a raised hand. "I've got to help him," he said, his tone brooking no argument.

She bit her bottom lip and nodded, knowing she wouldn't be able to change his mind. Grant was a physician, a healer by nature and training. His patients came first, and no amount of arguing on her part was going to sway him.

"At least wear a mask?"

"Of course," he assured her. Then he was off, striding down the hall after the man, already calling out orders to his team.

Avery stood rooted to the spot, still trying to process everything that had just happened. Her professional curiosity demanded she run to the equipment crate she'd brought and don the protective blue suit that would keep her safe. But her concern for Grant overrode the urgency she'd felt moments before. Would he be all right? Had the pathogen already jumped to his body, or could he still protect himself? Anger flared in her chest as she thought about the risks he was taking even now as he worked over the man. She heard the dim sound of his voice as he spoke to his team and pictured him leaning over the patient, checking vitals and completing the physical exam.

"Why do you have to be the damn hero?" she muttered. It would serve him right if she were to drag him away from the man's side and insist he put on the protective suit. But did it really matter now?

Avery turned with a sigh and headed in the direction of the crates she'd brought. She couldn't spend any more time worrying about Grant—only time would tell if he had escaped the bug. She comforted herself with the knowledge that he hadn't gotten sick yet. That, coupled with the fact that there had only been ten cases during the first outbreak, made her suspect the disease was not highly contagious. At least she hoped not.

Still, she couldn't shake the image of the man coughing with Grant standing right next to him, taking the brunt of it. Had he faced that kind of exposure while treating the first set of patients? Would today be the day his luck finally ran out?

Stop it, she told herself firmly as she opened the crate containing the protective equipment. *He's going to be fine.*

He had to be. There was too much unfinished business between them.

Chapter 7

Grant stared down at the patient on the gurney, a growing sense of resignation filling him as he realized the man was likely too far gone to save. It was just like before, when the first patient had come back to the hospital, coughing up blood. As if to punctuate his thoughts, the man emitted a deep, wet hack, and small beads of red appeared on his lips.

Grant adjusted his mask, hoping the flimsy fabric barrier would provide enough protection to see him through this. He glanced up at the nurse standing opposite him and noted the sheen of fear in her eyes.

"It's going to be okay." He tried to sound reassuring, but based on her jerky nod of response, he'd missed the mark.

He opened his mouth to try again, but the man moaned, cutting him off before he could speak.

"Hurts…"

"I know, buddy," Grant said. "Can you tell me where?" The man's ID badge lay flat on his chest, and Grant glanced at the name. "Talk to me, Richard." He needed to keep the man conscious if Avery was to have any hope of talking to him.

Richard stirred at the sound of his name, but his eyelids slowly drifted closed again. Grant checked over his shoulder, but there was no sign of Avery. He turned back to his patient, his mind made up. He'd start questioning the man himself—better to get some information than none at all.

"Richard, I need you to focus for me."

The man's eyes blinked open again, glassy with fever.

"How long have you been sick?"

He appeared to consider the question. Then he let out a sigh. "Started yesterday morning," he rasped out.

His response made Grant's heart seize. The first patients had initially presented with a mild illness and had taken days to decline to the point of Richard's symptoms. Either Richard had misunderstood his question or the disease was growing more virulent.

"Are you sure?" He hated to waste the man's waning energy on a repetitious question, but this was important.

Richard's eyebrows drew together. "Got a sore throat yesterday. Thought it was from working outside." He paused, gasped in a breath with a worrisome rattle. "Cough started last night."

Grant frowned. The man sounded lucid enough. "Did you do anything unusual the past few days? Eat

anything different, go to a new part of the base?"
He was grasping at straws, but maybe—*maybe*—
Richard would remember something that could help
Avery.

The man shook his head weakly. "No. Went to work.
Beers with the guys. Normal stuff," he wheezed.

Grant's attention snagged on the word *beers*. "Did
you drink at the bar?"

Richard blinked at him as if he were stupid. Then
he nodded once, apparently deciding not to waste energy replying to such an obvious question.

"When?" Grant leaned forward, not wanting to
miss his response.

Richard frowned again, clearly thinking. He closed
his eyes, and he was silent for so long Grant feared
the man had drifted into unconsciousness.

"Richard?" he prodded.

"Day before yesterday," his patient mumbled.

My God, Grant thought. The disease progression
was accelerating, and at an alarming rate. Still, he
couldn't dwell on that unsettling fact. There was
more he needed to know.

"Who were you with?" Were there other people
who had been exposed at the same time? Were there
other patients lying sick in their beds, too weak to
make it to the hospital?

"Tom. Bradley. Paul." Richard winced with each
name, the effort of talking clearly costing him dearly.

"Paul Coleson?" Avery came into view, her movements a little cumbersome in the thick blue plastic
suit she wore. Grant felt a flash of relief at her appearance. Now that she was here, he no longer had

to worry about wasting time by asking the wrong questions.

Richard's eyes flared wide as he caught sight of Avery, and he pushed at the mattress with his feet, trying to scoot away. Grant placed his hands on the man's shoulders to calm him.

"You're okay," he said softly. He couldn't blame Richard for his reaction—the lights turned Avery's face shield into a glaring pane, making it nearly impossible to see her face. Grant could only imagine how Richard's fevered brain had interpreted the unexpected sight of her lumbering form.

Richard stilled under his hands, but his pulse continued to beat wildly in his neck, betraying his fear.

Avery tried again, softening her voice. "Is the Paul you mentioned Paul Coleson?"

It was one hell of a leading question, but given the speed of Richard's decline, it was probably best to get directly to the point. Despite the nasal cannula delivering oxygen to his system, his saturation level was dropping fast. He'd probably pass out in the next few minutes, and Grant couldn't help thinking that was for the best.

"Yes." Richard's voice was fainter now as his grip on consciousness slipped. Avery made a small sound of frustration and Grant could tell she wanted to ask another question. He held up his hand to stop her, knowing Richard wouldn't be able to answer her.

"Thanks, Richard," he said, pitching his voice low. "You've been a huge help. Just rest now."

The man let out an unintelligible mumble and gave up the fight to stay awake, his body going limp on the gurney. Grant gave a few additional orders to the nursing staff and led Avery a few steps away so they could converse in relative privacy.

"Were you able to talk to him before I showed up?" There was hope in her voice, and he caught a glimpse of her face through the glare on her face shield. The look in her eyes was pure determination, as if she could beat this disease single-handedly if given half a chance. It made him feel better to see her fighting spirit, and once again, he found himself in awe of her.

"I got him to answer a few questions, but I don't think you're going to like his responses." Grant frowned, reality slamming back down on him as he recalled Richard's words. "He said he started feeling bad yesterday, and he'd shared drinks with his friends the night before that."

Avery grasped the issue immediately. "The course of the illness seems to be speeding up."

"Exactly." He glanced around to make sure no one had overheard them. The last thing he wanted was for this information to spread to the wider world. If the rest of the base were to find out, it would incite panic among the population. And while he didn't intend to withhold important information, Grant wanted a chance to verify the facts before issuing another warning that was sure to have a dramatic effect.

"Do you think it's true? Or do you think he's lost sense of time?" She glanced back at the prone figure, now being attended to by the nursing staff as they administered the medications Grant had ordered.

"I doubted that myself," he admitted. "But I asked him twice. He sounded pretty sure."

Avery made a thoughtful noise that he barely

heard over the whir of her portable air tank, which worked to both keep her suit inflated and provide her with oxygen to breathe. "Let's assume he's right, and that he was infected the day before yesterday. Either the pathogen has mutated to become more virulent, or perhaps he was infected with a higher initial dose. If more of the bug entered his body to begin with, it wouldn't take as long for this kind of damage to result."

Grant nodded, appreciating her logic. "How can we determine which scenario applies here?"

She frowned. "We can't. At least not yet. Jennifer is still working to isolate the causative agent. Once she does, we can sequence its DNA and compare it to samples isolated from the patients—that will tell us if there's been a mutation. In the meantime, there's no way to know for sure."

Fear trailed a cold finger down the hollow of Grant's spine and he shuddered. *Please, don't let this thing get out of control.* But he was afraid it was already too late.

"Are you going to interview Paul Coleson?"

Avery nodded. "He's my next stop. I have my fingers crossed he's the key to stopping this disease in its tracks."

"I hope so, too. I'll ask one of the nurses to log in to the system and find his job location for you."

"Thanks." The look on her face softened and her hand twitched, almost as if she wanted to touch him. "Are you going to stay here?"

Grant shook his head. "I have to try to find the other men Richard mentioned. The ones he shared a drink with before getting sick. It's possible they're ill as well and haven't made it in yet."

"Good idea. I pulled out a suit for you—if you help me get out of mine, I'll help you put on yours."

He smiled at her offer and almost made a joke of it, but decided now was not the time. "I appreciate it, but I think it's best if I don't wear it outside the hospital."

Avery opened her mouth to protest, so he held up a hand to forestall her response. "Can you imagine the reaction if people saw me wandering around in one of those? It's not exactly a subtle look, and I don't want to incite a panic on the base."

"Grant, you can't go out there unprotected. If you do find the men and they are sick, you'll need the proper equipment."

"I'll bring masks, gloves and disposable gowns. It'll be fine."

She frowned at him, her displeasure clear even through the thick, plastic suit. "You're playing awfully fast and loose with your safety. Why is that?"

A flash of irritation welled in his chest at her question. He didn't enjoy taking risks. But he was more worried about the bigger picture, which was the overall safety of the people on-base. If panic and paranoia were to set in, it would have disastrous consequences for everyone.

"The basics have served me well so far," he said, a little coolly. "I have no reason to think they will fail me now." *Besides*, he added silently, *if I'm already infected, all the biohazard suits in the world aren't going to help me.*

Avery looked as though she wanted to argue, but

she remained silent. After a tense moment, she nodded. "So be it. I'm going to go track down Paul Coleson. Good luck finding the other men. Is there some way we can stay in touch?"

"There's a set of walkie-talkies on a charger in the supply closet. Grab one on your way out the door. Set it to channel six."

"Will do." She turned and started to lumber down the hall but stopped a few feet away. "Grant?"

He glanced up, surprised to see a concerned expression on her face. "Yes?"

"Please be careful."

He nodded, touched at her words. "You, too." Just like that, his earlier irritation with her went up in smoke and in its place sprouted a reluctance to part company with her. Even though it had only been a few days, he'd gotten used to Avery's constant presence once again.

She held his gaze for a moment, then gave him a small smile. "Channel six."

"Channel six," he confirmed.

He took a moment to watch her until she rounded the corner and was out of sight. Then he let out a sigh and walked over to the nurses' station, where most of the staff was clustered in a tight knot. Worried faces turned to him, seeking guidance and reassurance. He met each person's gaze in turn, knowing the next few moments were vital. With the exception of the two nurses Avery had brought with her, no one had experience working in a hot zone with infected patients; it was only natural people were feeling worried and afraid. Grant had to instill confidence in his staff so they could continue to function. If they let fear get the better of them, they wouldn't be able to do their jobs, and the whole base was as good as dead.

"We have a new patient," he announced needlessly. "His symptoms suggest he's suffering from the same illness that affected the earlier group of people, so we're going to employ the same treatment strategy again."

"Where is the disease coming from?" asked Megan, one of the nurses.

"We don't know yet. That's why Dr. Thatcher and her team are here."

Karen, one of the nurse practitioners, spoke up next. "Do we even know the causative agent yet?"

Grant shook his head. "No. But I think the lab technician is getting close to identifying it." In truth, he had no idea if that was the case, but the white lie gave his team hope, which was what they needed right now.

"You've treated patients with this disease before, and although I know it's frightening, I have to ask you to do it again. Right now we only have one, but there could be more walking through our doors soon. We have to be ready."

"What about protective equipment? Dr. Thatcher was wearing a biohazard suit—should we be wearing those, too?" Megan's voice was high with worry, and Grant searched her face for any signs she'd overheard his earlier conversation with Avery. The standard gloves, mask and gown seemed like flimsy protection in the face of such graphic and terrifying symptoms, and if the disease was truly growing more severe, they might not do the job anymore.

"I'll ask what type of protective supplies the team

has brought with them. In the meantime, though, the standard gear kept us all safe while we treated the first round of patients." The tension of the group eased a bit as the truth of his words sank in, and several of the nurses nodded in agreement. Grant prayed he wasn't giving them false hope, but until he knew for sure why Richard had gotten so sick so quickly, he wasn't going to share his suspicions with the staff.

He nodded in the direction of Richard's bed, tucked away in one of the examination bays that doubled as inpatient "rooms" when necessary. "Keep an eye on our new patient. Page me if his status changes at all."

"You're leaving?"

"Not for long," he said. "Besides, it's not like I can go far." He winked at them, and his teasing words coaxed a few answering smiles from the group. He moved to leave, but one of the women held up her hand to stall him.

"Dr. Jones," Karen said, her gaze serious. "Do you think there are other cases on-base now?"

Grant pressed his lips together, carefully considering his response. "I'm not sure," he admitted. "But I'm going to find out."

Paul leaned back from his microscope and rubbed his eyes with a sigh. He'd been burning the candle at both ends lately, trying to get results for both his university-sponsored research projects and his shadow employers. While he was easily able to record his progress on the former endeavors, it was growing increasingly difficult to conduct experiments on the latter.

He could only infect so many people at a time using the vial of virus-saturated liquid, which meant the number of victims was limited. Furthermore, it seemed the disease itself wasn't very contagious; after the initial set of ten patients, he'd expected the illness to spread organically through the base population. The fact that it hadn't made him suspect the virus in its natural form wasn't going to be useful to the Organization. He wasn't naive—he knew they were hoping to find a new biological weapon. And while this bug was promising, it would take a bit of tinkering to be truly suitable in that regard.

What am I thinking? His professional curiosity was interested in the idea of genetically manipulating the virus to make it more lethal, but he shied away from actually contemplating the strategy he would use to do such experiments. He already felt like he was in too deep with the group—the last thing he wanted was to entangle himself even further in their web. "Just finish the job and go home," he muttered.

His kids needed him.

Just the thought of them made his heart twist a little, and not for the first time he kicked himself for taking this job so far away. It had seemed like a good idea at the time. He'd gotten the offer to work in Antarctica nine months to the day after his wife, Carol, died, and while his first thought had been to refuse, something had kept him from saying no. He'd taken a few days to consider it, and during that time he'd received a mysterious phone call proposing a low-risk, high-reward side project, with the promise of handsome compensation for his efforts. *That* had definitely gotten his attention—the stack of past-due hospital bills grew higher every day, and with no solution in sight, Paul had been considering filing for bankruptcy. Doing so would have gotten the creditors off his back, but his pride kept him from making the call. He didn't want his children to know how bad things were financially, not when they were still so distraught over the loss of their mother. So he'd kept quiet, trying his best to maintain the illusion that everything was all right, moneywise.

At first, he'd thought the offer was a joke. He'd listened politely, and both the euphemistic language used and the tone of the man on the other end of the line had raised all sorts of red flags. But desperation drove him hard, and so he'd held his nose and agreed to do the job.

One hour later, the first payment had arrived in his bank account. Seeing the new balance had loosened the ever-present band of tension around his chest, and he'd taken his first deep breath since Carol's diagnosis.

Of course, had he known then what he knew now, would he still have accepted the money? It was a question that haunted him at night as he lay awake in bed pondering what kind of man he'd become. This trip had changed him. There were moments when he didn't even recognize himself anymore, and he knew Carol would balk at the things he'd done. It made him ashamed to imagine her reaction, but also a little angry. He wasn't proud to admit it, but in the dark recesses of his mind, he blamed her for making him pick this course of action. If she hadn't spent so much time outside, basking in the sun's deadly embrace, she'd never have developed melanoma. And if she'd been more proactive about going to the doctor, perhaps they would have caught it in time to actually do something about it. If, if, if. The word plagued him, teasing him with possibilities that were, in fact, impossible. It was enough to drive a man insane.

He shook his head, trying to forcefully reset his thoughts. It wasn't productive to dwell on the might-have-beens and the what-ifs in life. This was his reality, and he had to figure out a way to move forward so he could go back to his kids and rebuild his family. There would always be a Carol-shaped hole in their lives, but with time and dedication he hoped the kids would emerge from their grief and find the strength he knew they had inherited from their mother.

"Hey, Paul."

He jumped, startled by the unexpected voice. His microscope was located in a small offshoot of the main lab, barely bigger than a closet, which meant he spent a lot of time alone. It was one of the reasons he enjoyed the work—he didn't have to make awkward small talk with anyone, didn't have to pretend like everything was okay when, really, the death of his wife had left him feeling adrift and lost.

He swiveled his chair around, moving carefully so as not to bump into the microscope. One of the graduate students stood in the doorway to his alcove, his hand on the jamb as he leaned forward to deliver his message. "Yes?"

"There's a woman here to see you. I didn't catch her name."

Paul frowned, the announcement catching him by surprise. Who would be asking for him? Then realization struck and his stomach heaved.

The investigator from the CDC. It had to be her.

He took a deep breath, hoping his fear didn't show on his face. The last thing he wanted was for word to get around that he was nervous about talking to the woman. "Ah, okay. Where is she?"

The young man lifted one shoulder in a casual shrug. "I sent her down to the break room. There's not really any place to talk in here."

"Good call," Paul said, his muscles relaxing a bit. He had a little time to get his emotions under control before facing her. "I'll be right there—I just need to shut this down first."

The student nodded and disappeared, and Paul turned back to the microscope, the wheels in his head turning a mile a minute. He'd expected this visit, just not quite so soon. He'd assumed it would take a lot longer to make the connection between himself and the victims. The fact that the woman was here now meant he'd underestimated her skills and perhaps overestimated his stealth.

Why hadn't Jesse warned him she was coming? He ground his teeth together, biting down hard on the urge to find his supposed assistant and shake the man. This was exactly the kind of situation Jesse was supposed to defuse. So why hadn't he? Was the man only pretending to help him? Once again, Paul had a sneaking suspicion Jesse was only in business for himself. *Thank God I didn't really tell him anything.* They hadn't had a chance to have a long conversation yet, which meant most of his secrets were still safe.

But for how long?

He shut down the equipment, his body moving on autopilot as he considered his options. It wasn't likely the woman knew the extent of his involvement in spreading the disease—if that was the case, she wouldn't have come alone. So she was probably here as a matter of course, rather than because she suspected him of something. He hadn't tried to hide the fact that he'd shared drinks with the men who eventually became ill, so she was most likely coming to talk to him in an effort to fill in the social history of the victims. If that was indeed the case, all he had to do was play along. If he was lucky, he might even be able to throw a few red herrings into the conversation to distract her and shift the focus of her investigation away from him.

And if she does know?

The thought sent a cold spike of fear through his belly and he shuddered, trying to shake off the disturbing sensation. *She doesn't*, he told himself firmly. She couldn't know. She'd only been here a few days; it wasn't enough time for her to have pieced everything together yet. But she would eventually.

And he had to be ready.

Chapter 8

Avery paced while she waited, studying the room as she walked in an effort to control her impatience. Shelves lined the walls, laden with items ranging from the ordinary toilet paper and tissues to more exotic chemicals likely used in lab experiments. A stray coffee cup and bowl stood forgotten amidst the supplies, testifying to the space's use as both storage and employee break room.

Where is he? Even though she'd only been waiting a few minutes, she was annoyed at the delay. Having a new patient present with symptoms of the mysterious disease only served to highlight the importance of her investigation. This was no academic exercise—people would die if she didn't figure out what was going on, and soon.

Her thoughts drifted back to Grant and his search

for additional victims. The initial outbreak had involved ten people, and based on the progression of
the disease, they'd all apparently been infected at
around the same time. If the same pattern held true
now, it was highly unlikely Richard was the sole victim in this flare-up. But would his drinking buddies
be affected, or would she have to search harder to
find the common connections between all the patients?

And what if Paul Coleson was sick? That would
certainly complicate matters—she couldn't hope to
isolate protective antibodies from his blood if he had
contracted the disease. On the other hand... If Paul
was also among the current batch of victims, it further supported her theory that the bar was somehow
involved in transmission of the agent. Either way, she
made a mental note to ask the base commander to
close the place down until further notice. Although
her current evidence was circumstantial at best, she'd
rather err on the side of caution. Annoying the base
population was a small price to pay if it meant controlling the spread of this disease.

Footsteps sounded on the scratched linoleum of
the corridor, and Avery stopped pacing and turned to
face the door. She ran her index finger along the edge
of the mask she'd brought as insurance—if Paul was
symptomatic, she didn't want to talk to him without
protection. She'd meant to ask the young man who'd
left her here, but he'd dashed off before she had the
chance. No matter. In a few seconds, she'd have the
answer firsthand.

She wasn't sure what she'd expected from Paul
Coleson, but the slender, bespectacled man who

walked into the room was a bit of a letdown. He paused just inside the room and blinked at her, his eyes wide behind the thick lenses of his glasses. "Uh, hello." It sounded more like a question than a statement, and Avery smiled, hoping to put him at ease.

"Mr. Coleson, I'm Dr. Thatcher. Thank you for speaking with me."

He nodded. "I recognize you from the base meeting." After an awkward pause, he thrust his hand out in a belated attempt at manners.

Avery declined with another smile. "I think given the circumstances, we can dispense with the handshake."

"Right." He let out a nervous laugh, plainly uncomfortable.

"I have a few questions, if you don't mind." She gestured to the small table and took a seat. After a brief hesitation, Paul walked over and sat across from her. His gait reminded her of a heron, long legs picking carefully over the terrain as he moved.

He pushed his glasses up, seemingly unbothered by the fact that they slid back down his nose as soon as he dropped his hand. He shifted his weight slightly, then reached up to smooth back a few wisps of light brown hair. It was a little on the long side, in an "I'm too busy to get it cut" kind of way. It was a style Avery recognized, as Grant had sported it all through college.

"There's no need to be nervous," she assured him. "I just want to talk to you about your activities over the past few days."

He frowned. "Can I ask why?"

"I'm investigating the disease outbreak that occurred earlier on the base." No sense telling him there was another victim yet—Mr. Coleson had a distinctly nervous air about him, and didn't seem like the type to take the news of a potential recent exposure to the pathogen very well. If he freaked out, Avery wouldn't be able to get any useful information from him. "Several of the surviving patients have told me they shared a drink with you before falling ill."

Guilt flashed across his face, there and gone in the space between heartbeats. It was an interesting reaction, but not all that unusual. In the aftermath of an outbreak, it was common for the survivors to feel somehow responsible for the deaths of others, even though there was often nothing they could have done to help. Given the limited population on-base and the fact that Paul had shared drinks with the men, it was likely they were all friends. He was the only one to escape the first outbreak unscathed, a fact that likely weighed heavily on his mind. Hopefully, Avery wouldn't have any trouble talking him into giving Jennifer some samples…

"Yeah." He placed his hands on the table, clasping and unclasping them. "I feel bad for the guys. One minute, they're fine. The next?" He shook his head, pushed up his glasses again. "Bam! Just like that." He met her gaze then, his light brown eyes full of concern. "Hard to believe, you know?"

Avery nodded. "I imagine it was quite distressing to hear they'd gotten sick. Did you feel any differently in the days after you shared a drink with them?"

"What do you mean?"

"Any headaches, muscle aches, sore throat, that kind of thing?"

Paul began shaking his head before she'd finished speaking. "No, not at all. And I was pretty paranoid about it, once I found out they were sick. I paid attention to every twinge, thinking it might be the start of something. I was so scared it could happen to me, too."

"It seems as though luck was on your side."

He seemed to consider her words for a moment. "Maybe so," he said softly.

Avery leaned forward, hoping the same could be said for her investigation. "When was the last time you had a drink at the bar?"

His eyebrows drew together as he searched his memory. "Day before yesterday. Why?"

Avery ignored his question in favor of her own. "Did you meet with anyone there?"

He nodded slowly. "Sure. Richard. Tom. Bradley. Just some of the guys. Why?" he repeated.

"Would you be willing to donate a few blood samples? We don't need much, just a couple of vials."

"I guess," he said, sounding a little hesitant. "What's this about? Why do you want my blood?"

"We're trying to identify the pathogen causing this disease. So far, you're the only person who seems to have been exposed multiple times without contracting the illness. I'm hoping we can study your blood and find something we can use to help the other victims."

"Multiple exposures," he said, almost to himself. He looked up, his eyes growing wide as the meaning of her words sank in. "Someone else is sick?"

Avery nodded. "I'm afraid so."

"My God." He slumped back in his chair, looking visibly deflated. Avery felt a swell of sympathy for him as she watched him process the news. It had to be tough for him to know his friends were falling ill while he remained healthy. She found it a little ironic that while Paul seemed completely unremarkable, so far as appearances went, it was quite possible his blood carried the secret to stopping this disease in its tracks. The thought made her own blood race, and Avery quashed the urge to grab him by the arm and dash back to the hospital so they could get started.

"How many people?" Paul's voice quavered slightly, but he was sitting up straight now, apparently recovered from the initial shock.

"Ah," Avery hedged. "One confirmed." Her thoughts flashed to Grant and his search—had he found the other men yet? Were they sick, too?

"Who is it?"

"I really shouldn't—" she began, but he cut her off.

"Please," he said, his tone pleading. "They're my friends."

She sighed. "It's Richard."

Paul merely shook his head. "Damn," he muttered under his breath. "He's such a nice guy."

Avery pushed back her chair and stood, hoping he would take it as a cue to do the same. "Let's get you back to the hospital so you can hopefully help him."

Paul rose, looking a little uncertain. "Do you really think my blood will tell you anything?"

Avery bit back an impatient reply and ushered him

to the door, feeling a bit like a shepherd dealing with a recalcitrant lamb. "We won't know until we look."

"Can I grab my phone? Just in case my kids try to call?"

She nodded, letting out a silent sigh. It would only take him a minute or two—not a huge delay in the grand scheme of things. Besides, could she really begrudge the man wanting to stay in touch with his children?

He scurried off down the hall, leaving her alone in the break room once again. Might as well use the time to check in with Grant and see how things were going on his end.

She reached for the walkie-talkie and picked it up just as it screeched to life. "Avery, are you there?"

"Yes. Did you find the other men?"

Static filled the line and she began to wonder if her response had been lost to the ether. Then the radio squawked and Grant spoke again. "Affirmative."

She could tell by the tone of his voice that something was wrong. Her stomach dropped, her earlier excitement evaporating as dread wafted over her. "Are they sick?"

"Affirmative," he said again. "It's bad."

Paul followed the woman back to the hospital, trailing along in her wake as she rushed down the main street, heedless of the other people walking nearby. He wasn't sure why she had such a fire in her belly—Richard was going to die, and there wasn't a damn thing she or anyone else could do to save him. He couldn't tell her that, though, or else she would realize he was not all he appeared to be. So he stayed quiet and tried to keep up, slipping and sliding a bit along the way.

The hospital was warm compared to the frigid temperature outside, and he paused just inside the door, welcoming the instant thawing of his exposed skin. He took a deep breath, warming his body from the inside out. The stink of disinfectant was heavy in the air, but he ignored it and drew in another breath.

Dr. Thatcher was a few steps ahead of him and turned back, clearly annoyed to see him lagging behind. "If you'll come this way, please?"

Paul nodded and started walking again, unbuttoning his coat as he went. Better to cooperate with her—he didn't want to give her any reason to examine his situation more closely. Hopefully, she would leave him alone once she realized there was nothing to be found in his system.

They moved deeper into the hospital, down a long hall that appeared to end in a large room. He expected her to take him there, but instead she guided him into a small enclave that reminded him of the closet that housed his microscope.

"Would you please wait here? I'll find a nurse to take your blood samples."

"No problem," he replied, but she was already gone, her footsteps beating out a rapidly fading tattoo on the tiled floor of the hallway.

He slipped his hand into his coat pocket and touched the vial he'd retrieved before leaving the lab. He didn't know why he'd brought a sample of the virus; he probably wasn't going to get a chance to dose her or anyone else with it. But Dr. Thatcher's visit had left him feeling more rattled than he'd like to admit. Carrying the virus gave him a sense of security and made him feel powerful and in control of the situation—a sort of biological security blanket. He scoffed at the thought, but it was the truth. Holding an agent of death was one hell of a boost to the ego, and it reminded him that no matter how smart this woman was, in the end he was the one who determined who lived and who died.

Another set of footsteps sounded, and he withdrew his hand from his pocket, leaving the vial safely tucked inside. After a few seconds, Jesse poked his head into the room and stepped inside.

"I'm here to draw a few vials of blood," he said, setting his supplies on the small table and pulling a chair close.

Paul waited for the other man to sit before speaking. "What the hell is going on here?"

Jesse met his eyes briefly, then returned to opening packages. "What do you mean?"

"I thought you had things under control here."

"I do."

"Then why is she asking me questions? I thought you were going to steer her in a different direction."

Jesse gestured for him to remove his coat. "She's not sharing her thoughts with the group. I didn't know she was going to talk to you."

Paul winced as Jesse pricked him with the needle. "Then how, exactly, are you helping me?"

Jesse ignored the question. "I have new instructions."

Of course. Paul silently sighed, wanting to strangle not only Jesse, but the man on the other end of the line who relayed all the orders.

"What?" he asked wearily.

Jesse filled one tube with blood, then switched it out for a fresh one, his movements smooth and practiced. "They want you to create a large batch of the agent and ship it off-base."

Paul bit back a question, knowing it was pointless to ask. Jesse was merely the messenger, not the brains of the operation. But could he really trust what the man was telling him? Perhaps this was just a ploy to get him to make a fatal error. After all, if he were to amplify the virus, it would increase the possibility that he would get caught, or that he might even contract the disease himself. Was that how they wanted to get him out of the picture?

His confusion must have shown on his face, because Jesse sighed impatiently. "They thought you might have doubts," he murmured. He pulled the needle from Paul's arm and pressed a cotton ball to the puncture wound. Then he fished in his pocket and withdrew his phone. He made a few quick taps on the screen and turned it around so Paul could see what he was looking at.

It took him a moment to register what he was seeing. Then the truth hit him with the force of a battering ram and he nearly doubled over in his chair.

Noah. They had his son.

The boy was tied to a chair, a red bandanna stuffed in his mouth. He squinted up at the camera through swollen, bruised eyelids, and a trickle of dried blood ran from his nose and stained his chin.

"No." Paul shook his head, denying the truth of what he saw. "No, no, no, no, no." The room began to spin and the air became too heavy to breathe. Black spots danced in his vision, but it didn't matter. The image of his son was burned into his brain, a nightmare he would never forget.

Jesse's hand clamped down on his arm, hard enough to bring tears to his eyes. "Stop it," he hissed. "Quiet down."

Paul bit his lip and the low, keening sound that had filled the air cut off abruptly. "That's my son," he said, choking out the words. He swallowed hard, trying to dislodge the painful lump in his throat. But it didn't help. Fear filled him, consuming him from the inside like a fast-growing cancer. How could he function, let alone do any kind of work, when his boy was being held captive?

Were they torturing Noah? It certainly looked like he'd been hurt. But had that been a onetime event, or was it ongoing? His brain shied away from the possibility, throwing up a wall in a pathetic attempt to protect himself from the image of his son in pain and suffering. Noah had always been a sensitive boy, a quality that had persisted even as he became a teenager. When so many young men sought to assert their independence and rebel, he'd been focused on his studies, working hard to maintain a perfect 4.0 grade point average. He had his sights set on an Ivy League school, and Paul and Carol had agreed to pay for his education if he got accepted.

He should be home, studying for his next exam. Not tied to a chair, bleeding onto a dirty rag.

Jesse shook him, and he realized the man was talking to him. He focused on his mouth, watched his lips move as he spoke again. "He's still alive."

That got his attention. "What?"

"He's still alive. Your boy. For now." The last words were said almost as an afterthought, as if Jesse couldn't be bothered to care one way or another. And why would he? It wasn't his child being threatened.

In that moment, Paul hated Jesse. Not just for his cavalier attitude regarding Noah's safety, but for all he represented. The Organization and the desperation that had driven him to accept their offer. His helplessness, stuck at the bottom of the world while his son was thousands of miles away, needing him in the worst way. And the blood that was on his hands, all thanks to them.

"Your mother thinks he's camping with friends," Jesse continued. "If I were you, I wouldn't let her know otherwise."

Paul flushed, the sudden surge of emotion warming him until he felt his skin might start to steam. The heat of his hatred tempered his fear, forged it into a weapon that he was determined to use against Jesse and all the others who had wronged him. The Organization had picked him because they'd thought he was an easy mark, a man they could manipulate to do their bidding. He had to show them how wrong they were.

"I don't understand," he said, pulling his arm free from Jesse's grip. "Why can't they amplify the virus off-base? I don't really have the equipment or facilities to do the job properly." It was the truth—the lab wasn't set up for generating a large batch of viral material. The chances of success would be much greater if he had access to the right equipment. Not to mention the safety concerns that went along with concentrating a dangerous pathogen. He'd been lucky so far, but given the lack of appropriate safety equipment, he was essentially playing with fire. Pretty soon he would get burned, and then how could he help his son?

"That's above our pay grade," Jesse replied, the latex of his gloves snapping as he pulled them off. "All I know is they want you to smuggle it back to the States on the supply ship. They want you to hide it in the equipment going for auction."

Paul's stomach churned as he connected the dots. One of the quirkier things the government did to raise money for the base was to send back furniture or equipment that was no longer needed and auction it off to the highest bidder. Since the items came from the US base in Antarctica, they weren't subject to rigorous inspections before entering the country. It would be child's play for a representative of the Organization to access the items in the US and retrieve the virus.

"How much?"

Jesse lifted one shoulder. "A liter. Two would be better."

"Fine." It wasn't an impossible task, but it would take some finesse to keep his activities secret from his coworkers in the lab. Still, his fear of discovery paled in comparison to his worry over Noah. "When will they release my son?"

"As soon as I verify the agent is on board, they will let him go."

Jesse looked away as he spoke, and Paul knew he was lying. But what choice did he have? If there was even a chance Noah was still alive, he had to do what they said. And there was also Lisa to consider...

"I need a week. Maybe a few days extra." There was no way he could make the process go any faster, despite his gnawing sense of urgency. Could Noah last that long? *Please, don't take my son from me, too...*

"I'll let them know." Jesse scooped up the vials of blood and the used supplies. "Oh, and one more thing."

Paul went still, his sleeve still partly rolled up his arm. "What?"

"I need you to dose the doctors. Get them out of the picture."

"Why?" He balked at the request. If the Organization no longer wanted him to infect people, it was highly likely his involvement in the outbreaks would remain a secret. It felt wrong to target the two who were doing their best to save others, especially when he wasn't acting in self-defense.

"They are too dangerous," Jesse said simply. "If Dr. Jones and Dr. Thatcher remain, they won't stop looking until they get answers to their questions. But if they are lost in the outbreak, the remaining medical staff will simply focus on survival. By the time other investigators are sent to the base, we'll be long gone."

His words made a sick kind of sense. Dr. Jones was a leader—he had displayed an easy confidence at the base meeting that made it clear he was a man who was comfortable with responsibility. And from what Paul had seen of Dr. Thatcher, she was an intelligent and determined woman. If the two of them were out of the picture, it would leave a void, one he could picture Jesse stepping in to fill.

Revulsion filled him at the thought. Despite his

earlier sins, Paul refused to do Jesse's dirty work for him. This was one bridge he wouldn't cross.

He finished unrolling his sleeve and rose to his feet. Without saying a word, he thrust his hand into his pocket and retrieved the vial of virus. He held it up for Jesse's inspection, then dropped it on the table, enjoying the quick flash of fear on the other man's face as the glass rattled against the wood. "Do it yourself."

Grant sank into a chair in the staff break room, his mind and body numb from the events of the morning. As if the shock of Richard's appearance hadn't been bad enough, Grant's little expedition to find the other two men had proved depressingly successful. Tom had been discovered in his bed, and given his body's state of rigor, he'd likely been dead for several hours. Bradley was still alive, although, given the severity of his symptoms, Grant wasn't sure if that was a good thing. The poor man was lying in the bay next to Richard, and both patients were struggling to breathe as their lungs filled with blood.

Grant and the team were trying everything to keep them alive, but deep in his heart he knew it was too late. If he'd gotten to them earlier, maybe they would have stood a chance. But the disease had progressed too far, and he was powerless to help. It was like re-arranging the deck chairs on the *Titanic*, and yet he couldn't give up. As long as they were breathing, he was going to fight for them.

"Hey." Avery's soft voice at his side broke into his thoughts, and he turned to find her staring down at him in concern. "You doing okay?"

He nodded mechanically, but inside he was a mess. When he treated the first round of patients, he'd been so wrapped up in the tension of the moment, trying to outwit the pathogen and save lives. He simply hadn't had time for fear. But now that he knew what was going to happen, terror seeped into his bones, nearly paralyzing him.

Am I infected? Is it only a matter of time before I get sick, too?

The questions circled round and round in his head, a broken record he couldn't turn off. The thought that he might be the next one lying in a hospital bed, drowning in his own blood, almost made him throw up. Beads of sweat broke out on his forehead, and he went hot, then cold, as he struggled for breath.

A loud *whoosh* sounded in his ears, overpowering the noise of the beeping monitors. He closed his eyes, retreating into himself as he fought for control of his own body. Something touched him; after a moment, he recognized it as hands grasping his shoulders, then his cheeks. He forced his eyes open and Avery's face filled his vision, so close he could feel the whisper of her breath against his lips. He focused on her eyes, their deep blue color as familiar to him as his own hands. How many hours had he spent staring into her eyes, dreaming of their future together? Her touch was gentle as she cupped his cheeks, and the roaring in his ears died down enough that he heard her soft words, meant for his ears alone.

"I'm fine." His voice sounded scratchy to his own ears, so he cleared his throat and tried again. "Really. I just needed a minute."

Avery studied him a moment, her gaze seeing far

too much. But she didn't push him. She leaned back, her hands sliding off his cheeks. The cool air hit his face, a poor substitute for her touch. But no matter how much he wanted to lean on her, no matter how badly he wanted to curl his body around hers and soak in the feel of her, this wasn't the place. He had to project a strong front for his team. If they had any idea how terrified he was, it would destroy what little morale they had left. It was bad enough they were facing this unknown pathogen. If he were to break down in front of them, it would make matters even worse.

"Did you find Paul Coleson?" he asked.

She nodded. "He's getting some blood drawn now. How are the patients?"

Grant shook his head. "Iffy. I'm not sure how much longer they're going to last."

"The antiviral medication we brought isn't helping?"

He shrugged. "It's too soon to tell." But he wasn't holding out hope. If he'd been able to administer it when the men's symptoms weren't so severe, they would have stood a better chance. Now he feared they were too far gone for anything to help.

She placed her hand on his shoulder and squeezed gently, and he felt some of her strength flow into him. "They're fighters," she said. "Give them a little time."

He wanted so badly to believe her, but watching people die from this infection had left him with a healthy amount of skepticism. "I hope so," he said noncommittally.

"Dr. Thatcher!"

They both turned as a woman stepped into the

room, her eyes wide with excitement. She clutched a notebook to her chest and made a beeline for Avery. *This must be the lab tech*, he thought, remembering he'd seen her unpacking boxes of supplies on the first day. If her demeanor was anything to go by, she must have found something. Grant felt a stirring of interest as the woman skidded to a stop next to Avery. Had she managed to isolate the pathogen already?

Apparently, Avery's thoughts paralleled his own. "Please tell me you have something good," she said, a note of desperation in her voice. They both needed some positive news right about now.

The woman placed her notebook on the table and flipped through the pages as she spoke. "I think we're dealing with some kind of flu."

Avery sucked in a breath and went very still. "Are you sure?"

The tech nodded and pointed to a set of photographs. They didn't mean much to Grant, but Avery leaned over and studied them as if they were the Rosetta stone. "The samples from the initial set of patients were pretty degraded, but I decided to test them anyway," the tech said. "I ran them through every rapid detection kit I had, and the only one that lit up was influenza."

Avery hummed thoughtfully. "But the signal isn't very bright," she observed. "Do you think that's because of the poor sample quality, or are we dealing with a virus that's related to flu but isn't actually an influenza virus?"

"I'm not sure," admitted the tech. "Without fresh samples, I can't make that distinction."

Grant snorted and the woman glanced at him,

frowning slightly as if just now realizing he was there. "You're in luck," he observed dryly.

She shot Avery a questioning glance. "There are two new patients," Avery explained. "I'm sure we can spare some blood for your tests."

"Oh." The woman appeared sobered by this news, but after a few seconds her mood shifted back to professional interest. "Once I get the samples, I can have an answer for you in an hour."

Avery nodded. "Excellent. I'll have one of the nurses drop off the samples."

The woman gathered up her notebook, clearly excited to get back to her lab. "Jennifer," Avery called out before the tech could leave. "Be careful."

Jennifer waved and headed out, stepping to the side to avoid bumping into one of the new nurses.

"Hi, Jesse," Avery acknowledged.

"Hey," he said. "Crazy out there."

"Any change in the status of our patients?" Grant asked. He held his breath, bracing himself for bad news.

Jesse shook his head. "Holding steady so far." He reached for the coffeepot, sniffed and grimaced. "I'm going to make a fresh pot. Want some?"

"That would be great, thanks," Avery replied. She turned to face Grant while Jesse busied himself with the coffee. "What do you think about Jennifer's results? Do they match with the clinical picture you've seen?"

"I'm not sure," he said. "I know the more virulent strains out there have a high mortality rate, but I've never encountered one in my practice before. It seems hard to believe the flu can take down a healthy man in a matter of hours."

"It happens more than people realize," Avery said. She was quiet for a moment, clearly thinking. "Jennifer's data isn't conclusive, but I think we can safely assume that we're dealing with something that is at least related to influenza. Do you think increasing the dose of the antiflu drugs I brought might help the men?"

He considered her question, mentally weighing the pros and cons of the approach. A higher dose of the medication might be the only chance the men had. But could they risk depleting their limited supply of the drug when there was a very good chance other people on the base were going to fall ill? How should he prioritize the needs of his current patients with the needs of the larger population, especially when there was no guarantee that increasing the dosage of drugs would help the men?

"Let's give them another dose and see what happens," he said slowly. "If they respond, we'll continue the therapy. But…" He trailed off, and Avery nodded.

"They might be too far gone to help," she finished.

"Exactly."

Jesse slid a cup of coffee in front of Avery. "Here you go, Doc," he said quietly. "Sorry it's not that hot. I think the machine is on the fritz."

"That's okay," she said. "Thanks for making it." She took a large gulp and shuddered. "It's really strong."

Jesse grinned. "Is there another way to make coffee?" He lifted his cup in salute and walked out of the room, leaving Grant alone with Avery once again.

She took another sip of coffee and studied him over the rim of the mug, her gaze surprisingly heavy. He could tell from the expression on her face that she wanted to say something, but she apparently wasn't sure how to express herself.

Join the club, he thought wryly.

He let her think, his own mind working busily as he tried to figure out what was troubling her. Did she want to talk about the patients and the resurgence of the outbreak? Or did she have something more personal on her mind? Were they finally going to talk about what had happened between them last night?

His stomach flipped over at the possibility, and he silently wished that wasn't the case. He knew it was cowardly of him, but the morning had been rough enough already—the last thing he wanted was to hear Avery reject him again.

There was a soft thud as she set the ceramic mug on the table, and she drew a breath as if preparing herself to walk into the lion's den. "I have an idea, and I want you to really think about it before you reject it outright."

That was an interesting preamble. Grant's curiosity prickled and he sat forward, meeting her gaze. "All right," he said slowly. She'd never started a conversation like this before. What was she going to say, and why did he get the feeling he wasn't going to like it?

She took another deep breath. "I want you to start taking the antiflu medication."

"No." His refusal was reflexive and instant, the word leaving his mouth before he'd fully considered the idea.

Avery lifted an eyebrow and stared at him archly. "You said you'd at least consider the idea."

He nodded. "You're right. I did." He waited a beat, then said again, "No."

Now her expression turned obstinate. "You're not thinking clearly," she began, but he cut her off.

"Avery, I'm not going to take medicine away from my patients. It's my duty to care for them, and I can't do that if all the medication has been wasted."

"You can't take care of anyone if you're sick," she snapped. "And given your recent exposures, it's in your best interest to take a few prophylactic doses. It might save your life."

Grant opened his mouth to argue, but she made a good point. He had taken a few risks when caring for the first set of patients, and he'd definitely been exposed to the pathogen when helping Richard. He shuddered as he recalled the man's hot breath on his cheek as Grant had struggled to keep him upright. Was the virus now in his system, silently multiplying as he sat here thinking?

If there was a chance the antiflu drugs could keep him healthy, it would be foolish to refuse to take them. But would there be enough left for the team and the rest of the base if necessary?

Avery's words echoed in his mind: *You can't take care of anyone if you're sick.* She was right, of course, but was his life really worth more than the life of another person on-base? If he took some of the drugs from the limited supply, was he dooming a patient to a horrible death? What gave him the right to make that decision?

But on the other hand, if he did die, who would be

left to help people? The nursing staff was top-notch, but there were limits to their capabilities. If he were to fall sick or even to die, it would drastically impact the hospital's ability to treat patients—not just those with the mystery pathogen, but people with any condition or injury. Maintaining the supply of antiflu drugs seemed like the immediate right decision, but could he ethically take such a risk, knowing it might result in more harm than good?

He glanced at Avery, who sat silently, sipping her coffee. He appreciated the fact that she wasn't trying to pressure him or rush him into making a decision. But he would have to make one soon.

Grant ran a hand through his hair, wanting suddenly to talk things over with Avery. She'd always been his moral center, and there were many times he'd turned to her for advice and insight. She always seemed to know the right thing to do, and more important, she'd always helped him find the courage to act accordingly. He'd missed her guidance over the past ten years. One more thing he'd lost thanks to his careless words…

He pushed aside the thought and focused on the question at hand. He hated the idea of potentially depriving patients of medication, but the alternative was much worse. The fact that the greater good demanded he act a little selfishly was a bitter pill to swallow, but it really did seem to be the best solution.

"You're right," he said quietly. "I'll take them."

Avery nodded, her expression serious. "Thank you," she said, her voice barely louder than a whisper. She held his gaze, relief and gratitude shining in her eyes. A surge of warmth rose in Grant's chest, and for a moment, the years of separation melted away and it was like they'd never been apart. He wanted so badly to touch her, to fold her into his arms and feel the weight of her against his chest. She belonged in his arms—no one else fit him quite the way she did.

The silence was broken by a whisper-soft gasp as Avery drew in a breath between her lips. Awareness flickered across her face, and for a second, Grant could have sworn she wanted him, too. But then she looked away, and the moment dissolved like ice in the sun.

"I—uh—" she stammered, clearly shaken. She pushed away from the table and stood, then swallowed the last of her coffee and took the mug to the sink. "I'll just go and grab the drugs now."

"Sounds good," he remarked. But he doubted she heard him as she practically ran from the room.

Grant leaned back in his chair, toying with the urge to smile. Being around Avery again was like a dream come true, and he couldn't ignore the feelings she'd reignited or his need to set the record straight between them. But the timing couldn't possibly be worse. As much as he wanted to focus on his own needs and desires, he had a job to do. And as long as the people on-base were in danger from this mystery pathogen, his personal life had to take a backseat. He'd taken an oath as a doctor, and he wasn't about to start ignoring his promise now.

No matter what his heart demanded of him.

Chapter 9

Avery stood in the middle of the bar, surveying the room with a critical eye. It wasn't big, so far as square footage went, but she did have a lot of samples to take. And since everyone was busy taking care of the two new patients, she was on her own.

The fact that the men had survived the night was a minor miracle, and it gave her hope they might go on to make a recovery. The antiflu drugs hadn't triggered a dramatic improvement in the patients, but their symptoms hadn't worsened, either. At this point, Avery considered maintenance of the status quo to be a victory, and she knew Grant felt the same way.

She walked over to the bar, her movements awkward in the bulky blue suit. She'd worn it out of deference to Grant, who had insisted she take every precaution. His concern had touched her, and she hadn't wanted to argue with him. Jennifer's latest results had confirmed they were dealing with a new strain of flu, and given what she knew about that pathogen, it was unlikely an active, intact virus had survived in the bar. But it was better to be safe than sorry...

Working carefully, Avery organized her sample collection tools and began to methodically swab surfaces and gather material for testing. "Where are you hiding?" she muttered as she worked. The virus had to be somewhere, and all the evidence she had to this point suggested it was coming from the bar. But how? Hopefully, these tests would provide some answers.

The base commander hadn't been happy about shutting the place down. On one level, Avery understood his frustration. The people here worked hard, and they didn't have a lot of options when it came to socializing. The bar was almost like the heart of the base, hosting trivia nights, dart competitions, movie screenings and a lot of other activities that brought people together and gave them a way to unwind and have fun. Closing the place down was going to make for a disappointed group of residents. On the other hand, the enforced social isolation might save lives. Still, the commander had made it clear that unless she found a smoking gun, the bar wasn't going to stay closed for long.

Avery moved around the room, the whir of the fans on her back loud in her ears. The battery-powered pack kept her suit inflated, but the noise drowned out any ambient sounds and made carrying on a conversation next to impossible. Fortunately, she didn't have that problem, but a part of her wished Grant was here working by her side.

Yesterday's events had left her more shaken than she wanted to admit. Seeing Grant helping Richard had triggered a burst of fear in her chest that had temporarily blacked out all other thoughts. She'd experienced a visceral, instinctive response to protect him, and even now the memory of their encounter was enough to make her shiver, despite the warmth of the plastic suit.

Arguing with him about the medication hadn't helped her nerves, either. It was only through sheer force of will that she'd managed to sit quietly while he thought over her suggestion. If she'd given in to temptation, she would simply have forced the pills down his throat and fought about it after the fact. But she'd respected him enough to let him make up his own mind, or so he thought. Grant didn't know it, but the entire time he was silently mulling over her suggestion she'd been scheming about ways to dose him with the drugs if he'd refused to take them. Adding them to his coffee, crushing them in his food—she would have found a way to make sure he was protected, even if he refused to protect himself.

It surprised her, this fierce need to keep him safe. The emotional magnitude of her response to him was almost the same as when they'd been dating, a fact that should have worried her. Instead she found it interesting, viewing it as a development that merited further investigation.

Really, the whole thing was all Mallory's fault, she decided as she slipped a tube into the plastic rack and pulled out a fresh one for another sample. Her reply to Avery's panicked email had made her look at the situation from a different angle.

I think it's time for you to forgive the stupid mistake of a dumb kid. I can't understand the pain you went through losing the baby, but holding on to your anger is only hurting you. You loved him once, Avery. I have to believe there was a reason for that...

Mallory was right, of course. And Avery had no doubt that Olivia would say the same thing, if she asked her. She *had* loved Grant once, and if she let herself think about it, she didn't have any trouble remembering why she'd fallen for him in the first place.

The simple truth was that Grant was a good man. She'd known it ten years ago, when it had been easy to see the promise of his potential in the boy he'd been. But being around him now drove home the realization that he had matured into a selfless, thoughtful man. He truly cared about his patients, putting their welfare above his own. He hadn't hesitated to help Richard, despite the man's telltale symptoms when he'd staggered into the hospital. And he'd really struggled with the decision to take some of the antiflu drugs for himself, knowing that to do so might leave them with a reduced supply if other people on-base fell ill. She'd watched him yesterday, seen the emotions flickering across his face as he debated what to do. How many people would care so much about others, especially when their own safety was at stake?

Not many, she admitted. She swabbed the nozzle of one of the beer taps and made a mental note to check with the bartender if there were any filters in the line connecting the tap to the kegs. Disassembling the whole system would take time and would create more work for her, but she couldn't afford to cut corners. She sighed and lifted her hand to her face, wanting to rub her temples to ease the growing pangs of a developing headache. But the plastic shield blocked her and she dropped her hand with a muttered curse. The long days were catching up with her, and the desiccated, cold air didn't help—her sinuses burned and her eyes were so dry they stung every time she blinked.

Grant had warned her it might take some time to acclimate to her new environment. Since Antarctica was essentially a frozen desert, he'd advised her to increase her water intake and to take it easy for the first few days. But she'd been so busy working she hadn't had the luxury of relaxing, and unless coffee counted as water, she'd fallen woefully short in that respect, as well. She'd just have to snag a bottle when she got back to the hospital to drop off these samples.

And after that, she was going to find Grant.

Did he still want to talk? Or would he take a page from her book and shut the conversation down? It was no better than she deserved, but she hoped he would at least listen to her. She owed him an apology, and it was ten years overdue.

Did he ever think about their baby? She pondered the question as she finished packing up her supplies. Part of her hoped so—the idea that she was the only one who missed that little life struck her as wrong somehow. Even though the baby had been there and gone in the blink of an eye, it had left an indelible mark on Avery's soul.

The first few months after the miscarriage, her thoughts of the baby had drowned out everything else, leaving her unmoored in the sea of her grief. But as time had passed, she'd found her footing again and moved forward. She still thought of the baby often, almost every day, in fact. But now she didn't feel a stab of pain every time she considered the life he might have lived. And she always imagined "him," picturing a little boy with Grant's hazel eyes and mischievous smile.

She could see him now, playing catch with Grant, the afternoon sun warming them both as they tossed a baseball back and forth in the yard. Grant would make a great father, and she knew without a doubt he would have been excited and eager to teach their son all the things a little boy should know, like how to fish, how to camp, and how to catch bugs and other creepy crawlies. The thought of the pair of them— one tall and broad, in the prime of his life, one short and slender with the promise of strength to come— made her smile, and the soft weight of contentment settled over her.

It would have been a great life, she mused. Grant probably would have been happy, as well. But fate had had other plans for them, and while she wasn't unhappy with her current situation, there was a family-shaped hole in her heart that could only be filled by a husband and kids. But if she was being honest with herself, not just any husband would do; Grant was the man for her, and it was time she stopped fighting that fact.

If she thought about the situation logically, it was clear she was only setting herself up for further heartbreak. She had no way of knowing how Grant felt about her—it was entirely possible he'd moved on and didn't want anything more to do with her. Sure, he'd kissed her the other night. But that might have been just a physical response on his part. Much as the idea bothered her, he might have kissed her to scratch an itch, not because he still had feelings for her.

But…he'd been so tender and gentle. The kiss had started out with an almost frantic edge, as if he couldn't stand to be apart from her for another second. But as the minutes had ticked by, their embrace had transitioned into something that went beyond the mere physical. The sweet pressure of his mouth on hers, the soft, almost hesitant caress of his hands… Those weren't the actions of a man who was only after the pleasure of release.

Avery had to believe Grant still cared about her. Even though she'd done her best to forget him and move on with her life, she hadn't been able to remove him from her heart. Given how serious they had been about each other, it wasn't unrealistic to think Grant might have a soft spot for her now. And even though her rational mind knew there was no way they could be together—thanks to his nomadic lifestyle and her need for stability—at the very least she could ask his forgiveness and they could part on good terms. She'd carried around her hurt and anger for too long. It was time to set them aside and truly move on.

It wasn't going to be an easy conversation, and her stomach tightened a little at the thought of giving voice to feelings she'd buried long ago. But she owed it to herself, and to Grant, to bring the old pain to the surface. She'd punished them both long enough with her silence.

"Dr. Jones? I have the latest test results."

Grant took the folder from the nurse with a smile of thanks and pushed the computer keyboard forward to make room on his desk. He already had an idea of what the numbers would look like, but it would be nice to have confirmation for the report he was writing for the base commander.

Richard and Bradley were holding steady, and he had noticed small signs of improvement in their conditions when he conducted his morning exam of the men. Their breathing seemed less labored, and their oxygen saturation levels had gone up compared to yesterday's numbers. They still had a long way to go before Grant would feel comfortable pronouncing them on the road to recovery, but it was important to celebrate any positive change, incremental though it might be.

He glanced over the test results, happy to see improvements in their blood chemistry. The chest X-rays also showed a subtle reduction in the amount of fluid in the men's lungs. Overall, they were headed in the right direction, and if they kept it up, Richard and Bradley might just survive their brush with death.

As long as he didn't run out of the antiflu drugs.

There was no denying the medication was having a positive effect—Grant was convinced it was the only reason Richard and Bradley were still alive, as their initial clinical presentation had been almost identical to that of the men who had died during the first outbreak. Grant hadn't had a stockpile of anti-flu medication then, and he was forced to wonder if something so simple could have saved the four patients he'd lost.

He finished typing his report and sent it off to the base commander. The man had asked for frequent updates on "the situation," as he called it, and Grant was happy to comply, even though it created more work for him. The last thing he wanted was to antagonize the commander. General Anderson had final say over all incoming and outgoing base traffic, and Grant needed the man on his side so they could bring in additional shipments of medication.

Speaking of which… He started a new email, putting in an official request for more antiviral medication. He didn't think there would be any delay in the approval process but given the unpredictable nature of the weather, it might be several weeks before a shipment could arrive.

I hope we can wait that long…

"Hey."

He glanced up to find Avery standing in the doorway, her hair still damp from the shower. She and the rest of her team had implemented a rudimentary containment strategy in the hopes of preventing the spread of the pathogen to uninfected people, and part of the plan involved showers after patient encounters or any work that might involve the pathogen. He knew she'd spent the morning collecting samples from the bar. Had she found something already?

"Hey, yourself," he said, rising from his chair and waving her inside. She took the seat across from his desk and he sat again, noting the lines of fatigue around her eyes and the pale cast to her skin. She was clearly exhausted, but was that the only thing going on?

His clinical instincts tingled and he took a closer look at her face. Her lips looked dry and cracked, and her eyes had a slightly glassy sheen that signaled fatigue. "Are you feeling okay?"

She nodded, brushing aside the question. Grant frowned, then rolled his chair over to the small refrigerator in the corner where he kept a personal stash of drinks and snacks, for those times when the cafeteria was closed. He grabbed a bottle of water and placed it on the desk in front of Avery. "You look dehydrated. You should drink more."

A faint smile flickered across her lips as she eyed the bottle. "Thanks," she said. "I was actually just thinking about that while I was collecting samples. Being in the suit always makes me thirsty."

"Great minds think alike," he said lightly.

She twisted the cap off and took a sip. "I ran into Jesse on my way to your office. He said our guys are holding steady."

"So far, so good."

"Do you think they'll make it?"

Grant lifted one shoulder in a shrug, the casual gesture belying just how worried he was. "I don't know. But I'm cautiously optimistic."

Avery fiddled with the label on the bottle, sliding a fingernail under one of the corners. "Still no sign of any new cases?" She began to peel the label off in thin strips and placed the paper on his desk, making a tidy pile of small curls. She seemed nervous, but why?

"None that I'm aware of," he responded.

She frowned, clearly unsatisfied by his answer. "You seem disappointed," he observed.

"I am," she said. "I mean, I'm glad no one else is sick," she hastened to clarify. "But something about the pathogen transmission seems off to me."

"What do you mean?" Grant leaned forward, a frisson of unease tickling his spine. He had assumed the lack of new patients meant they had gotten lucky, but Avery made it sound like something unnatural was going on. But what could that be?

"Don't you find it a little odd that there hasn't been a single instance of person-to-person transmission in either of the outbreaks?"

"I suppose," he said slowly, considering her question. "I just figured the bug must not be very contagious."

"Maybe it isn't," she said, leaning back in the chair. "There are some strains of avian influenza that are highly lethal but not very transmissible. But even with those strains, there are still a few cases that develop due to contact with the patient. Why aren't we seeing that here?" She lifted her hand and rubbed her forehead, wincing a little as if the contact caused her pain.

"I'm not sure." Worry began to gnaw at the edges of his thoughts—maybe things weren't as under control as he had thought. "What exactly are you saying, Avery? I thought the lack of spread on the base was a *good* thing. Why are you second-guessing that?"

She was silent a moment, staring at the water bottle as if it held all the answers in the world. Then she shook her head. "I'm not sure. It just doesn't feel right to me, for some reason. But I'm pretty tired," she added, giving him a halfhearted grin. "So maybe I'm just tilting at windmills here."

Grant opened his mouth to respond, but she went on. "Anyway, that's not what I wanted to talk to you about."

"Oh?" He blinked, a little put off by the sudden change of subject. "What's on your mind?"

Avery returned her focus to the water bottle and began attacking the label again. Her nervousness was back, and Grant found himself wanting to hug her. He didn't know what had her twisted up inside, but he hated to see her worried.

"The other night, after we…kissed." Pink spots of color appeared on her cheeks, and he felt his own skin warm at the memory.

"Yes?" Was she going to tell him why she had started crying? He had been meaning to ask her about it, but between Richard's appearance and the discovery of the other patient, there simply hadn't been time.

"You said you wanted to talk. Did you mean about our breakup?" She met his gaze, a guarded look in her blue eyes as if she was afraid of his response.

"Well…" For a split second, he debated lying to her. If talking about their past was going to hurt Avery, he didn't want to do it. But if she didn't want to have the conversation, why had she brought up the topic?

"Yes," he said, deciding to take a chance. "That, and other things."

Avery nodded, as if he'd confirmed her suspicions. Her fingers stilled on the bottle, and she took a deep breath. "I owe you an apology."

Grant simply stared at her, refusing to believe his ears. *She* was apologizing to *him*? It was so outside the realm of what he had expected her to say that for a moment he couldn't respond. Given the circumstances surrounding their breakup and the nature of her parting words to him, he'd assumed she would be angry with him forever. Never in a million years had he thought she would be able to see the situation from his side, much less recognize that she had hurt him deeply.

"I was hurting, and I lashed out at you without stopping to think. I shouldn't have."

Her voice jarred him out of his thoughts, and Grant leaned forward. "Avery," he breathed. "You don't have to apologize for that. I can only imagine how much pain you were in, both physically and emotionally."

A shadow crossed her face, and for a split second he was back in her apartment, watching the woman he loved suffer while he stood there, helpless. She shook her head, shattering the illusion.

"Be that as it may, I overreacted. I was running on emotion, pure and simple."

Grant stood and rounded the desk to kneel next to her. "I never meant to hurt you," he said, staring up into her face. "Please believe me, I didn't mean what I said about the baby. I was sick, and I said the first thing that popped into my head without stopping to think how it sounded."

She smiled faintly. "I know that now," she said

softly. "Seeing you again has reminded me of what a good man you truly are. I know you would never wish for me to lose the baby, or that you would dismiss the miscarriage so easily. But at the time, I wasn't capable of thinking rationally. I just reacted."

Relief flooded him, making him feel suddenly light-headed. He had felt the weight of her condemnation for so long it had become a part of him, like an arm or a leg. Over the years, he'd questioned whether she might be right about him after all—what kind of man felt a shadow of relief upon learning the love of his life was losing their baby? It had taken time, but he'd gradually come to forgive himself for his knee-jerk reaction, viewing it as a moment of weakness brought on by youth and the aftereffects of his illness-induced fatigue. He had moved on, but part of him had always ached to think that Avery would never know just how badly he wanted to take back his thoughtless words.

It looked like today was his chance to tell her.

Avery's forgiveness was a balm for his soul, an absolution he had hoped for but never thought to receive. But he had wronged her, too. He had left her alone in the darkest moments of her life, walking away when she'd needed him the most, despite what she had said. Mere words would never be enough to tell her how sorry he was.

But he had to try.

He reached out and placed his hand on her arm, needing to touch her while he spoke. But her skin felt wrong; it was much too hot, and had the strange, almost waxlike quality of illness.

"Avery," he said, alarm creeping into his voice.

"You're burning up." He slid his hand up her arm to her neck, her forehead, then her back, searching in vain for a sign to prove him wrong. But her body gave off heat like a furnace, and he now recognized her glassy eyes were due to fever, not fatigue.

"I'm just still warm from the suit," she protested, trying to wave off his grasp.

"No, you're not." He put his fingers on her wrist, feeling for a pulse. Nice and steady; that was good. Keeping one hand on her shoulder, he reached back to grab his stethoscope off the desk.

"Grant," she protested. "Really, I'm fine. Nothing a little sleep won't fix."

He ignored her and focused on the sound of her breathing, searching for any signs of fluid in her lungs. They sounded clear, thank God.

For now.

"I want to get you started on the antiflu drugs," he pronounced, rising to his feet. Fear began to bubble up in his chest as he considered possible diagnoses. Avery could just have a case of the base crud—it was still circulating, and she had been talking to a lot of people during her investigation. It was a logical and likely explanation. But Grant couldn't shake the sense that this was something more.

When you hear hoofbeats, think horses, not zebras. It was an old adage from medical school, meant to encourage young, excitable clinicians from excluding a basic, common diagnosis in favor of something flashy but rare. Grant knew he was taking a leap to assume Avery was suffering from something more than a seasonal illness. But given the events on the base over the past few weeks, he wasn't so quick to dismiss his instincts. Especially not where she was concerned.

If, heaven forbid, she did have a case of this new flu, it seemed he was catching it early. Her only symptom so far was the fever; that meant her lungs weren't damaged yet. If he could get her started on the drugs now, hopefully he could stave off the worst of the illness and she'd make a full recovery.

He tuned in to realize she was talking to him. "I really think you're overreacting," she said. "Why don't I just take some aspirin and see if that helps? Save the drugs for the patients who need them most right now."

"Avery—"

She lifted her hand, cutting him off. "I'm going to head back to my room now and catch a nap. I'll check in with you later." She stood—or rather, she tried to. As soon as she made it to her feet, her face drained of what little color it had, turning a bone white that sent a nasty shiver down his spine. Avery lifted a hand to her forehead and swayed, letting out a soft "oof!" of surprise. Grant lunged forward and caught her just before she fell, maneuvering her back into the chair so she didn't hit the floor.

"I don't think so," he muttered. But it was clear Avery hadn't heard him. Her head lolled on her neck, and the bottom dropped out of his stomach as he realized she'd passed out.

"I need some help in here!" he yelled. Moving quickly, he gathered her into his arms and carried her to a cot a few steps away. He needed her to lie flat to help restore blood flow to her head, and he wasn't about to put her on the floor. As gently as he could, Grant placed her on the folding bed, then applied his fingers to her neck to find her pulse. Fast, but steady. Fair enough.

Jesse stepped into the office. "Everything okay, Doc? I thought I heard you shout…" He trailed off when he saw Avery on the bed. "What happened?" He rushed forward, his face a mask of worry.

"She's febrile. Tried to stand and fainted. I need you to bring a gurney, please, and let's get an IV started. Normal saline, ibuprofen. And the antiflu drugs."

Jesse stilled, his body going tense. "Do you think she has the virus?" His voice was very quiet, as if he was afraid of being overheard.

Grant placed his hand on her forehead. She felt even hotter now, and his certainty rose another notch even as his heart sank. "I'm afraid so."

Chapter 10

Darkness surrounded her.

She lay still, trying to assess if moving would be worth the effort. Her body felt leaden, almost as if she was buried in a vat of sand. She took a breath, fighting against the pressure on her chest. But something felt…off. She tried again, turning her focus inward in the hopes of identifying the problem. After a split second, she realized the issue: the pressure was coming from *inside* her chest.

Claustrophobia slammed into her, adding to the weight that kept her immobile. Panic scrabbled at the edges of her awareness, closing in on her consciousness. She tried to gasp for air, but her lungs refused to cooperate. Her heart pounded in her chest, the beat of it echoing in her ears until she felt like she was drowning in the noise.

Move, she had to move. Somehow she knew on an instinctive level that if she didn't regain control of her body she would die. She could feel it now, a sense of slipping away, as if she were in a boat approaching a waterfall. If she didn't do something, she would go over the edge and be lost.

Momentum built as the current of the river picked up speed, pushing her faster toward the drop-off point. She struggled against it, searching the banks for something to grab on to, an anchor to hold her in place. But it was no use. Every time she made contact with the edge, her grip was too tenuous to withstand the forces dragging at her. She kept slipping, at the mercy of the elements and totally helpless to change course and avoid her fate.

No! Her scream drowned out the sound of her heartbeat, and for a second she felt herself slow down. But the reprieve didn't last. The boat picked up speed again, roaring toward the falls ahead. The *whoosh* of the rushing water wrapped around her, cocooning her in a sound that should have been soothing but instead was terrifying.

No, she thought again, but she was losing the will to fight. What was the point? Helplessness stole over her, and as she surrendered to the river, the weight on her body lifted.

She took one deep, unhindered breath, reveling in the sensation of her lungs opening up to the cold, crisp air. Then the boat tipped over the ledge, launching her into the sky. She hung there for one brief, thrilling moment and felt the urge to laugh from the delight of weightlessness. She settled for a smile, and dropped like a stone.

* * *

"Pulse rate is dropping."

Grant bit his lip to keep from firing back a retort. He was watching the damn monitors, thank you very much. He didn't need a verbal play-by-play of Avery's deterioration—he was already well aware of the gravity of the situation.

"Don't even think about it," he muttered to her. He didn't know if she could really hear him—in medical school, they'd said hearing was the last sense to go—but he liked to think she could feel his presence and his determination to get her through this.

She just had to fight.

It was too early for the cough to have set in, but scans had revealed fluid was already starting to accumulate in her lungs; she'd developed a little hitch in her breathing that tugged at his guts with every inhalation. Could he stop it from getting worse?

Raising his voice, he barked out a series of orders. The nurses jumped into action, bringing him medication and tools in a carefully choreographed dance borne of training and clinical experience. He moved on autopilot, adjusting this, injecting that, tweaking what variables he could to pull Avery out of the free fall and bring her back from the brink. Anyone looking at him would see a calm professional doing the job he loved.

Inside, though, he was falling apart.

He could not lose her. Not again. And not like this. They had finally—finally!—started to repair the rift between them. And even though it hurt his heart to consider it, if Avery wanted to walk away again when this was over, he would respect her choice. But he wasn't going to let her die. If she left him again, it would be because it's what she wanted, not because some freak infection had stolen her life.

And just what are you going to do about it? whispered the voice of doubt in his mind. Because as much as he hated to admit it, the outcome wasn't really up to him. This virus had taken patients from him before, and it could do it again. The pathogen didn't care that Avery was different, that she meant so much more than a random patient. If he could use the brute force of his will to keep her alive, she would be safe, but medicine didn't work that way.

After a few tense moments, her heart rate evened out again and her vital signs stabilized. Grant stared hard at the monitors, holding his breath as he waited for any sign that the improvement was temporary. But she held steady, and after what seemed like an eternity he let himself relax.

"That's my girl," he murmured. She wasn't out of the woods yet, but if she could just hold on a little longer, give the drugs time to work…

He leaned down and put his mouth next to her ear. "Hold on, Avery," he whispered. "Just hold on."

Avery jerked to a sudden, painful stop.

She cast about with her senses, trying to determine what had broken her fall. But there was nothing, save the darkness. One minute, she was falling down, down, down into the depths. The next minute she was suspended in the air, hanging over the abyss. Even though she couldn't see it, she could *feel* it yawning beneath her, hungry for her body.

She did not want to surrender. Not just yet.

Time stretched on. She tested the tether that kept her dangling over the void. It was thin and tenuous, too fragile to hold her for long. But as she studied it, it grew a little thicker, a little bit stronger. Curious, that.

She heard a noise in the darkness and her senses prickled. There was something about it…something familiar. She struggled to make a connection, but it was too exhausting. Better to let it wash over her instead, a low, crooning sound that was soothing to her battered soul.

Colors flashed across her vision. A vibrant blue pulsed in time with the sound. Now a dark green, a different color for a different noise. That one was higher, softer. Then a brassy yellow sunburst exploded, triggering a wave of revulsion so strong she turned away, curling inward to protect herself. The buzz echoed around her, growing louder and louder until she thought she might burn from the intensity of the color. But then the blue voice returned, chasing away the noxious feeling like a cleansing rain. She unfurled her limbs, stretching and opening to soak up the light.

The blue wrapped around her, a soft warmth that made her feel safe. Her body began to tingle as the light and sound strengthened the harness that kept her in place. Slowly, so slowly, she felt herself rise, bit by bit.

But what was pulling her up? She focused on the sensation, but fatigue slammed into her and she slipped down, snapping the cord taut. She hung there for a breathless second, hardly daring to move lest she snap the tether and be lost.

Gradually, carefully, she forced herself to relax and cleared her mind. The sound returned, bringing with it another pulse of blue light. The healing ripples washed over her, and once more, she began to rise.

"How's she doing?"

Grant looked up to find Karen, one of the nurse practitioners on staff, standing on the other side of Avery's bed. Her expression was a mix of pity and concern, and he couldn't tell if she was more worried about Avery or his recent behavior.

He sat up, wincing a little as the stiff muscles of his back protested the movement. He'd parked himself next to Avery once she stabilized, and he hadn't moved for the last several hours. Some of the nurses had tried to entice him to take a break with offers of food or drink, but he'd refused them all. It wasn't just stubbornness on his part—he physically couldn't leave Avery's side. It made his palms sweat just thinking about her lying here alone. What if she woke up? What if she needed him? He simply couldn't take the chance that he would let her down.

And so he'd sat, holding one of her hands between his own, keeping one eye on the monitors as he crouched forward and spoke into her ear. He kept his voice low so as not to broadcast his words to the whole team. What he had to say was for Avery's ears only.

He'd apologized for his careless words all those years ago. He'd told her what he'd really felt that day, and in the days after—how his heart had broken and he'd worried he'd never find love again. And he told her what his life had been like without her: how he'd managed to build a life for himself, but now that he'd seen her again he realized his accomplishments paled in comparison to being with her. He bargained with her, offering her whatever she wanted if she would just open her eyes and come back to him. Then, because he didn't want to make her too depressed, he told her funny stories of his childhood and embarrassing stories from his early years as a doctor, when he'd been the new guy the staff had pranked relentlessly.

He talked about everything and nothing, but the words really didn't matter. He just wanted her to hear his voice. Some small, scared part of him feared that if he stopped talking to her, he would lose her for good. It wasn't very scientific of him, but Grant liked to think Avery was trying to find her way back to him, and if he kept speaking, she could use the sound of his voice as a guide. He'd already done everything he could for her, medically speaking. This constant stream of chatter was the only thing he had left to offer.

"She's holding on," he said, casting another look at the monitors. They confirmed his statement, and he exhaled softly. So far, so good. She wasn't showing marked signs of improvement—*yet*, he added silently—but she was no longer declining. It was almost as if she was in limbo, trying to decide which way to go. Hopefully, the sound of his voice would encourage her to choose the path of life.

Karen studied Avery's face for a moment, then nodded. "She's a fighter," she said softly. "If anyone can make it, she will."

Grant nodded, his throat too tight to speak. It was

the truth, and he was glad to know someone else realized how special Avery was.

"Some of the men who recovered from the infection are here. They'd like to speak to you."

Grant shook his head. "Tell them I'm busy."

"I figured you'd say that," Karen said. "But I thought I'd ask anyway." She turned to walk away, but Grant held up a hand.

"Do you know what they want?"

Karen lifted one shoulder and glanced pointedly at Avery. "They want to help."

"News travels fast, I suppose."

"It's a small world, Dr. Jones. And with three new patients and one man dead in his bed, there was no way this was going to stay secret for long."

Grant dropped his head, a wave of guilt washing over him. He should have been the one to break the news to the base and answer people's questions. But as soon as Avery got sick, his entire awareness had compressed down to her alone and he'd lost sight of his larger responsibilities.

"I'll tell them you're busy," she said, taking a step back.

"No, wait." He stood slowly, his mind whirring with possibilities. "You said the survivors are here?"

Karen nodded, eyeing him curiously. "Yes. I think everyone else is too afraid to come here. They don't want to accidentally get exposed to the pathogen."

Grant waved off her speculation, unconcerned with their motivation. All that mattered was that they wanted to help.

And he might have figured out a way for them to do just that.

* * *

Pain.

A stinging pinch, enough to get her attention. Anxiety prickled, making her skin crawl. The light surrounding her flickered and her unease mounted. Was she going to be left in the dark again? She tensed, but before panic could truly take hold, the blue resumed its steady glow. She relaxed back into its embrace, her concerns receding with every beat of her heart.

But the respite was short-lived. A new sensation demanded her attention, a tingling effervescence that was not altogether unpleasant. It started small but soon spread throughout her body until she felt like she was melting away.

Then the voice was back, strengthening the intensity of the blue light until it was blindingly bright. She turned away but could still feel the rays soaking into her body, fortifying her tissues with every pulse.

The intensity of the sensations mounted, driving her higher and higher toward some point she felt but could not see. Energy flooded into her, building to a crescendo too violent for her body to contain. Just as she began to shake from the effort of holding herself together, she broke through an invisible barrier and launched into a new plane of awareness.

It was an assault on her senses as sounds, scents and light battered her from all sides, the input immediately familiar and yet somehow foreign after her absence. Her brain began to catalog everything, the pace sluggish at first as she adjusted to her new level of consciousness.

The sharp, slightly stinging scents of bleach and alcohol invaded her nose. A steady, droning beep pierced the air, a counterpoint to the lower, constant thrum of the heater. Shadows and light played across her eyelids as people moved around her, and she was struck by a pang of longing for the comforting blue glow that had been her companion in the darkness. She tried to open her eyes but the task proved too difficult.

What happened? It was her first coherent thought and it echoed throughout her mind, urgency building with every repetition. She struggled to think, feeling like her brain was filled with honey. The answers were there, but she couldn't access them—at least not quickly enough to suit her. But the harder she reached for the thoughts, the faster they scuttled away. Recognizing the futility of her efforts, Avery relaxed and was finally rewarded as bits of memories gradually bobbed to the surface and she began to piece things together.

The hospital. The outbreak. And Grant.

Clearly, she was sick. But how had it happened?

The last thing she remembered was talking to Grant. He'd given her a bottle of water, and the cool liquid had felt so nice sliding down her parched throat. But that's where her memories ended. Everything after his office was a mystery.

Grant will know. The thought brought some measure of comfort and she relaxed, only to feel the cold grip of fear with her next heartbeat.

What if Grant was sick, too? Or worse, what if he had fallen over the edge and was truly gone? She had been lucky; something had grabbed her before she'd gone too far into the abyss. What if Grant hadn't been so fortunate? It was a possibility almost too terrifying to contemplate.

Avery channeled all her energy and tried to move. She needed to find Grant, to reassure herself that he was fine. She fought against the weakness of illness and the mental fog that still hovered over her, but her body wouldn't respond to her commands. She tried to speak, but something was lodged in her throat, paralyzing her voice.

"She's waking up!" a voice called out.

Hands descended, touching her here, then there, pushing lightly on her shoulders and trapping her hands. Avery's heart pounded hard in her chest, and she felt the echo of each beat thrum through her limbs. She struggled harder, fighting to cast off her restraints and get back to herself.

"Avery."

His voice was low and clear in her ear, and her body relaxed before her mind had fully recognized him. Grant. He was here.

"You're okay," he continued. "Try to stay calm for me. You're intubated—that's why you can't talk. We need you to stay quiet for a little longer, so I'm going to give you a little something to help you relax. I'll be here with you the whole time."

He slipped her hand between his own as a trickle of warmth traveled up her arm and a bitter taste flooded her mouth. Her limbs grew impossibly heavy, and she felt like she was sinking into quicksand. It was a claustrophobic sensation, but the comforting sound of Grant's voice in her ear helped keep the fear at bay. She focused on his touch and let herself drop, trusting him to be there to pull her back up again.

Chapter 11

Grant leaned back in his chair and watched Avery sleep, the tension slowly leaching from his body with every breath she took. He should have been happy, but he was too drained for that. The last few days had left him feeling raw and fragile, as if the disease that had attacked Avery had burned through him, as well.

For a brief, terrifying time he'd thought he was going to lose her. She'd been circling the drain, moments away from death, and he'd stood there, paralyzed by fear. After an endless pause his training had kicked in and he'd shoved his emotions to the side so he could do what needed to be done. He'd administered drugs, giving her anything he thought might help. He'd tracked her progress with tests and scans, poring over the results in search of any sign her condition was improving. And when the survivors had volunteered to help, he'd taken their plasma and injected it into Avery, hoping their antibodies would help her fight the disease.

Against all odds, his efforts had worked.

He still wasn't sure how she had survived—the disease had progressed quickly and her symptoms had grown worse with each passing hour. Her breathing had worried him the most; the amount of bloody fluid in her lungs had increased at an alarming rate, and he'd made the decision to put her on a ventilator to help her breathe. He had practically felt her life draining away and he'd tried to make peace with the idea of losing her. But no matter how bad she looked, he hadn't been able to accept that she was dying.

Maybe it was his unwillingness to give up on her. Maybe it was Avery's stubborn streak. Or maybe it had simply been luck. Whatever the reason, she had rallied, and he wasn't too interested in questioning their good fortune.

She stirred on the bed and moaned faintly. The sedative was wearing off, and he was anxious for her to wake up. Even though all her test results and vital signs showed improvement, he needed to hear her voice and watch the emotions play across her face before he could really trust that she was going to be okay.

"Avery." He spoke softly so as not to startle her. Some patients came out of sedation confused and agitated, and he didn't want to make the process any harder on her. But he wanted her to know he was there, that she wasn't alone.

She turned her face toward him and blinked slowly, clearly trying to wake up. He took her hand

and squeezed gently. "I'm here," he said. "Just take your time. I'm not going anywhere."

"Grant?" Her voice was barely more than a mumble, but it was music to his ears. His heart lightened at the sound, and he couldn't keep from smiling.

"Yes, it's me. I'm here."

She focused on him, her blue eyes bleary but growing more alert by the minute. Her fingers moved in his, her palm turning so she could grip his hand. There was an edge of desperation to her touch, as if she was afraid he would let go. *Not a chance*, he thought. *Not ever again.*

"What happened?" The words came out a little slurred but they were clear enough. "How did this…" She trailed off and closed her eyes again, clearly worn out from the effort of speaking. But she didn't lapse back into unconsciousness. After a second of rest, she opened her eyes and fixed her gaze on him with an expectant air.

Grant debated his answer. Should he tell her everything he knew, or just the basics? He didn't intend to keep anything from her, but he knew from experience patients needed a little time before the mental fog of sedation fully cleared. It was probably best to provide simple answers so as not to overwhelm her— they could have a more in-depth conversation later.

"You got sick," he said.

Despite the lingering effects of the drugs, Avery still managed to shoot him a piercing look. "You don't say."

Grant laughed at her unexpected sass and shook his head, feeling a little rueful. Truth be told, his answer was lame even to his own ears. So much for trying to spare her an upset.

"Fair enough," he said, secretly pleased at her display of attitude. She must be feeling better if she had energy to spare for sarcasm. "Five days ago you fainted in my office when you tried to stand. You were febrile, and tests showed early signs of blood accumulation in your lungs. Your condition worsened, but fortunately the drugs and supportive care kicked in and you began to improve. We gave you a boost two days ago, and now here we are."

Avery frowned as he spoke, and he could tell she was working hard to listen and process what he was saying. He wanted to tell her to save her strength, but he knew she was too stubborn for that.

"Was it the pathogen?" She phrased it as a question, but he could tell by her tone she was making a statement. Still, he nodded in confirmation.

"How?"

It was the same question that had been haunting Grant since she came to his office. How had Avery contracted the virus? As far as he knew, she hadn't been around any sick people, with the exception of Richard. But she'd been wearing full protective gear while talking to him, so she couldn't have gotten it that way. She might have been exposed while collecting samples from the bar, but again, she'd taken proper precautions. Furthermore, the timing didn't match up—she'd sampled the bar only hours before falling ill, which didn't fit the clinical profile of this disease. No, she had to have picked it up some other way, and until they knew how, he was going to second-guess everything they knew about this bug and how it was transmitted.

"I don't know yet," he said. "But I'm going to find out."

She nodded slightly, her eyes closing. "Anyone else?"

"No," he assured her. That was another odd piece of the puzzle. Aside from Richard and Bradley, Avery was the only one who had fallen ill recently. He'd expected additional cases to pop up after she got sick, because it stood to reason that when Avery had been exposed, other people had been, as well. But the disease had remained quiet...

She shook her head slowly, the furrow between her eyebrows deepening. "Doesn't make sense," she mumbled. "This is all wrong..."

Grant agreed with her, but now wasn't the time to discuss it. Avery needed her rest, and frankly, so did he. He'd been surviving on catnaps at her bedside, but now that she was out of the woods he could let himself collapse for a few hours.

She was so still he thought she'd gone back to sleep, and he rose quietly. But before he could take a step, she spoke again. "The others?"

Richard and Bradley, she meant. Unfortunately, they hadn't fared as well. "They're both still unconscious," he said. "Their condition hasn't really changed much in the last few days." Which was a mixed blessing—he was glad they didn't seem to be declining, but they should have started to improve by now, especially after the administration of plasma from the survivors. The fact that the men were still so ill meant there was a very large chance they weren't going to pull through. But he wasn't willing to give up hope just yet...

"They'll make it," she said, her voice surprisingly certain despite its weakness. Grant wondered at her confidence—maybe experiencing the illness herself had given Avery special insight into surviving it. Or maybe she just had more faith in his abilities as a physician than he did. Either way, he hoped she was right. He'd had enough of watching people suffer. He was no stranger to death in his line of work, but that didn't mean he had to like it.

"I'll tell them you said so." He leaned forward and brushed a strand of hair off her forehead. The corners of her mouth turned up as his fingertip grazed her skin, and his heart fluttered to see her response. Never in his wildest dreams had he imagined there would come a time when Avery welcomed his touch again. It both humbled and exhilarated him to realize how far they'd come in such a short period of time.

"Get some rest," she said softly. "You look like hell."

"I thought that was supposed to be my line," he teased.

She smiled but didn't reply, her body going lax as she sank back into sleep. Grant watched her for a moment, oddly reluctant to leave her side. Logically, he knew she would be fine and there was no reason for him to stay. But something about the situation nagged at him, like a hangnail he couldn't stop bothering. Right before she'd passed out, Avery mentioned the outbreak seemed strange. Although Grant didn't have a lot of experience dealing with disease epidemics, even he could see she was right. He wasn't quite sure what to make of recent events, but until he knew exactly what was going on, he didn't want to leave Avery alone when she was still so vulnerable.

Feeling a little ridiculous, Grant walked over to the nearest empty gurney and unlocked the wheels, then manhandled the unwieldy bed into place next to Avery's. He grabbed the edge of the privacy curtain and tugged, pulling the rough fabric along the tracks in the ceiling to create the illusion of a room. The gurney squeaked in protest as he climbed on and he froze, casting a glance at Avery to see if he'd woken her. But she slumbered on undisturbed, her expression peaceful and no longer marred by the strain of sickness.

With a sigh, Grant arranged his long frame on the narrow bed and closed his eyes. The bright fluorescent lights overhead made it difficult to fully relax, but despite the annoying glow he could feel sleep cast its seductive spell on his body. After a final glance at Avery, he surrendered to the pull and sank into the restorative depths of oblivion.

Paul dialed the phone with shaking fingers, hoping his contact would answer. He'd tried to call several times over the past few days, but the man hadn't deigned to pick up. Every unanswered call had twisted the knot in Paul's gut a little tighter, and now it was on the verge of snapping. He had to find out what was happening with his son; he couldn't take the silence any longer.

His mother still thought Noah was staying with a friend, and Paul didn't have the heart to tell her otherwise. She was getting on in years and had already been overwhelmed by the daily demands of life before he'd left the kids with her. But he hadn't had any other options, and Noah and Lisa were old enough to mostly fend for themselves. Lisa was savvy enough to know something didn't quite add up with her brother's absence, but Paul had lied to her and said he'd spoken with Noah. The last thing he wanted was for his daughter to start asking questions. The Organization was clearly keeping tabs on his family, and he knew it wouldn't hesitate to take his other child if she became a liability.

The ringing tone grated harshly in his ear as he held his breath, silently counting along with the pulses. Ten... Twenty... Thirty... He tightened his grip on the phone, his hope waning as the time stretched on. Forty... Fifty... He wasn't going to pick up.

Just as Paul lowered the phone from his ear, a low voice came on the line.

"You're a very persistent man, Mr. Coleson."

Paul scrambled to bring the phone back up to his ear, nearly dropping it in his haste. "Yes, I—uh—I needed to speak with you." His heart pounded as he spoke, hard enough that he felt every beat in his fingertips.

"Were your instructions not clear?"

"No." Realizing his mistake, he hastily added, "I mean, no, I understand what you want me to do."

"Then why do you continue to call?" The man's tone made it clear that even though he hadn't answered, he had nonetheless been disturbed by Paul's frequent attempts to connect. A tendril of fear curled around Paul's heart and began to squeeze. Would they take their displeasure with him out on his son?

He considered his next words carefully. It wouldn't go over well if he sounded too demanding. He had to make it clear they were still in charge, or else they might try to punish him by hurting Noah.

"I was hoping you could give me news of my son," he said, trying to keep his tone deferential. "I've been worried about him."

"Have you, now?" Amusement laced his contact's words, and Paul felt a surge of white-hot anger build in his chest. What he wouldn't give to be able to reach through the phone and strangle the man on the other end!

"Please," he said, nearly choking on the word. "Please let me know how Noah is doing."

"I can assure you he is fine," the man replied briskly. "He continues to enjoy our hospitality and will do so until you have fulfilled your end of the bargain."

It was the first time the Organization had confirmed what Jesse had told him regarding Noah's release, and Paul seized on the words. "So you'll let him go once the virus is loaded onto the ship?" He brightened a little at the thought—he'd been working nearly nonstop since finding out about Noah's abduction, and he was almost done amplifying the virus. It was a matter of days now until he'd have the quantity they'd asked for, and it wouldn't take long to smuggle it aboard the ship. This nightmare would be over soon...

"Something like that," the man replied smoothly.

Paul kept his mouth shut, but he was no fool. He knew in that moment they weren't going to release his son. He could send them a million gallons of the virus and they still wouldn't let him go. Noah's fate had been sealed the moment they kidnapped him, but Paul had been too stupid to realize it.

What was left of his heart snapped into pieces and the pain of it made him double over. He was going to lose his son, if he hadn't done so already. His firstborn, the young man who would always be a baby in his mind. He sucked in a ragged breath and was assaulted with the scent memory of Noah's soft, wispy hair, fresh from his first bath in the hospital. He clenched his fist, feeling the ghost of Noah's small hand tucked trustingly in his own as they walked to the park. So many memories, so many small scenes that made up Noah's life. Despair filled Paul's chest, and tears stung his eyes. It wasn't enough—Noah was still so young, with so much potential yet to be realized. He had barely begun to experience life; he deserved so much more before he came to the end.

"No." His voice broke on the word. "Please, let him go. Take me instead."

"Perhaps we will," his contact said shortly. "In the meantime, continue to do your job. Should you find your motivation flagging, remember you still have a daughter and a mother, too. It would be a shame to involve both of them, as well."

Sensing the man was about to hang up, Paul blurted out, "Can I talk to him? Please, can I just hear my son's voice?" If he knew Noah was still alive, he might be able to find a way to save him. It was a long shot, but he couldn't give up on his son without trying anything and everything possible to bring him home.

There was a pause, and for a moment Paul feared the man had already disconnected. Then he heard the man sigh and knew he was considering the request. "He is not nearby," he said finally. "But I will see what can be arranged."

"Thank you," Paul said, but he was talking to a dial tone.

He pocketed his phone, his mind a million miles away. Noah must still be alive—he had to believe it. Surely he would know if his son had died already. Wouldn't he have felt the ripples in the universe if Noah was no longer here? But how could he save him?

He could call the authorities. Maybe if he explained everything, they could track Noah and find where he was being held. It was a long shot, but it might be the only chance his son had...

Paul ran his finger over the phone, preparing to dial the numbers that might save Noah's life. But before he could press the first digit, Lisa's face flashed in his mind. Could he risk the safety of his daughter and his mother, knowing the chances of finding his son were infinitesimally small?

But could he live with himself, knowing his failure to try had condemned Noah?

Paralysis overtook him and he stood frozen in place, trapped between two horrific choices. He had already lost his wife. Would he have to bear the loss of his children, too?

Noah's situation was dire, and Paul understood the chance of losing his son was unbearably high. Lisa was safe—for now. But Paul knew it was only a matter of time before the Organization targeted his daughter. Never mind that she had no knowledge of his work; ignorance was no guarantee of safety, and she would never stop asking questions about her brother's disappearance.

Were they watching her even now? They had to be. They must have been spying on his family all along, hiding in the shadows until it was time to strike. He still wasn't sure why they'd taken Noah in the first place. Had he asked them too many questions or seemed too reluctant to carry out their orders? Or perhaps this had been their plan all along. Either way, he was running out of time to save his kids.

There was only one thing he could do—he had to call the authorities and confess everything. He would probably spend the rest of his life in prison for his crimes, but it was a small price to pay for the lives of his children.

Assuming they believed him.

The thought made his blood run cold, and a trickle of fear slid down the valley of his spine like a rivulet of ice water. What if he called the FBI or Homeland Security and no one believed his confession? They had to get hundreds, if not thousands, of crank tips a week. What if his story was too fantastical to be believed? After all, he was talking about an all-powerful terrorist organization operating in the shadows of a well-respected international charity. It was the stuff of movie thrillers, not real life. He would probably be laughed off the phone, and even if he wasn't, it would take time for them to confirm his story.

Time his children didn't have.

Paul sank into his chair, panic starting to set in as he realized he held no power over this situation. One of the reasons he'd agreed to work for the Organization was because he'd assumed that if things got really bad, he could always expose them to the world via the police or the press. He'd thought of it as his "nuclear option" and had figured it was a kind of insurance policy that would ensure that the Organization treated him fairly. What a fool he'd been!

Now he realized he only had two options: call his mother and tell her to pack up Lisa and run, or say nothing and hope the Organization left her alone. If he warned his mother, she would at least be aware of the danger they were in. But it would probably only make things worse. His mother wasn't capable of protecting Lisa, and the thought of her trying to outrun the Organization would be comical if the situation wasn't so serious. Furthermore, if he did reach out, the Organization would know and it wouldn't hesitate to punish Lisa. At least if he kept silent they wouldn't have a reason to target his mother and daughter.

He should leave well enough alone. It was the smart thing to do, considering how completely outflanked he was.

But he was tired of being smart. And he was tired of being scared.

He'd had more tragedy in his life than he deserved. First, he'd lost his wife. Now he was losing his son and would likely lose his daughter, as well. He was done being a passive victim of fate. It was past time for him to step up and fight for the things that mattered to him.

Starting with his family.

He dialed the numbers before he could lose his nerve. It was only after the phone started ringing that he realized he had no idea what time it was back home. Would anyone be there to answer?

"FBI. How may I direct your call?"

He swallowed hard and took a deep breath. "I want to report a kidnapping."

Chapter 12

Avery sat in bed and stared at her laptop screen, but no matter how many times she read the email, the words didn't change.

I'm relieved to know you are recovering from your illness, Harold wrote. I've managed to arrange transport off the base, which will bring you back to Atlanta. I'll feel better once we get you into a fully equipped hospital, and hopefully your antibodies will shed further light on this virus. Safe travels. See you soon.

She couldn't deny the suggestion of home was comforting—she still felt weak from the virus, and the thought of slipping into her worn flannel robe and curling up in her own bed was unmistakably appealing. She was also touched by Harold's concern. Based on his previous emails, she knew that he'd pulled a lot of strings to get a plane arranged on such short notice, and it was a testament to his loyalty to her that he'd persisted in the face of bureaucratic resistance. Avery knew she should be grateful for his efforts, and she was. But despite all the reasons she should be counting the hours until the plane arrived, she wasn't quite ready to leave.

Part of it was professional pride. She'd never left an investigation before it was finished, and doing so now felt like admitting defeat. Her ego demanded she stay and see the case through to the end, regardless of the lack of meaningful progress. None of the samples she had gathered at the bar had tested positive for the virus, which meant she was back to square one in terms of finding a common source for the outbreaks. It was a frustrating setback, but it made her all the more determined to solve the mystery. This was proving to be the most difficult case of her career to date, and she hated the thought of leaving early simply because she'd been unlucky enough to contract the disease. Thanks to the efforts of Grant and his team, she had survived. Now she owed them answers. This wasn't just a matter of professional curiosity anymore—it was personal.

Speaking of personal... Grant's face flashed in her mind, and she couldn't help smiling. Her memories before passing out were a little fuzzy, but she did recall their conversation in his office. Forgiving him had felt good, as if she'd cast off some emotional hobble and was now free to fully experience life again. It was amazing how much of a difference she noticed, despite the lingering effects of her illness. All that anger and hurt she'd held on to had shaded her perceptions, casting the world in shadows. Now that she had released the burden of her pain, things looked bright again, as if she'd taken off dark sunglasses. The color was back in her life, and it was truly beautiful.

She needed more time with Grant. This truce between them was still so new. She wanted to nurture it, to strengthen it, and see where it would lead them. They had ten years of catching up to do—there was no way to accomplish that in the two days she had left on-base.

Maybe she could take a leave of absence, she mused. She certainly had a good reason for it. As much as she hated to admit it, it would be a long time before she felt back to her old self again. Harold would understand if she wanted to take some personal leave to deal with the physical and psychological aftereffects of coming so close to death. Perhaps Grant could visit her in Atlanta, or she could meet him somewhere and they could get to know each other again. Now that they were on good terms once more, she wanted to discover if there was still anything worth resurrecting between them.

The more she thought about it, the more she liked that idea. The next time she saw Grant, she'd ask him about it. His response would reveal a lot about his feelings on the matter, as well. If he was excited about the plan, she'd know they might still have something. If he was lukewarm to the idea, well…it would be disappointing, but better to find that out now before she fell all the way in love with him again.

In the meantime, though, she needed to turn her full attention to the investigation. Grant had insisted she stay in her room and rest as much as possible, going so far as to bring her meals so she didn't have to get out in the cold. He had even tried to take her files, saying they would be a distraction and she needed to conserve her energy. It was only after she'd told him she would hike over to the hospital in her bare feet to get them back that he'd relented and left all her notes and patient records. She closed her laptop and turned to them now, hoping that by looking at the information again she'd find some new detail she'd previously missed that would prove to be the salvation of this sinking investigation.

Avery immersed herself in the data, trying to examine it with fresh eyes. She ignored all her previous analyses and started from scratch, thinking that maybe a new approach would reveal the proverbial smoking gun. The work proved harder than she cared to admit. Her bout with the virus had taken a lot out of her both physically and mentally, and once more she recognized how lucky she was to be alive.

She lost all awareness of time as she worked until a knock on the door interrupted her focus. She blinked and cast a quick glance at the alarm clock on the bedside table, surprised to find that three hours had flown by. Not that she had anything impressive to show for it…

Anticipation fluttered in her belly as she shoved the paperwork to the side and climbed out of bed. Only one person came to her room, and even though she had seen Grant when he'd brought her lunch, she was looking forward to seeing him again.

She crossed to the door and had the sudden realization she must look terrible. She'd thrown her hair in a ponytail this morning and hadn't bothered with makeup since falling sick. It was silly to be so vain when Grant had seen her at her worst, but a small, girly part of her wanted to look nice for him. She smoothed a hand over her hair with a sigh. Maybe next time.

The scent of food wafted into the room, and her stomach rumbled appreciatively. Apparently, Grant had heard the sound—she opened the door to find him grinning down at her, his arms full of bags.

"Hungry?"

"Starving," she replied. She hadn't noticed her empty stomach while working, but now that she'd taken a break she was becoming aware of her body's needs again.

"That's a good sign," Grant said. He stepped into the room and nudged the door shut, then put the bags on the narrow desk and began pulling food from their depths. "I brought soup, sandwiches, drinks and, if you're very good, dessert."

Her ears pricked at that. "What kind of dessert?" Avery craned her neck to see over his shoulder, but his body blocked her view of the food.

Grant laughed and placed one of the paper bags on the floor, making sure to fold it shut before he did so. "It's a surprise," he said. "You have to finish your dinner first."

"You sound like my mom," she grumbled. "That was always her line when I was a kid."

If the comparison bothered him, he didn't show it. "She sounds like a wise woman," he said with mock solemnity.

Avery rolled her eyes. "Well, she always liked you, so I'm not sure what that says about her judgment."

Grant clapped a hand to his chest and staggered back a step. "You wound me!" he declared dramatically.

"I'm sure your ego will recover," Avery said primly.

He returned to the table and pulled out her chair, gesturing for her to sit. "I'm sure you're right," he said with a wink.

Avery reached for a bottle of water and unscrewed the cap. "You seem in an especially good mood."

Grant sat next to her and pushed a carton of soup and a cellophane-wrapped sandwich in front of her. "I'm having a cozy dinner with a beautiful woman. What more could a guy ask for?"

His compliment made her glow a little inside, and she smiled. "Good day at the hospital?"

He nodded, holding up a finger that told her he had something to say as soon as he finished chewing. Excitement burned bright in his eyes, and Avery leaned toward him, eager to hear his news.

Grant swallowed with an audible gulp. "Richard woke up," he announced.

The news was so unexpected Avery nearly choked on her spoonful of soup. "That's wonderful! What about Bradley?"

"Still unconscious. But I'm not giving up hope yet."

Avery nodded, and they ate in silence for a few moments. "Do you think Richard feels up to talking yet?"

Grant chuckled softly, and she tilted her head to the side, sensing she was being teased. "What?"

"I was waiting for you to ask me that," he said, taking another sip of soup.

"Glad I'm so predictable," she responded wryly.

Grant winked at her. "Just another one of your charms."

"Indeed." She set down her spoon and reached for the water bottle. "But seriously, when do you think I can talk to him? I have more questions, especially since none of the samples at the bar gave us anything, and Paul's blood was a big miss, as well."

Grant lifted one shoulder and considered his sandwich. "We'll see how he's doing tomorrow. You might be able to ask him a few questions if you keep it short. I don't want to wear him out." He took a bite and spoke through a mouthful of food. "What's the rush?"

Avery took a deep breath, hating to be the bearer of bad news. She'd thought Grant would already be aware of her upcoming departure. The base commander certainly knew to expect the arrival of a plane, and she figured he would have told Grant about it. Apparently, that wasn't the case.

He slowly lowered his sandwich to the table and swallowed. "What's going on? Why do you have that look on your face?"

The question distracted her, and she smiled. "What look is that?"

"It's the same expression you wore in college when my mom made you tell me the dog had died."

"In her defense, she was very broken up about it," Avery began, but Grant cut her off.

"I'm sure she was. Now spill it."

There was no sense in beating around the bush— he knew her too well for that. "I'm leaving in two days."

He went totally still, freezing in the act of lifting

his water bottle to take a sip. He held it in midair, his thirst apparently forgotten for the moment.

"Oh?" The casual note in his tone sounded forced, and Avery knew he was more upset by the news than he was letting on. He took a drink from his bottle, then placed it back on the table and carefully re-capped it, avoiding her eyes the whole time.

"It wasn't my idea." It was important for him to understand that. Avery didn't want him to think she was running away from him, or that she no longer wanted to see him.

"My boss arranged it," she continued. "He wants me back in Atlanta, wants me to get checked out at the hospital there."

Grant's shoulders relaxed and he met her gaze. "He's right. You should finish recovering at home."

"I don't see why," she retorted, suddenly annoyed. What made the men in her life feel like they knew what was best for her? It was nice of Harold to have arranged transport off the base, but he could have at least warned her before taking the initiative. And Grant of all people should know that she was now on the mend. "I can rest here, and I'm not done with my investigation."

"I'll feel better knowing you have access to unlimited medical care," Grant began, but she cut him off.

"Don't sell yourself short," she said. "You're an amazing physician. You're the reason I'm still alive, the reason any of the victims of this disease are still alive."

Spots of pink bloomed on his cheeks and he looked away. "I got lucky," he said gruffly.

"No, you didn't," Avery said softly. "You saved

me." As she spoke the words the memory of the warm blue light filled her and everything clicked into place. "You sat by me, didn't you? While I was unconscious. You were there." It had been his voice, his touch finding her in the darkness. He had been the one to stop her fall, to bring her back into the light when she would have been lost.

Of course, she thought. *It's always been him.*

Grant's eyes widened, but he nodded. "Did one of the nurses tell you that?" He sounded almost embarrassed, as if his vigil had been something he wanted to keep secret. But why? Did he think she wouldn't appreciate his sacrifices?

Avery shook her head. "No one told me. I heard you."

He scoffed, but when he saw she wasn't kidding he grew serious again. "Really?" There was doubt in his voice, as if he couldn't quite bring himself to believe her. But underneath that was another note: hope.

"It's the truth. I felt like I had fallen over the edge of a waterfall, and I was sinking fast into darkness." Her voice trailed off as the memory asserted itself, and a hollow feeling opened up in her stomach as she relieved the terror of the free fall. Panic was a thick band around her chest, growing tighter with each breath. She closed her eyes, trying to summon the strength to break free, but it was no use. She was back in the darkness, alone and scared.

Something touched her, and she opened her eyes to find Grant's hand on hers, his eyes full of concern. She squeezed his fingers, silently assuring him she was okay. And she was—now. Once again, he had brought her back from the edge.

She took a deep breath and continued the story. "So there I was, falling into the abyss, my stomach in my throat. Then something grabbed hold of me before I was lost, and it slowly started pulling me back up." Avery traced the bones of his hand with her fingertip, avoiding his gaze. "I didn't know what it was, but now I realize you were the one to find me in the dark. You were the one who pulled me back and kept me from dying." She looked up then, blinking against the sting of tears. "It's always been you, Grant. There was a time when I didn't want to need you, and I hated the fact that I did. But I learned the hard way that didn't change things."

"Oh, Avery." He spoke her name with reverence, as if it was something precious. "You are too good for me. I don't deserve your heart."

She tilted her head to the side as she studied him, seeing the emotion play across his face. "Why would you say that?"

"I should have been there for you." He saw her look of confusion and held up a hand to forestall her question. "Before. With the baby."

"Oh." The reminder of her loss gave her pause, and she braced herself for the usual jolt of pain that accompanied thoughts of the miscarriage. But they didn't come. She felt an ache as she pictured the child that had been a part of her life, if only for a brief moment. But it was the dull throb of a healing bruise, not the fresh sting of a raw wound. There would always be a part of her that grieved the loss, but it no longer overshadowed her life.

"I was so selfish," Grant continued. "I should have been there for you, supported you like a true partner.

But all I could think about was how the miscarriage affected me. I let you down, and I've never forgiven myself for it."

Avery was silent for a moment, trying to decide what to say. If she rushed to reassure Grant that she no longer blamed him, he wouldn't believe it—he would think she was just trying to be nice. If she wanted him to let go of the past, she was going to have to try a different tack.

"I spent a lot of years blaming you for your reaction," she said finally. "I won't lie—it hurt me badly to think you didn't want the baby. At times, I thought you were almost happy to be off the hook." Grant made a small sound of distress and she touched his arm, silently asking him to let her finish. "I know now that you weren't, but at the time I was too short-sighted to see otherwise."

"I was never happy about the miscarriage." He paused, clearly weighing his words. "But I won't lie—I did feel a little lighter, as if a burden had been lifted from me." He dropped his head. "I tried to put on a brave face for you when you told me about the baby, but inside, I was terrified at the thought of becoming a father. When I found out you were losing it, it was almost like the universe had hit Pause for me, and was giving me more time to become the kind of man who deserved a child."

"Maybe it did," Avery said softly.

Grant jerked his head up. "How can you be so understanding? Don't you hate me for what I just told you?"

Avery's heart swelled with compassion, and she leaned forward to put her hand on his shoulder. "No," she said simply. "You can't help how you felt, and I'm not going to punish you for being honest with me. Especially because I know what kind of man you were then, and what kind of man you are now."

"I…I don't understand." His voice was thick with emotion and disbelief.

"I loved you for a reason, Grant," she explained patiently. "You were a good man. I couldn't have been with you otherwise. And being around you now has shown me that hasn't changed. I've been watching you, the way you interact with your staff and your patients. The care you take with the people around you. The burden you carry as you try to do right by your patients. Those are the actions of a man with integrity, with honor and with goodness in his heart. I'm not going to let one moment ten years ago define how I think about you. Not any longer." She paused to let her words sink in. "And neither should you."

He was still a moment, so still she wondered if he had heard her. Then he shot out of his chair and grabbed her, pulling her up and pressing her against his chest.

"Do you have any idea how much I've missed you?" Avery opened her mouth, but he didn't wait for a response. "You were my whole life," he continued. "Nothing worked without you, did you know that? You ruined me for anyone else."

His confession sent a thrill down her spine, and pleasure bloomed in her chest. She shouldn't feel happy at the news that Grant had also been stuck in limbo since their breakup, but her heart was anything but logical right now. A giggle bubbled up and broke free before she could contain it, and Grant leaned back to look at her.

"Laughing at my pain?" he grumbled. But there was a note of humor in his voice, and Avery knew he was teasing. She didn't try to stop the grin tugging at the corners of her mouth.

"Yes," she replied.

His eyes softened and soon he was smiling, too. She giggled again from the sheer joy of being in his arms, and he chuckled, his chest vibrating pleasantly against hers. Then they were both laughing, leaning against each other as all the emotion poured out of them in wave after wave of chortles, snickers and snorts.

Several minutes later, Avery managed to catch her breath. "Oh, man," she said, wiping the tears from her eyes. "I haven't laughed like that in ages." Her stomach ached from it, the muscles of her torso sadly out of use in that respect.

"I know what you mean," Grant said. "It feels good." He reached out and traced the line of her jaw with his fingertip. The light touch made Avery's blood heat, and she was suddenly very aware of Grant's nearness and the warm smell of his skin. "I've missed you so much," he whispered.

"I've missed you, too," she said, her throat tight with need.

His gaze zeroed in on her mouth and his hazel eyes darkened. "Would you cry if I kissed you again?" he said.

The question made her body rejoice, and she felt a zing of anticipation low in her belly. She lifted her hand and threaded her fingers through the short, soft hair on the back of his head.

"I'll cry if you don't."

Desire flickered in his eyes, but before he could say anything, Avery pulled him down and kissed him.

Chapter 13

Grant sucked in a breath and froze, half afraid that this was all just a dream that would vanish if he moved. But Avery's mouth was warm on his, and he tasted the lingering flavors of tomato and basil left behind from her soup. This was real—*she* was real. And she was giving him a second chance.

He had imagined this moment in so many ways over the years, but the reality far surpassed any of his fantasies. Her lips were supple and a little rough, their slightly chapped condition a lingering testament to her illness. She linked her hands behind his neck and pressed her body flat against his chest, the strength of her grip leaving no doubt as to her intentions.

His body rejoiced, all too happy to reciprocate her interest. He spread his hands across her lower back, then slowly ran them up her sides. His fingertips encountered the dips and projections of her ribs, another reminder of the toll the virus had taken on her body. A shiver ran down his spine at the visceral reminder of how close he had come to losing her, and he wrapped his arms around her, his arousal momentarily eclipsed by the need to reassure himself that she was okay.

Avery seemed to sense his need; she broke their kiss and laid her head against his chest with a little sigh. It was a sweet, trusting sound, an aural confirmation that she had opened her heart to him again. It was the greatest gift he'd even been given, and he silently vowed to be a man worthy of her regard.

He idly stroked her hair, the strands smooth against the skin of his palm, her orange-spice scent strong in his nose. Life was just about perfect, he mused. The woman he loved was in his arms; he was warm; his stomach was full. What more could a man ask for?

Grant wasn't sure how long they stood there, lost in each other's arms. It didn't matter—he would never get enough time with her. Eventually, Avery stirred and he loosened his hold enough to let her lean back. It was late, and she was likely tired. She was still recovering, and he should leave so she could get some rest.

But when he saw the look in her eyes, Grant realized sleep was the last thing on Avery's mind.

A mischievous smile lit up her face and she placed her hand flat on his chest, giving him a little shove. It was unexpected, and he stepped back to catch his balance. She followed, pushing again, and he took another step back. His knees hit the edge of her bed and he sat, his eyes growing wide as he stared up at her.

Avery moved to stand between his legs, her smile growing heated. She reached out and placed her hands on his shoulders, her touch warm through the fabric of his scrubs. His heart skipped a beat as she leaned down and brushed her mouth against his. Once… Twice… She moved in for a third kiss, and he reached up, catching her face in his hands before she could make contact again.

He read the question in her eyes and answered it with one of her own. "What are we doing?" he whispered.

She laughed, a low, sexy rumble that sent his blood pooling low in his belly and almost made him forget his own question. "Isn't it obvious?" she teased. Her hands traveled across his chest, her touch simultaneously gentle and taunting.

He struggled to stay focused, but it was growing increasingly difficult to ignore his body's responses. "Uh…" he stalled. There was something he'd wanted to say, but what was it? She continued to touch him, first here, then there, each caress taking him further away from logical thought. He grabbed her hands, stilling them as he made one last attempt to remember what had seemed so important only seconds ago…

It came to him in a jolt, and he snapped his head up to look at her. "You need to rest," he said firmly. "You're still recovering, and I don't want you to have a relapse."

"I'm fine," she assured him, leaning forward to

kiss him again. For a second, he let himself get caught up in the feel of her, but then his rational side made one final attempt at resistance.

He pulled back, breathing hard. A flicker of exasperation crossed Avery's face. "What now?" she asked.

"I just don't want to rush into anything. We spent the past ten years apart—are you sure this is what you really want?" It was true. While his body was more than happy to continue this journey, he didn't want to sleep with her if she was going to immediately regret it. Grant wanted this peace between them to last; he wanted a chance at a real relationship with her again. And while scratching a physical itch would feel amazing, it wasn't worth it if it would only push them apart again.

She smiled warmly as she looked down at him. "I'm sure," she said softly. "I'm leaving in two days. I don't know when I'll see you again. I don't want to waste any of the time we have left together." She kissed him gently, first his mouth, then his cheeks, and finally his forehead. "I have missed you for too long. I'm not going to miss you any longer."

A wave of love washed over him, stealing his breath. He recognized the same emotion in her eyes and could only nod, not trusting his voice. What could he even say in response? He was no poet, and his emotions were so intense that mere words failed him. He would just have to show her how he felt.

Grant rose to his feet and placed his hands on Avery's upper arms. Using gentle pressure, he steered her movements until they had changed places and she stood in front of the bed. In an echo of her earlier actions, he pushed her down onto the mattress.

She stared up at him, her expression so trusting, so loving it made his heart ache. Grant ran his fingers along the curve of her cheek, traced the line of her jaw, then down her neck into the dip of her collarbone. She shivered and closed her eyes, leaning in to savor his touch.

He took his time, every touch, every kiss a reunion. At first, they were content to leisurely explore each other, to take their time becoming reacquainted after so many years apart. But soon their needs took on a desperate edge, one that could not be satisfied by gentleness.

Grant pulled away, gasping. In unspoken agreement, he and Avery quickly stripped off their clothes, their hands moving frantically over buttons and zippers, arousal making their movements clumsy. Finally, free of the last barriers between them, they came together again. The feel of her bare skin against his own was intoxicating—every place they touched sent tingling waves of sensation through his body, making him feel like he was in danger of coming apart at the seams. Holding her like this again was at once familiar and strange, and her warm scent unlocked a flood of memories that threatened to overwhelm him.

Avery's voice was low in his ear, bringing him back to the present. "I always loved it when you touched me like this."

"You mean here?" he teased. He moved his hand and she squirmed against him, letting out a little squeal that made him grin.

"Grant!"

"Or what about here? I seem to recall you liked that, too."

She moaned, her body going limp as she melted against him. "That's what I thought," he said softly, pressing a kiss to her temple.

Avery let out a sigh, then lazily began to move first one hand, then the other until he was gasping for breath. She laughed, a sultry, satisfied sound that nearly drove him over the edge. "You're not the only one who remembers things," she said, her voice hot in his ear.

Grant grabbed her hips and rolled, flipping them over and landing on top of her. She laughed and wrapped her arms around his neck, urging him closer. He was all too happy to comply, but a belated sense of caution made him pause.

Avery noticed his hesitation. "What's wrong?"

"I don't have a condom." Of all the times to be caught without protection! He silently cursed himself and his luck, hating that this part of his reunion with Avery was going to have to be postponed.

"It's okay," she said. "I'm protected."

His spirits lifted at her words, but on the heels of his celebration came a potential complication. "How?" he asked bluntly. "We didn't give you any birth control pills while you were sick, so if that's what you were using you're not covered right now." He began to move away, but Avery locked her arms, holding him in place over her.

"IUD," she said simply.

"Oh." Relief slammed into him, and he grinned stupidly. "Really?"

She smiled back. "Really. Now get back over here so we can finish what we started."

Grant leaned down to kiss her again. They shifted together, their bodies joining in one smooth movement that made them both sigh. Grant lost all awareness of their surroundings and gave himself over to sensation. There was only Avery and a profound sense of rightness that filled him with peace. The restlessness that had plagued him for the past ten years vanished as together they celebrated the connection that he had only ever found with her. Avery was home to him. She was his everything. His past. His present.

And hopefully his future.

He buried his face in her hair as they moved, trying to catalog as many sensations as possible. The heady scent of her skin, like oranges drizzled with honey. It was the smell he'd always associated with her, familiar and intoxicating all at once. The taste of her mouth, still faintly seasoned with the spices from her soup. The warm feel of her, liquid and boneless one moment, powerful and playful the next. He wanted to soak it all in, to burn it on his brain and in his heart. He didn't know what the future held for them, and if this was their only night together he wanted to remember every second of it.

"Let go," Avery whispered in his ear. "You're thinking too much. Just feel."

"I can't," he gasped. "I don't want to lose a moment with you."

"You won't," she assured him. "Trust me."

After a second's hesitation, Grant relaxed his mind

and surrendered to the pleasure he'd been keeping at bay. The time for thinking was over. He ceded control to his body, content to let his base instincts lead.

Avery gripped his hips, her fingernails digging into his skin with little nips of pain that were soon borne away on another wave of pleasure. Her body tensed for one endless second and then she relaxed, shuddering slightly from the force of her release.

Grant felt the tension of his arousal build and knew his own satisfaction was close. Avery seemed to recognize it, too, as she moved under him, her touch helping him close the distance. He was almost there, his release beckoning like a shining star he could pluck from the sky. But something was holding him back, and no matter how hard he tried, his completion remained just out of reach.

Suddenly, Avery's voice was in his ear, soft and sweet. "I love you," she whispered.

Her words broke the barrier holding him back, and Grant's climax shattered over him like a blizzard of sparks, his body going cold, then hot as all his nerve endings seemed to fire in unison. His heart pounded against his breastbone with such force he was half afraid it was going to beat right out of his chest.

Moments later, after the world stopped spinning and he felt like himself again, Grant gathered up his courage. "Did you mean it?"

Avery turned to look at him and he held his breath, a little apprehensive of her response. He wanted so desperately for her declaration to be real and not just the product of passion, but he braced himself for disappointment. Ten years was a long time to be apart.

And while his love for her had merely lain dormant, perhaps it had not been the same for her...

"I did." Her voice was quiet, but her words were clear. Grant held them in his mind, imagining them as two precious gems that were almost too beautiful to look at. A surge of emotion threatened to choke him, and he had to clear his throat several times before he felt like he could speak.

"I'm glad to hear you say that." He turned to face her, smiling despite the tears welling in his eyes. "Because I love you, too."

Avery sank into the worn chair in the hospital break room, grateful for the chance to sit down. The trek over from her dorm room had taken more energy than she liked to admit, and she wanted a moment to recharge before she went in search of Grant. If he saw how tired she was, he'd insist that she go back to her room and rest.

"Although," she murmured to herself, "it's his fault I'm tired in the first place."

Last night had been...magical. That was such a clichéd description, but in this case it really fit. Being with Grant again had made her feel truly alive for the first time in years. His touch had rescued her from the emotional purgatory she'd inhabited for the last decade. The sex they shared had transcended the mere physical—they had made love, joining not only their bodies, but their hearts and souls, as well.

Even now, hours later, just the thought of last night made Avery's skin tingle with the memory of Grant's touch. The look on his face as he'd entered her was fixed in her mind, and her heart swelled as she recalled the yearning, hope and love in his expression. His tenderness had unlocked the last gates protecting her heart, and she had confessed her love for him without a second thought.

In hindsight, she probably could have timed it better. Those three little words carried a lot of weight, and while she had absolutely meant them, she didn't blame Grant for wondering if her declaration had merely been a cry of passion.

Fortunately, he had believed her assurances. And his answering response had filled her with a deep and abiding sense of peace that lingered even now.

He loved her. She loved him. It was that simple.

And that profound.

She hugged the words to herself, feeling torn between her desire to broadcast the news to the world and wanting to keep it a secret celebration between the two of them. She would tell Olivia and Mallory, of course. They were her best friends and had helped her so much in the aftermath of her breakup with Grant. But she liked the idea of keeping the wider world at arm's length for now. What she and Grant had still felt too new, too fragile, and she didn't want to deal with the scrutiny of outsiders before they'd had a chance to nurture their relationship.

"Penny for your thoughts?" His voice was low and intimate in her ear, his breath hot on her cheek. Avery smiled and leaned back into the solid wall of his chest as Grant slid his arms around her.

"Only a penny?" she teased. "I think they're worth

more than that. Especially because they're of a scandalous nature."

"Oh, my," Grant said, affecting a breathless tone. "Then I really want to hear them."

He pressed a quick kiss to her cheek and rounded the table, taking the seat across from her. "Seriously, though, how are you feeling today?"

"Never better," she replied. And it was the truth. Even though she felt like she could sleep for a month, her spirits were high. In fact, the only dark cloud on her mood was the still-unfinished investigation and her incipient departure...

"You look a little tired," Grant said, not unkindly.

"And whose fault is that?" she fired back.

His cheeks flushed, but the grin he sported was pure masculine satisfaction. "We had to make up for those lost years, didn't we?"

"I'd say we got a good start." Avery leaned forward and lowered her voice, just in case one of the nurses was walking by. "But don't think I'm done with you yet."

A flash of arousal warmed Grant's eyes, and butterflies of anticipation took flight in Avery's belly. "I'm glad to hear you say that. I feel the same way."

The look on his face made Avery flush, and she was half tempted to suggest they go back to her room and continue getting reacquainted. But the files on the table taunted her, and she could no longer ignore her duty. Her illness had hampered her efforts on the investigation, and since she was leaving tomorrow, she needed to focus all of her efforts on doing what she could while she was still here.

Grant sensed the shift in her mood and nodded at the files. "Back to the grindstone?"

Avery sighed, trying not to feel discouraged. "Yeah. The clock is ticking, and I can't just walk away without giving it one more try."

"Understandable." Grant watched her spread out the papers. "Do you remember the conversation in my office? Before you collapsed?"

"Yes. What about it?"

He shrugged. "You said you thought something was off about this outbreak. What did you mean by that?"

Avery frowned, trying to find the words to properly describe what amounted to a gut feeling. "There's just something about the way these cases have popped up," she began, choosing her words carefully. She was a scientist, and as such she relied on data and evidence, not amorphous sensations. But there was something different about this job, and she wasn't going to be able to rest until she figured out what made it so unique.

"What do you mean?" Grant asked. His expression was open and curious, and Avery felt her muscles relax. He was a good sounding board; he wouldn't judge her for listening to that nagging voice in her head that insisted she pay attention.

"I don't have any proof—" she began, but Grant waved her concern away.

"I'm not your boss," he said. "You don't have to submit a list of supporting references for everything you say to me."

She smiled, appreciating his support. "Well," she

said, "preliminary results suggest this virus is related to influenza, perhaps even a strain we've never seen before. Those viruses tend to be very contagious and spread rapidly through a vulnerable population. But that's not what happened here—the outbreaks were very contained, very focused."

Grant's eyebrows drew together as he considered her words. "True," he said slowly. "But I thought there were some cases of a new avian influenza virus that didn't show a lot of person-to-person spread."

"You're correct." Her respect for him went up another notch. It was unusual for an emergency room physician to be so well versed on the ins and outs of flu appearances over the years. It seemed Grant had been paying attention...

"That virus came out of China, and scared us all to death." Avery shuddered at the memory—it had been a few tense months for the public health community as they raced to determine what was going on with the virus and if it presented a pandemic threat. Fortunately, it hadn't spread and humanity had dodged a bullet. Would they be so lucky next time?

"Even though that virus wasn't terribly contagious from person to person, we still understood how it was spreading. People had direct contact with infected poultry. That's not the case here."

"So you're still wondering about the source?" Grant asked.

"In a way. The only thing the victims of this disease seem to have in common is a person."

"Paul Coleson," Grant supplied.

Avery nodded and drew in a breath. This was where

her thoughts departed from the facts and veered off into conjecture. "Exactly. And for a person to be the common element… It almost suggests…" She trailed off, not wanting to give voice to the possibility.

"You think he might be deliberately spreading the virus?" Grant's voice was low, but Avery glanced around to make sure no one had overheard. Fortunately, they were still alone and there were no sounds from the hallway.

She nodded. "I hate to even suggest it, but I keep coming back to the idea that someone is responsible. It fits the pattern of transmission we've seen—all the victims recall sharing drinks with Paul right before falling ill. Since they all work such disparate jobs, it's unlikely there is another common source. And we tested the bar itself—nothing."

Grant was silent for a moment, his expression unreadable. A knot of anxiety formed in Avery's stomach. The idea that someone—Paul, in particular—was deliberately spreading the disease was a very serious charge. It required evidence, the kind she didn't have. Which was exactly why she was reluctant to discuss her feelings. She knew Grant wouldn't judge her on a professional level for voicing these concerns, but it still made her uncomfortable to accuse a man of doing something so heinous based on nothing more than a hunch.

"Let's say you're right." His tone was neutral, careful, as if he, too, wanted to give the man the benefit of the doubt. "Where would he get the virus? It's not the kind of thing you can pick up at the base store."

"I don't know," Avery admitted. "That's why I haven't said anything before."

They were both silent a moment, lost in their own thoughts. Avery let her mind wander, trying to make the connection between Paul and the virus. Where had it come from? Infectious agents weren't conjured out of thin air—there had to be a source. But where? The germ of an idea formed and she had a sudden feeling of déjà vu. She shook her head, and Grant saw the gesture. "What?" he asked.

"I'm not sure. It's probably nothing."

He lifted one eyebrow and stared at her. "At this stage, I don't think we can afford to dismiss any ideas."

"It's just…" She focused, trying to pull up a mental image of the news article she had read a few years ago. "I remember reading a story about a research group who worked with ice core samples. They were trying to determine what kinds of microbial life were present millions of years ago, or something like that."

"And?" Grant urged. He leaned forward, placing his forearms on the table.

"They found a prehistoric virus in one of their samples, something previously unknown to science. It infected algae, so it wasn't a threat to humans or animals. But I remember thinking it was a cool discovery." She caught sight of Grant's face and paused. "What is it?"

He swallowed, looking like a man who had been forced to eat a rotten egg. "Ice core samples, you said?"

"Yes." His reaction was making her nervous and

she put a hand over her stomach to quell the unpleasant tingles. "What's wrong?"

"Paul's group studies climate change." He swallowed again and clasped his hands together on the table. "Using ice core samples."

A chill skittered down her spine and the fine hairs on the back of her neck stood at attention. "Oh, my God," she whispered. "Do you think—"

Grant nodded grimly. "I do. Where else could it have come from?"

Avery rubbed her forehead with a grimace. "I'm going to need caffeine to really process this."

Grant jumped out of his chair. "I'll make us some coffee."

Avery remained seated, feeling a little gobsmacked. How could someone deliberately infect others with a pathogen? Where did that kind of hatred come from? And what made Paul even think to do this in the first place?

A growing sense of horror dawned on her as she followed that thought to its logical conclusion. It took a lot of effort to isolate a new virus from ice samples and to amplify it so there was enough to carry out infections. This wasn't an accidental discovery gone off the rails—it was premeditated and methodical. If their suspicions were correct and Paul was responsible for these outbreaks, he had known exactly what he was doing.

But was he working alone? Or were his efforts just the tip of the iceberg of a much bigger plan?

Her thoughts were interrupted when Grant slid a cup of coffee in front of her. He rounded the table and sat again, his mouth drawn in a tight frown.

"I just can't believe it," he said softly, almost to himself.

"I think you have to," Avery said, just as softly. "But there's something else we need to consider."

Grant's shoulders stiffened, as if he was bracing himself to take a hit. "What's that?"

"Paul might not be working alone."

"You think someone else on-base is helping him?" Grant sounded miserable about the possibility, and she couldn't blame him. He'd spent a lot of time with these people and probably thought he knew them fairly well. To have not one, but two or more, bad apples in the barrel was a disappointment to say the least, and if Avery were in his shoes, she'd be forced to question her instincts when it came to judging people and their intentions.

"I don't know if anyone else here is involved," she said, reaching across the table to touch his hand. "But I think we need to look hard at Paul's contacts. It's possible he's working in collusion with someone off-base, someone who is setting things up in the US or maybe another country. Why stop at infecting a contained population here when there's a big, wide world full of potential victims?"

Grant nodded, biting his bottom lip thoughtfully. "You think this is merely a test run so they can see how the virus behaves."

Avery nodded. The idea made a sick kind of sense, much as she hated to admit it. Find a new virus, throw it into the human population to see how it behaves. If it doesn't cause illness, keep looking. If it starts killing people, all the better.

"It's the perfect candidate for a new biological

weapon," she mused aloud. "The virus has been frozen for millennia. No one alive has any kind of protective immunity to it, so everyone on earth would be vulnerable to infection. It would spread like wildfire through the population."

"Except it hasn't," Grant pointed out. "We haven't seen any person-to-person transmission here."

She nodded. "That's the only flaw with this virus, isn't it? I think that's why there were two outbreaks—he started the second one after the first round of patients failed to infect anyone else."

Grant closed his eyes and shook his head. "How did I miss that?"

"You were a little busy trying to keep people alive," Avery said smartly. "Don't you dare go blaming yourself for this. You had nothing to do with it—you saved the lives of most of the people he infected. That's not a small thing. Try to focus on that instead of the might-have-beens and what-ifs."

He smiled at her, and her heart kicked hard in her chest. "You always had an answer for everything."

"You should listen," she said with a wink. She picked up the coffee mug and took a large gulp, then immediately spat the coffee out with a muffled curse.

Grant's eyes went wide. "Is everything okay?"

Avery dabbed at her chin and blinked away tears. "The coffee is hot." Her tongue felt like she had used a flaming sword to scrape it raw, and her cheeks ached from the assault.

"Ah, yes." Grant's tone suggested he was mentally sizing her up for a straitjacket. "Coffee generally is."

"The last time Jesse gave me a cup of coffee, he said it was cold because the machine is on the fritz."

Grant frowned. "I don't think so. It's been working fine for as long as I've been here."

"Why would he give me lukewarm coffee?" Avery mused. Then the pin dropped, and everything fell into place. "Oh," she said dumbly, seeing things clearly for the first time.

"Oh, what?" Grant echoed, one eyebrow lifted in curiosity.

"I know how I got sick."

Chapter 14

"Grant, slow down! We need to talk about this."

"No," he said flatly. The time for talking was over. Action was the only option now.

"Grant," Avery said, a note of warning in her voice. She huffed after him, her breathing labored as she tried to match his pace. He slowed, immediately feeling guilty. She should be in bed recovering, not exerting herself by chasing after him.

Besides, he didn't want her to see what happened next.

The realization that someone had deliberately infected people with a pathogen was bad enough. But to know that they had targeted Avery, too? That made it even worse. They had already lost ten years of their lives, and to come so close to losing her forever after they had started to patch things up? It was a sin he simply wasn't willing to forgive.

The urge to do violence leached from his bones and thrummed in his muscles. Never before had he felt such an intense need to inflict harm and cause someone pain. It was a heady, almost intoxicating sensation that threatened to completely override his self-control.

It was a good thing he hadn't found Jesse. After Avery realized he must have slipped the virus into her coffee, Grant had leaped into action. His first instinct had been to hunt him down and beat the man to within an inch of his life. But a quick search of the hospital had proved disappointing, and so Grant had taken aim at the next man on his list: Paul Coleson.

Avery slid to a stop next to him and grabbed his arm, wobbling a bit on a slick patch of ice. It had started snowing soon after they'd stepped outside, and the initial fat, fluffy flakes were now morphing into small, cold pellets of slushy ice. It was the kind of weather that drove even hardened researchers indoors, and Grant wanted Avery to go back to her dorm and burrow under the covers until he returned. She had no business being out in this cold, especially in her condition.

He put his arm around her shoulders and pivoted on his heel. "Come with me," he said, steering them toward the living quarters.

"I don't think so." She dug in her heels and slipped out from under his support. He turned to find her standing with her hands on her hips, a mulish expression on her face.

"Avery—" he began, but she cut him off.

"No. I'm not going to let you stash me in my room while you go off half-cocked and confront Paul and Jesse. Do you think I'm stupid?"

"Of course not. But—"

"If you want to talk to them, you're going to have to take me with you."

Grant's patience stretched to the breaking point and he took a deep breath. "Can we have this conversation inside, please? You don't need to be out in this weather."

Avery narrowed her eyes. "I'm fine. And while I appreciate your concern, I am not a porcelain doll that needs to be coddled and protected. I am a grown woman who can take care of herself."

Grant held up his hands in defeat. "Okay, have it your way. I just thought it would be nicer if we argued someplace warm. But if you're happy standing out in the cold, so am I." He crossed his arms over his chest and stared down at her, willing himself not to shiver. If she wanted to stand out in the cold, then that was what they'd do. He wasn't about to let her win this one, even if it meant risking exposure.

The look she shot him was pure annoyance. "I'm fine with going inside. But don't think you're going to leave me there while you run off to chase the bad guys."

"I wouldn't dream of it," he said dryly.

He ushered her inside the closest building, gritting his teeth when he realized they were right outside the cafeteria. There was a steady stream of people entering in search of breakfast and just as many leaving to face the day, cardboard coffee cups in hand. He couldn't have picked a worse location to have a private talk, so Grant grabbed Avery's hand and led her past the entrance and down the hall. He stopped at the small nook that led to the back door of the kitchens—

there would be no traffic here, and the thick metal door should muffle their conversation. Even if they were overheard, the workers in the kitchen were too busy with the breakfast rush to eavesdrop, so this was his best option.

"Talk."

Avery blinked up at him. "Excuse me?"

"You wanted to talk to me. So talk." He knew he was being short with her, but he was too wound up to care.

If she noticed his tone, she didn't show it. "We need a plan."

"I have a plan. You just don't like it."

She arched one eyebrow, silently communicating her exasperation. "Do you honestly think roughing up Paul Coleson is going to solve anything?" He opened his mouth to respond, but Avery held up her hand, stalling his reply. "Think, Grant! You're a smart guy. We don't actually have any evidence, remember? Just speculation and conjecture. If you go in there and start hitting the man, he's going to shut down. There's no way you'll get the truth from him that way."

As much as it pained him to admit it, Avery was right. Punching Paul Coleson would give him immediate satisfaction, but it wouldn't help them solve the larger mystery—why had he done this, and was he working alone? "What did you have in mind?"

"For starters, is there any kind of security force on-base that can apprehend Paul and Jesse?"

Grant shook his head. "No. It's such a small community, there's only one US Marshal posted here. Crime has never been an issue. Until now."

"Oh." She deflated a little. "I was hoping someone else could arrest them so you don't have to put yourself in danger."

Her concern for his safety warmed his heart, and he reached out to touch her arm. "I'll be okay," he said. "If it makes you feel better, I'll make sure the one officer on-base goes with me."

She harrumphed at that but didn't press the issue. "I think we should talk to Paul first before we try to arrest him."

Grant's first instinct was to reject her proposal. His emotions demanded he take action to avenge Avery's near-death, and since he wasn't going to be able to beat the man, the least he could do was see him thrown into the jail on-base. "I'm not interested in talking to him right now."

Avery took a step closer, practically vibrating with urgency. "I'm not saying you have to let him get away with what he's done. But we need more information if we want to convince people the outbreaks were deliberate. If we go to Paul's lab and talk to him, he might let something incriminating slip."

"It's possible," Grant allowed.

"And," Avery continued, warming to the subject, "while we're there, we can take a closer look at his workspace. See if there's anything out of place, or maybe find some evidence that shows he isolated and amplified the virus. Once we have that, we'll have grounds for an actual case against him."

"Do you really think he has a big flask labeled 'virus' just sitting on his desk?"

Avery ignored his sarcasm. "There are a lot of subtle signs we can look for. Lots of empty supply bottles in the trash. An incubator with a 'do not use' sign on the door. Even the smell of the lab can reveal if there's stuff being grown in the room."

Grant considered her points. She made a good case; they really did need more than theory to prove Paul's guilt in all this. Without solid evidence, Grant would have a hard time convincing the base commander and the US marshal that Paul needed to be arrested, which would give the man more time to cover his tracks.

But they needed to move quickly. The seasons were changing, and the base was gearing up for the mass exodus of researchers that occurred every winter. Paul would undoubtedly be one of the people leaving in the next few weeks to go back to the States, so unless they could pin this on him before Avery's departure tomorrow, he was going to get away with murder.

"You're right."

"I'm sorry?" Avery held her hand up to her ear and leaned forward, blinking innocently. "I couldn't quite hear you. What did you say?"

Grant resisted the temptation to roll his eyes. "You're better than this," he said, mildly exasperated.

Her grin was pure amusement. "Not today. Now, you were saying?"

He sighed, smiling despite the residual fog of his earlier anger. She'd always had that effect on him— he never could seem to hold on to a bad mood when Avery was around. It was just one of the many reasons why he loved her. "I believe I said you were right."

"I'm glad you realized it," she replied, straightening with a nod. Her gaze was questioning as she searched his face. "In all seriousness, though, are you ready to do this?"

"Yes. Don't I look ready?"

Avery tilted her head to the side. "To be honest, you still look angry. You've calmed down a lot, but I need to know that seeing Paul won't push you over the edge."

"They tried to kill you," he reminded her, heat creeping back into his voice. Why wasn't she more upset by that fact?

Maybe the experience had been easier on her, he mused. Sure, she'd been the one to struggle through the illness firsthand, and she'd felt the brush of death as it winged by. But it was one thing to be sick yourself and quite another to have to watch the ones you loved suffer, knowing there was nothing you could do to save them. He had so much knowledge and skill, and yet he still hadn't been able to spare Avery the pain of sickness. The fact that she had survived was likely due to a combination of luck and her sheer determination; he certainly didn't have the power to decide who lived and who died.

But he did have the power to bring her would-be murderers to justice. Determination filled him, pushing aside his petty need for immediate gratification. He took a deep breath, trying to erase the emotions from his face.

"You should probably be the one to ask him questions," he said after a moment. "It would be less suspicious that way, since you're still investigating the outbreak."

Avery nodded. "That sounds reasonable to me. Are you ready?"

Grant looked into the eyes of the woman he loved, the woman he'd already lost once and come so close to losing again. He was most definitely ready, for so many things—ready to find a new job in a nice, normal location, ready to put this outbreak behind him, ready to settle down, with her.

Ready to start their life together.

But rather than say all that, he merely nodded and stuck out his hand. Avery slipped her hand in his, like it was the most natural thing in the world. Her touch made his heart sing and banked the fires of his anger. He focused on the feel of her skin against his, and turned his mind to the task ahead. It wasn't going to be easy, but he knew one way or another, they would find the answers they sought.

Together.

He was almost finished—just a few steps left and then it would be ready.

Moving carefully, Paul poured the last of the liquid from the flask into the thermos Jesse had given him. The nurse had instructed him to use this as the transport container for the virus, and Paul hadn't bothered to argue with the man. He just wanted this whole thing to be over with; the sooner, the better.

The last drop slid into the thermos, and he screwed the cap on, his hands shaking only a little. Then he exhaled and slumped against the table, the metal cold against his palms.

Nothing was going according to plan. As if there had even been a plan in the first place! Still, he could say objectively and decisively that his life had fallen apart. Even when he'd tried to do the right thing, it had blown up in his face.

The FBI hadn't believed him. He'd spelled it all out for them, right down to the details of his project for the Organization. But it hadn't mattered; they'd treated him like a crank call, like some nutty conspiracy theorist who couldn't be trusted. He couldn't really blame them—no one knew about the Organization. Paul didn't even know the real name of the group. And his rising panic over the fate of Noah hadn't exactly made him coherent.

Recognizing defeat, he'd hung up, taken a few deep breaths and called the local police to report his son missing. But that conversation hadn't gone much better. They refused to file a missing person's report on the basis of a phone call, especially once they found out he was thousands of miles away.

At that point, Paul had given up. All the fight had left his body and he'd fallen to the floor, the phone forgotten in his hand. He had failed, in every aspect of his life. For the first time, he was actually glad Carol was dead so she couldn't see how badly he had screwed things up. And not just his life, but the kids', as well...

He shuddered, recalling the heavy sense of finality that had stolen over him as he sat on the tile, the chill seeping through his clothes and into his bones. The room had been silent except for the drone of the dial tone from the disconnected call, the sound harsh and unforgiving as it rattled around in his brain.

He was out of moves. The Organization had beaten him, and there was nothing he could do about it.

For a brief, desperate moment, he'd considered sabotaging the project. Why should he continue to work for them when they had so thoroughly wrecked his life? But he couldn't bring himself to do it. Not when Lisa's fate was still undecided. Bad enough he had lost Noah—he couldn't sign his daughter's death warrant, as well.

Suicide had beckoned, a siren's call that even now he found hard to resist. It was so tempting to surrender, to end the worry and despair and absolute sense of defeat that plagued his every breath. It would probably be better for his family; the Organization would lose interest in Lisa and his mother if they could no longer use them as leverage.

The only thing stopping him was fear. Despite everything, he was still too much of a coward to take his own life. At least not until he knew for sure that Lisa would be safe. And the only way to do that was to complete the job at hand.

He glanced at his watch. Jesse was running late—where was he? The man had been maddeningly difficult to get a hold of over the past few days, and this plan of his had too many loose ends for Paul's liking. He still wasn't sure how they were going to smuggle the virus onto the ship; it wasn't like they could just waltz on board without attracting notice. No matter how subtle they tried to be, the crew would likely notice them wandering about in search of the agreed-upon hiding spot.

Unless the crew was in on it, too, he thought sourly. Nothing would surprise him at this point. The small, logical part remaining in his brain recognized he was being paranoid, but that didn't mean he was wrong…

Footsteps sounded in the hall, coming closer. That would be Jesse. Finally.

He waited until the footsteps stopped and he sensed someone behind him in the doorway. "You're late."

"I'm sorry," said a woman's voice. "I didn't know we had an appointment."

Paul's stomach twisted and he closed his eyes, cursing silently. What the hell was *she* doing here? And how could he get rid of her quickly?

He took a deep breath, hoping his thoughts didn't show on his face. "We don't," he said, turning to face Dr. Thatcher. His heart rate spiked when he saw she wasn't alone. Dr. Jones was with her, his expression unreadable. Paul turned his attention back to her and offered up a smile. "I'm sorry—I was expecting someone else."

"Ah." She stepped into the lab, trailed by Dr. Jones, and Paul felt his body tense. He didn't know why they were here, but he needed them to leave before Jesse arrived. He didn't have a good excuse for meeting the other man, and it would only trigger the doctors' suspicions if they saw them together.

"We won't stay long," she continued. "I just had a few follow-up questions for my investigation." She glanced around the lab as she walked, her gaze flicking from one spot to another as if she was searching for something. Trying to keep his movements casual, Paul shifted so his body blocked her view of the thermos on the counter and the empty flask sitting next to it.

"How can I help?" Hopefully, he could take care of this issue quickly and dispatch the both of them.

She came to a stop in front of him, Dr. Jones trailing in her wake. They were an interesting team—while she hadn't stopped looking around since entering the room, Paul noticed Dr. Jones had kept his gaze fixed on him the whole time. The man's stare was probing and intense, and Paul fought the urge to squirm. Had he noticed Paul's attempt to hide the flask and thermos with his body? Was he going to say anything, or just stand there in silent judgment?

"I don't know if you heard, but your blood samples tested negative for the virus."

He hadn't actually been worried, but a wave of relief washed over him nonetheless. "That's good, right?"

She inclined her head in a small nod. "For you, yes. Unfortunately, it leaves me with more questions than answers."

"I'm sorry to hear that." He struggled to keep the impatience out of his voice. Would she just get to the point already?

Dr. Jones made a low, rumbling sound of disbelief, and Dr. Thatcher shot him a quelling look. There were clearly some undercurrents between them, and Paul felt the hairs on the back of his neck rise. This visit was more than just a chance for her to ask him additional questions. Something bigger was going on here. But what?

"Can you tell me a little more about your work?"

Paul frowned. Had she made a connection between his research and the virus? Or was she merely fishing for information? "I'm part of a group that studies climate change," he said. "Why do you want to know?"

Dr. Thatcher shrugged. "Just curious. I'm trying to get a better idea of your potential exposures, see if they overlap with any of the disease victims."

Her answer made sense, and Paul relaxed a little. Either she was a good liar or she really didn't suspect him of any wrongdoing. He slid a glance over to Dr. Jones, who was eyeing him as if he were something stuck on the bottom of his shoe. Paul quickly looked away and shifted slightly, wanting to get away from the man. But he couldn't move without exposing the flask and thermos behind him, so he was just going to have to endure the man's continued scrutiny.

"What kind of experiments do you perform?" Dr. Thatcher's question drew his attention away from Dr. Jones, and he blinked at her, trying to decide how to answer her question. Should he throw out a red herring to send her in another direction? It might be his best option. He was due to go home at the end of the week, so if he could find a way to shift her focus until then, he might be able to get away...

"I'm responsible for analyzing ice core samples," he said. "I look for trapped gases and other evidence of prehistoric climates, and I track how those parameters change over time."

Her eyes lit up. "Sounds fascinating," she said. "Do you collect the samples, as well?"

He shook his head. "No. I just stay in the lab. We have some field workers who do the actual drilling. In fact," he said, inspiration striking like a bolt of lightning, "I should really put you in touch with one of the guys. His name is Tex and I think he might be able to help you with your investigation."

"Oh, really?" She leaned forward, sounding interested. "How is that?"

"Well…" Paul glanced around, pretending to be worried about eavesdroppers. "He has a, uh, relationship with one of the women who works at the bar. She's married, so they're trying to be discreet about it, but this place is too small for secrets. Anyway, he told me the other day that Suzy—that's his lady friend—she said she saw someone fiddling with a tray of drinks before they were served." He raised his brow, as if to emphasize the importance of this revelation. "Maybe that's how people are getting infected."

Dr. Thatcher nodded thoughtfully. "It's a possibility. I'll definitely want to talk to Tex and Suzy. In the meantime, can you tell me if you have any microbiology experience?"

Her question was unexpected, and Paul's stomach did a little flip. Even though her pleasant demeanor hadn't changed since she'd walked in the door, Paul began to suspect Dr. Thatcher was asking him questions not because she didn't know the answers, but because she wanted to see his reaction.

"Uh, no," he lied. "Not really."

"Mmm." She nodded again, then tilted her head to the side. "Tell me, then, why does it smell like you've been growing cells in here? And why is there an empty flask behind your back?"

"Excellent questions, Doctor," said a voice from the doorway. "But I'm afraid you don't need to know the answers."

Paul glanced over, relieved to see Jesse had finally arrived. But the emotion curdled in his gut when he saw the snub-nosed pistol in the man's hand and the sick, triumphant smile on his face.

He's going to kill them, Paul realized with a small shock. *And he's going to enjoy it.*

Chapter 15

Avery only caught a glimpse of Jesse before Grant stepped in front of her, blocking her view with his body. But she'd seen the gun and the expression on his face, and her knees began to tremble as the danger sank in.

He's going to kill us. The thought registered with perfect clarity, a cold, logical realization that had the ring of absolute truth. She was going to die today.

But she wasn't going down without a fight.

Determination filled her, cutting through the numbness of her earlier shock. She placed her hand on Grant's back and felt a swell of love so powerful it almost knocked her off her feet. His first thought had been to shield her, to protect her from the threat with no regard to his own safety. It was the act of a man who was good down to his core, and for a brief second she wondered how she'd ever questioned that about him.

Moving slowly so as not to startle Jesse into pulling the trigger, Avery stepped to the side, away from the shelter of Grant's body. If Jesse wanted to hurt her, she wasn't going to let Grant get caught in the cross fire.

"What are you doing?" she asked quietly. Clearly, her earlier suspicions were correct. But this was one hell of a way to get confirmation that Jesse and Paul had deliberately infected people with the virus. What was their plan now? Was Jesse just going to shoot her where she stood, despite the fact that they were in a building crawling with researchers?

She glanced at Paul, but his bewildered expression made her think he hadn't expected this show of force. Great. That meant Jesse was operating off-script. The man could be capable of anything.

Her heart thudded hard against her ribs, each beat a visceral reminder of the life that was once again in danger. A thread of anger began to vibrate deep inside her chest, the emotion growing more intense as she stared at Jesse.

He glanced at her, his expression dismissive. "Tying up loose ends."

What did that mean? Had he come here deliberately, knowing he would find her and Grant? Or was Paul the real target, and Jesse had decided to seize the opportunity to do away with them all in one fell swoop?

"Where did you get the gun?" Grant said, his voice a little hoarse. "Weapons aren't allowed on-base."

Jesse's features twisted in an ugly sneer. "Do I

look like a Boy Scout to you?" He directed his gun toward Grant, and Avery's heart caught in her throat.

"Wait!" Paul exclaimed. He took a step forward, his hands raised in a placating gesture. "Don't shoot."

Jesse lifted an eyebrow but didn't lower his arm. "Why not?" He sounded genuinely curious, as if he couldn't come up with a single reason not to kill them.

"There are too many people around." A note of exasperation crept into Paul's voice, making him sound like a tired parent. Plainly, there was tension between the two men, and Avery held her breath, hoping Jesse would listen to his partner.

"We can't just let them go," Jesse pointed out.

Paul walked around Grant and approached Jesse, apparently deciding to make his case from a closer distance. Jesse lowered the gun, and Avery felt the tight band of panic around her ribs loosen a bit. Grant's shoulders sank as he exhaled, and she used the distraction of Paul's movement to touch Grant's back. He was solid and strong under her palm, and she wanted so badly to press herself against him so they could draw comfort from each other. But any movement might set Jesse off, so this hidden touch would have to suffice.

Paul and Jesse spoke in urgent whispers, apparently trying to decide what to do now. Avery let her gaze wander around the room as they spoke, searching for something she might be able to use to defend herself and Grant. Labs often had scissors or even box cutters lying around to open packaging, but the black tables were frustratingly bare. A glint of silver by the door caught her eye, and she squinted to bring the object into focus.

It was a small screwdriver, the kind that was no bigger than a ballpoint pen. It lay forgotten next to a centrifuge that looked as if it had seen better days. It wasn't much, as far as weapons went, but it was better than nothing.

Now she just had to find a way to get it.

Paul's voice cut through her thoughts. "Give me the gun."

Jesse shook his head. "No. It's mine."

Avery almost rolled her eyes at his response. He'd seemed like such a normal guy before—how had he kept this side hidden for so long? Was she that bad at judging other people? Or was Jesse just that good at pretending to be someone he wasn't?

"You are jeopardizing this operation," Paul hissed, clearly impatient. "If you shoot them here, people will come running. How exactly are you going to explain the bodies, hmm? Dr. Jones is practically a god on this base— I don't think people will take too kindly to finding him dead."

"What's your plan, then?" Jesse sounded defensive, and Avery started to tense up again. He seemed to be running off emotion, which made him unpredictable.

"Bring them with us. We'll dispatch them on the ship."

Ship? Her ears pricked at the word, and realization dawned. A few days ago, a large vessel had docked and there had been a steady stream of activity to and from it ever since. Grant had told her it was the garbage boat, delivering the last of the winter supplies and loading up the waste from the base. It was due to sail back to the US, where the cargo would be processed and disposed.

What do these two want with the ship? No sooner had the question formed in her mind than the answer presented itself: they were going to use it to smuggle the virus back to the States.

Of course. It was so simple. No one would think to take a close look at the garbage. If they had a co-conspirator at the landing dock in the US, it would be easy to retrieve the virus without anyone being the wiser.

And once the pathogen was Stateside, they could deploy it anywhere.

She made a fist, crumpling Grant's shirt and dragging her fingers across his back as she tried to silently communicate her realization. He nodded once, indicating he understood.

Paul and Jesse couldn't be allowed to smuggle the virus aboard that ship. They had dodged a bullet here on-base—the virus was deadly but not contagious. But if the pathogen reached the US, it would take an unprincipled microbiologist a matter of weeks to fix that flaw. And once that happened, the virus would burn across the globe in no time at all.

Avery shuddered, imagining the scenario all too easily. Millions, if not billions, of people would die. Entire cities, wiped out in a matter of days. The world's poor would be hit the hardest—they always were—but no one would escape the effects of the pandemic. It would change humanity and the course of civilization forever, and not for the better.

Suddenly, Avery's concerns for her personal safety

seemed small and selfish. She didn't want to die, but she might have to sacrifice herself to keep the virus out of the wrong hands. The realization stung, but what was one life compared to the millions she would save?

A flash of movement caught her eye and she glanced over to see Jesse stuff the gun into the waistband of his pants. It seems Paul's admonitions had worked. For now, at least.

"Let's go." Jesse pulled the edges of his coat together and nodded at the door. "You two take the lead. And don't try anything." He patted his waist, the threat clear. "If you do, I'll kill you both and infect everyone on this base. Is that clear?"

Avery and Grant both nodded, but she could tell by the set of Grant's shoulders he was itching to make a move. She gave his back a subtle rub that was part warning, part sympathy. She understood his need to act all too well, but now was not the right time. They had to choose their moment, or it would all be in vain.

"Get the stuff," Jesse instructed Paul. Then he turned his gaze back to Avery and Grant. "You guys, start walking."

She began to shuffle forward, moving at an angle to get closer to the lab table with the screwdriver. Fortunately, Jesse's attention seemed to be fixed on Paul and the viral culture. His distraction wouldn't last, which meant Avery would get one shot at this. She took a deep breath and glanced at Jesse out of the corner of her eyes as she moved past him. He was still watching Paul, but for how much longer?

There was no way to know. Her heart in her throat, Avery stared straight ahead and tried to walk normally. As she passed the table, she reached out and grabbed the small screwdriver, tucking it up into the sleeve of her shirt. Her shoulders tensed in anticipation of a bullet or a blow, but neither Paul nor Jesse spoke.

"Nice job," Grant said, the words in so low a voice she might have imagined them. She felt the ghost of his touch across the back of her neck and a sense of peace began to spread through her, smothering the panic and distress that had ruled her since Jesse's arrival. No matter what happened, she and Grant were a team and they would fight to the end.

Together.

It took everything he had to remain calm and collected as Grant marched through the icy drizzle with Avery by his side and two psychopaths at his back. His instincts were screaming at him to do something—to defend himself and Avery by attacking the men when they were distracted by the cold and the slippery ground. But he knew the time wasn't right. He wasn't a fighter by nature, and even though he had the benefit of adrenaline and anger, he couldn't take on two men at once.

Especially when one of them was armed.

A chill skittered down his back as he relived the moment Jesse had pointed the gun at him. Grant had never found himself on the business end of a gun before, and he didn't much care for the experience. The fact that the weapon was now tucked in the waistband of Jesse's pants didn't make him feel much better; the man seemed far too eager to start shooting, regardless of any potential witnesses.

He tried not to look at Avery as they made their way to the ship. He didn't want to draw attention to her, nor did he want Paul and Jesse to know the nature of their relationship. He'd heard the rumors floating around the hospital, sparked by his constant vigil by Avery's side as she battled the virus. But he'd never confirmed anything, and he wasn't about to do so now. Jesse seemed like the kind of man who would hurt Avery to get Grant to cooperate, and he didn't want her singled out that way.

Grant racked his brain, trying to come up with a way to disarm Jesse without getting himself or Avery killed. As much as he hated the idea, it was better to wait until they were alone again—if he tried to overpower the man now, he risked a stray bullet hitting an innocent bystander.

The ship loomed large as they approached, their footsteps crunching in the thin layer of icy sludge that was growing thicker by the moment. Grant held his breath as they stepped onto the gangway; the textured metal walkway was coated in a clear layer of ice, and the going was treacherous. He concentrated on each step, knowing that if he fell and hurt himself here, he'd be unable to protect Avery once they were inside. And even though he still didn't have much of a plan, his goal was crystal clear: keep her safe.

Getting on board the ship proved disappointingly easy. No one challenged them or asked what they were doing there. Given the weather, the crew were probably all indoors, trying to stay warm. *It's for the best*, Grant thought resignedly. It would have been nice to have a potential ally, but Grant didn't want to give Jesse any additional targets...

Paul and Jesse herded them down a series of corridors, speaking only to tell them when to turn left or right. Grant quickly became disoriented—everything was painted battleship gray, and there were no windows or other identifying markers to help him mentally map out where they were. Escaping would be difficult, but hopefully he and Avery could make enough noise to attract the attention of the crew.

Finally, Jesse pointed them through a door that opened into a cavernous room. Grant glanced up and saw that the ceiling was actually a large set of doors that could open to allow access to the deck of the ship. This must be the main cargo hold, he realized. His suspicions were confirmed as he registered the large crates lining the walls, stacked from floor to ceiling. Was this where they planned to hide the virus?

Someone shoved him from behind, and Grant took a step forward so he didn't land on his face. Something small and hard pressed against his lower back, and he realized Jesse had drawn his gun again.

"Move."

He forced Grant and Avery over to a large metal shipping container sitting against one of the walls of the cargo hold. *So this is it*, Grant thought grimly. *He's going to shoot us and stuff our bodies inside.*

Grant turned to face Jesse and Paul and planted his feet. He wasn't going to die without a fight, but he would only have one real shot at defending himself and Avery.

"Open it," Jesse ordered Avery. When she hesitated, Jesse cocked the gun and pointed it at Grant. Grant's heart leaped into his throat and he bit his lip to keep from showing his fear. Avery let out a small sound of distress and reached for the metal lever that controlled the doors of the container. She pulled hard and the hinges squealed in protest. The doors opened slowly, revealing a collection of tables and chairs stacked inside.

"In you go."

Grant glanced at Paul, who had remained silent since leaving the lab. The other man met his gaze and looked quickly away, as if he couldn't stand the contact. Interesting. Back in the lab, Paul had seemed like the mastermind behind this operation. But now he appeared content to defer to Jesse. What had changed? Was he starting to feel guilty, and could Grant somehow use that to his advantage?

"You don't have to do this," he said, directing his comment more toward Paul than Jesse. Paul stared at the floor, the walls, anywhere but at Grant and Avery. Jesse merely rolled his eyes.

"If we could just skip the part where you beg for your life, I'd appreciate it. I have a lot to do today, and I'm running out of daylight." Jesse gestured for Grant and Avery to enter the container, careful to stay several feet away from them both.

The kernel of a plan began to form in Grant's mind. He nodded to Avery, and they both stepped inside the metal crate. "No matter what happens," he whispered to her, "stay back."

She glanced up at him, her eyes wide. He raised one eyebrow, and she nodded once.

He gestured for her to go deeper into the container. If she could take cover behind some of the furniture, she would be a little more protected if the bullets started flying.

Grant turned to face Jesse. "What now? Are you going to shoot us both like the coward you are?" He leaned forward a bit, balancing himself on the balls of his feet. As soon as Jesse raised his arm to fire, Grant was going to spring…

"Pretty much," said Jesse, his mouth twisting in a cruel smile. He took a step toward Grant, and Grant drew in a deep breath. One more step, just one more…

"No." Paul spoke quietly but with authority. Jesse paused and turned to look at him, his expression incredulous.

"What do you mean, no?"

"We can't alert the crew. Just lock them inside."

"Someone will find them!"

"No, they won't," Paul said calmly. "The cargo has all been loaded. The crew won't come here for days, by which time they'll both be unconscious or dead from dehydration. No one will find them until the ship docks and this container is opened, weeks from now. And once that happens, no one will connect their deaths to us." He shrugged. "It'll be written off as a tragic accident."

"I suppose you're right," Jesse grumbled. He lowered the gun but shot Grant a hateful look. "Guess it's your lucky day."

You have no idea…

Jesse pointed the gun at Grant again. "Step back," he said, apparently unwilling to come closer until Grant moved farther into the container. Grant obliged, backing up until he hit a chair. He tested his weight against it and was pleased to find it held strong. Good—that would come in handy soon.

Jesse swung one door shut and began to close the other, intending to seal them in darkness. As soon as Grant lost sight of Jesse, he braced himself against the furniture and pushed with all his strength, launching himself forward.

He hit the door hard, shoving his way back out into the cargo hold. Jesse hadn't been expecting any resistance, and Grant felt a satisfying thud as the door hit Jesse's shoulder. The other man stumbled back with a yelp and his gun clattered to the floor.

Grant's momentum kept him moving and he grabbed Jesse, dragging the man down. They landed in a heap, and Jesse immediately began to buck and kick, trying to dislodge Grant. Grant gritted his teeth and held on, landing several blows to the other man's ribs and head. He couldn't let up; if Jesse managed to get away, he'd grab the gun and start shooting, witnesses be damned.

Suddenly, a loud shriek rang out and Grant felt a rush of air as something streaked past him. Avery. What was she doing? He'd told her to stay inside the container!

He glanced over, trying to determine where she was. It was all the distraction Jesse needed. The man punched him in the nose and Grant's head exploded, a million stars filling his vision as a lightning bolt of pain sank deep into his brain. He scrabbled to hold on to Jesse, but the man shoved him off. By the time Grant's vision had cleared, Jesse was standing in front of him, the gun pointed at his head.

"I should have done this from the start," he sneered.

"You and that bitch doctor just had to get in the way. Not anymore." He cocked the gun and Grant closed his eyes, offering a silent apology to Avery.

I tried.

Hopefully, she had managed to escape. The idea gave him comfort and he clung to it, glad that his last thoughts were of her.

Grant tensed, waiting for the shot. He opened his eyes, determined to look his murderer in the face as he died. Instead he saw an angel.

Avery stood behind Jesse, the screwdriver clutched in her hand and her arm raised high. Her expression was one of pure determination, and her arm didn't falter as she brought the screwdriver down, stabbing Jesse in the shoulder.

He screamed and dropped the gun, falling to his knees. Grant sprang forward, batting the weapon away with his hand so Jesse couldn't grab it again. Then he tackled the man, pulling hard on his injured arm to keep him incapacitated.

Satisfied Jesse was no longer a threat, Grant glanced up at Avery. Relief drenched him when he saw she was whole and unharmed, making him feel a little light-headed. "I thought I told you to stay inside the container."

She arched one eyebrow. "You're welcome," she said dryly.

"You could have been killed," he pointed out.

"So it's okay for you to risk your life, but I can't do the same?" she fired back.

"Well…yes," he said, at a loss.

Avery rolled her eyes but she smiled at him. Grant rose to his feet and yanked Jesse up, as well.

"Let him go."

He froze at the sound of Paul's voice. Damn! He'd assumed the other man had taken off as soon as the fighting started, but apparently Paul had merely hid until the scuffle was over. Now it seemed he had found his courage again, along with Jesse's gun.

"Shoot him!" Jesse yelled. Paul pointed the gun at Grant, but his hand trembled a bit.

"It doesn't have to be like this," Grant said. "Let's just all calm down and talk, okay?"

"Shoot him!" Jesse screamed again.

"Paul," Grant said, raising his voice to be heard over Jesse's shouting. "This isn't you. You're not the kind of man to shoot someone in cold blood." At least he hoped not. Paul hadn't hesitated to deliberately infect people with the virus, but shooting someone seemed more personal. Hopefully, Paul would be too squeamish to pull the trigger.

"I want to help you," Grant continued. "I think you're a good guy who got caught up in a bad situation. Let me and Avery help you out of it."

Paul's features twisted with despair, and after an endless moment, he lowered the gun. "I'm sorry," he said, his voice barely audible.

"You bastard," Jesse said, his voice full of venom. "You're useless, just like your son. Turning traitor won't bring him back, you know."

Paul's head snapped up. "He's gone?"

"Of course," Jesse replied. "And now you'll never find him."

Paul blinked and his face went blank. Then he calmly closed the distance between them, and before Grant realized what the other man was doing, he shot Jesse in the chest.

Jesse crumpled, his deadweight pulling Grant down as he sank to the deck. Grant rolled the man onto his back, but it was too late. He was gone in a matter of seconds, his mouth open in a silent scream of protest.

Grant whirled back, expecting to find Paul pointing the gun at him or Avery. But the other man merely stood in place, staring down at Jesse's body in a detached sort of manner, the way one might look at an uprooted tree after a storm.

"Paul," Avery said cautiously. "Give me the gun, please."

Her words broke the spell he was under, and Paul looked down at the gun in his hand, surprise flickering across his face. He studied it for a moment, then raised his arm and pointed the weapon at his own head.

"Paul," Grant said, reaching out to pull Avery back. "That's not necessary. Please don't."

Tears streamed down the other man's face. "Don't you understand? My son is gone. It's all been for nothing."

"I'm sorry," Avery said softly. "I truly am. But don't do this. Don't let Jesse win."

Rage flashed across Paul's face, and Grant's breath caught in his chest. For a split second, he thought Avery had said the wrong thing, pushing the man over the edge instead of bringing him down. Then he sank to his knees, dropping the gun as he began to sob in earnest.

Grant picked up the weapon and tucked it into

the waistband of his pants. He exhaled heavily and his body started to shake as the adrenaline left his system. He glanced over at Avery and didn't know whether to laugh or cry. He opened his mouth to speak but found that he physically couldn't form words. Too drained to care, he simply held out his arms.

She stepped into his embrace, pressing her body against his. She was reassuringly warm and solid and *alive*, and he rejoiced in the feel of her.

He wasn't sure how long they stood there, wrapped in each other's arms. He was dimly aware of the arrival of some crew members, who had been alerted to their trespassing by the gunshot. People began to arrive, some to ask questions, some to deal with the situation, some just to gawk. But through it all, Grant and Avery clung to each other, drawing strength from their newly reforged bond.

"Thank you for being here with me," she whispered during a break in the questioning.

Grant looked over at her and smiled. "As long as I'm with you, there's no place I'd rather be."

Epilogue

Six weeks later

Olivia Sandoval let out a long whistle and leaned back from the computer screen. "Damn, girl. You really do need a vacation!"

Avery grinned at her friend's reaction. "Told you I wasn't kidding."

"I'm just glad you're okay." Even though her friend was hundreds of miles away in DC, her concern came through loud and clear.

"Me, too," Avery said. "And I could say the same about you." Olivia had dealt with her own adventure in Colombia a few months ago, and Avery got goose bumps every time she thought about how close she had come to losing her friend.

"We must have been born under a lucky star," Olivia said.

"Maybe so," Avery said. "And I think we should celebrate by getting together. I want to meet this new guy of yours, and I want you to meet Grant."

"Sounds good. What did you have in mind?"

"I'm thinking we need to go on a cruise," Avery suggested with a smile.

Olivia smiled back. "I know a good company," she said.

"Do you think Mallory would mind?"

Olivia shook her head. "Nah, I bet she'd be thrilled. It would be like a working vacation for her."

"Excellent." Excitement sparked in Avery's belly, and she reached for her phone to pull up her calendar. "It's kind of short notice, but can you guys go next month? I know Mallory is working the launch of a new ship."

"I'll talk to Logan, but that should be fine," Olivia replied. "It'll be so great to see each other again!"

Happiness flooded her system, making her feel lighter than air. "I can't wait!"

"Me, neither. I'll let you go so you can finish unpacking, but I'll call in a few days so we can start ironing out the details."

"Great! Love you, O."

"Love you, too, A."

Avery leaned forward and closed her laptop, then let out a happy sigh. Everything was really coming together, and she was glad to put the events in Antarctica behind her.

The aftermath of the shooting was still a bit of a blur. She and Grant had spoken to the US marshal on-base, General Anderson, and a whole host of law enforcement personnel via webcam. Fortunately, it hadn't taken much effort to convince Paul Coleson to talk. The man had told them everything, from his first contact with the mysterious Organization to his efforts to isolate and purify the virus, and his deliberate infection of people on the base. It was almost too fantastical to believe, and while she questioned the existence of the all-powerful Organization, his actions were not in dispute.

She shuddered, the memory of his words making her blood run cold. Paul and Jesse had come so close to smuggling the virus off the base. And while she understood Paul had acted out of grief and fear, she still couldn't forgive his actions.

Harold had been happy to see her, and thanks to her efforts, she was part of the team working to characterize this new virus. It was an exciting professional development, one that filled her with pride. They were learning so much about the pathogen, and hopefully their work would translate into better therapies for regular influenza outbreaks.

But the best part of all? Grant had found a job at Emory University Hospital, which was practically across the street from Avery's office at the CDC.

"Start looking for a house," he'd said right before she'd boarded the transport plane in Antarctica. "I'm moving to Atlanta as soon as I get back."

"Are you sure?" The idea thrilled her, but she didn't want him to uproot his life without really considering all the consequences.

"My life is with you, Avery," he'd said softly. "I don't care where I live, as long as we're together."

And so she'd put her condo on the market and found a little bungalow just outside the city. It hadn't taken Grant long to find a job—with his experience, he had his pick of hospitals. And even though they weren't going to be working side by side like they had in Antarctica, she liked knowing he would be so close.

Grant had driven up from Miami a few days ago with a trailer full of his things, and they had worked steadily to get it all unpacked. It had been a bit of a challenge to combine her stuff with his, but she enjoyed seeing their lives come together.

A pair of strong, warm arms slid around her from behind, and she leaned back into the solid mass of Grant's chest.

He buried his nose in her hair and kissed her temple. "Did I hear you say something about a cruise?"

She nodded. "I thought it would be a nice getaway, and a good opportunity for you to meet my friends."

"Does that mean you're keeping me?" he teased.

Avery turned in his arms until she was facing him. "That depends," she said. "Are you going to keep that coffee table?"

He let out an exaggerated sigh. "There is nothing wrong with that table," he began, but she held up her hand.

"Bottle-cap tabletops are no longer in style," she said.

"I don't think they ever were," he quipped. "But the guys and I had fun making it in college. Can I at least keep it in the garage?"

"Fine," she relented. In truth, she didn't care about the coffee table. She'd live under the thing if that was the only way to be with Grant, and he knew it.

"Thanks, baby." He pressed a kiss to the tip of her nose and she smiled.

"Ready to finish unpacking?" There were only a few boxes left to tackle, and then they could sit back and relax.

"I thought we might take a break first," Grant suggested.

"Weren't we just on a break?" Avery asked. His hands stroked her back, drifting lower in a clear suggestion. "Oh, you mean *that* kind of break," she said.

He grinned. "The best kind."

She rose on her tiptoes and kissed him, threading her fingers through his hair in a caress that was part tenderness, part need. "Sounds like a good idea to me," she said after a moment. "We've got a lot of breaks to catch up on."

Grant cupped her cheek with his hand, love shining in his eyes. "And the rest of our lives to do it."

"You've got a visitor."

Paul sat up on the thin mattress and swung his legs over the side of the cot. "Who is it?" *Please, not Mother...* Her first, and so far only, visit had been a disaster. The last thing he wanted was to be confronted with her tearful admonitions again. She blamed him for Noah's death, and rightly so. But what she didn't understand was that her anger and disappointment paled in comparison to his own self-hatred.

The guard rolled his eyes. "Do I look like your social secretary? Come on, let's go."

Paul walked over to the door and presented his hands for cuffing. The guard escorted him from his cell and through a series of corridors until they reached one of the visitation rooms, a spartan space that he knew from experience contained only a metal table and two chairs.

They entered, and Paul got his first glimpse of his visitor. It was a man he'd never seen before, and the bottom dropped out of his stomach.

Today's the day, then.

The guard fixed his cuffs to the loop on the table and took a step back. The man glanced at him. "I'd like some time alone with my client, please."

The guard pursed his lips but nodded. "I'll be just outside if you need anything."

As soon as the door clicked shut behind him, the stranger took the seat across from Paul. "Do you know who I am?"

"No. But I can guess." Paul tilted his head to the side, expecting to feel scared, or worried, or maybe even relieved. But there was nothing. He felt empty, drained of all emotion.

The man nodded, apparently satisfied by this answer. "Your failure to complete your mission has been a bit of an inconvenience."

"I did my job," Paul replied quietly, his pride stung by the rebuke. "It's not my fault you sent some psycho with poor impulse control to assist me."

"That was…unfortunate," the man said delicately.

"Are you here to punish me for killing him?" The question was blunt, but Paul didn't want to waste time with this man. He'd rather sleep in his cell than continue with this cryptic conversation.

"No. We would have been quite happy to let the

civil authorities handle the matter. I'm here because you ran your mouth."

"For all the good it did me," Paul said bitterly. He'd confessed everything after his arrest for Jesse's murder—the Organization, his orders to search for potential new biological weapons, his instructions to test the virus he had found on the base population. He hadn't held anything back, but they hadn't believed him. The Organization had planted enough evidence to make him look like a deranged loner who had snapped after the death of his wife.

Noah's body had been found a few days after he returned to the US. The police had characterized his case as a runaway after they found a series of angry emails on his laptop. The authorities believed Paul and Noah had gotten into a heated argument and Noah had left home and had been living rough on the streets. It didn't matter that Paul denied ever sending the messages—no one believed the word of a murderer.

"Regardless, your actions have consequences." The man reached into his pocket and slid a small red pill across the table.

Paul eyed it. "What if I refuse?"

The man shrugged. "You still have family."

His stomach twisted as Lisa's face flashed in his mind. "How do I know you'll leave them alone if I cooperate?"

"You don't."

Paul was silent a moment, but did he really have a choice? If he defied them, Lisa would suffer. If he cooperated, they might forget about her. There was only one thing he could do.

He reached out, took the pill and popped it into his mouth.

The stranger nodded and rose.

"None of this would have happened if you'd left my son alone."

The man paused on his way to the door. "I appreciate your perspective, and your desire for revenge. But you should know, all your efforts have been for naught. We have people everywhere. Eyes and ears all over the world. As I said, you caused us an inconvenience, but we will soon move past it. There are other targets—planes, trains, ships. Nothing is safe."

Paul was beginning to feel a little light-headed and he leaned forward, bracing his hands on the table for support. "Why? Just tell me that. Why do you do it?"

The man lifted one shoulder in a careless shrug. "Why not?"

* * * * *

*If you enjoyed this exciting romance
by Lara Lacombe,
don't miss the first volume in
the DOCTORS IN DANGER miniseries,
ENTICED BY THE OPERATIVE,
available now from Harlequin Romantic Suspense!*

REQUEST YOUR FREE BOOKS!
2 FREE NOVELS PLUS 2 FREE GIFTS!

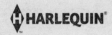

ROMANTIC suspense

Sparked by danger, fueled by passion

YES! Please send me 2 FREE Harlequin® Romantic Suspense novels and my 2 FREE gifts (gifts are worth about $10). After receiving them, if I don't wish to receive any more books, I can return the shipping statement marked "cancel." If I don't cancel, I will receive 4 brand-new novels every month and be billed just $4.74 per book in the U.S. or $5.49 per book in Canada. That's a savings of at least 12% off the cover price! It's quite a bargain! Shipping and handling is just 50¢ per book in the U.S. and 75¢ per book in Canada.* I understand that accepting the 2 free books and gifts places me under no obligation to buy anything. I can always return a shipment and cancel at any time. Even if I never buy another book, the two free books and gifts are mine to keep forever.

240/340 HDN GH3P

Name	(PLEASE PRINT)	
Address		Apt. #
City	State/Prov.	Zip/Postal Code

Signature (if under 18, a parent or guardian must sign)

Mail to the **Reader Service:**
IN U.S.A.: P.O. Box 1867, Buffalo, NY 14240-1867
IN CANADA: P.O. Box 609, Fort Erie, Ontario L2A 5X3

Want to try two free books from another line?
Call 1-800-873-8635 or visit www.ReaderService.com.

* Terms and prices subject to change without notice. Prices do not include applicable taxes. Sales tax applicable in N.Y. Canadian residents will be charged applicable taxes. Offer not valid in Quebec. This offer is limited to one order per household. Not valid for current subscribers to Harlequin Romantic Suspense books. All orders subject to credit approval. Credit or debit balances in a customer's account(s) may be offset by any other outstanding balance owed by or to the customer. Please allow 4 to 6 weeks for delivery. Offer available while quantities last.

Your Privacy—The Reader Service is committed to protecting your privacy. Our Privacy Policy is available online at www.ReaderService.com or upon request from the Reader Service.

We make a portion of our mailing list available to reputable third parties that offer products we believe may interest you. If you prefer that we not exchange your name with third parties, or if you wish to clarify or modify your communication preferences, please visit us at www.ReaderService.com/consumerschoice or write to us at Reader Service Preference Service, P.O. Box 9062, Buffalo, NY 14240-9062. Include your complete name and address.

HRS15

"Your time would be better spent coming up with answers
regarding our dead woman," she said in a no-nonsense tone.

Our.

Her slip of the tongue was not lost on Chris. The grin on
his lips told her so before he uttered a word. "Our first joint
venture. We should savor this."

"What I'd savor," she informed him, "is some peace and
quiet so I can work. Specifically, some time away from you."

The expression that came over Chris's face was one of
doubt. "Now, if we spend time apart, how are we going to
work on this case together?" he asked, conveying that what
she'd just said lacked logic.

Suzie had only one word to give him in response to his
question. "Productively."

With that, she went back to doing her work, but that
lasted for only a few moments. A minute at best. Though she
tried to block out his presence, he still managed to get to her.

He was standing exactly where he had been, watching
her so intently that she could feel his eyes on her skin. It

caused her powers of concentration to deteriorate until they finally became nonexistent.

Unable to stand it, she looked up and glared at him. "What do you want, O'Bannon?" she muttered. It took everything she had not to shout the question at him. The man was making her crazy.

Chris never hesitated as he answered her. "Dinner."

She clenched her jaw. "You can buy it in any supermarket," she informed him coldly.

He sidestepped the roadblocks she was throwing up as if they weren't there.

"With you."

This time Suzie was the one who didn't hesitate for a second. "Not at any price. Now please go before I take out my manual on workplace harassment and start underlining passages to get you banned from my lab."

"It's the crime scene lab, not yours," he reminded her pleasantly, taking a page out of her book. And then Chris inclined his head. "Until the next time."

"There is no next time," she countered, steaming even though she refused to look up again.

"Don't forget we're working this case together," he told her cheerfully.

He thought he heard Suzie say "Damn" under her breath as he left the lab.

Chris smiled to himself.

Don't miss
CAVANAUGH IN THE ROUGH by Marie Ferrarella,
available February 2017 wherever
Harlequin® Romantic Suspense books
and ebooks are sold.

www.Harlequin.com

HRSEXP0117

Turn your love of reading into
rewards you'll love with
Harlequin My Rewards

**Join for FREE today at
www.HarlequinMyRewards.com**

Earn **FREE BOOKS** of your choice.

Experience **EXCLUSIVE OFFERS** and contests.

Enjoy **BOOK RECOMMENDATIONS**
selected just for you.

PLUS! Sign up now
and get **500** points
right away!

MYR16R

HARLEQUIN®

A Romance FOR EVERY MOOD™

JUST CAN'T GET ENOUGH?

Join our social communities
and talk to us online.

You will have access to the latest
news on upcoming titles and special
promotions, but most importantly,
you can talk to other fans about your
favorite Harlequin reads.

Harlequin.com/Community

 Facebook.com/HarlequinBooks

 Twitter.com/HarlequinBooks

 Pinterest.com/HarlequinBooks